CW01091320

Swedish Folk Tales

SWEDISH FOLK TALES

Illustrated by John Bauer

Floris Books

This edition published in 2004 by Floris Books
15 Harrison Gardens, Edinburgh
www.florisbooks.co.uk
Sixth printing 2014

The acknowledgements on page 240 form part of the copyright agreement.
English version © 2004 Floris Books

British Library CIP Data available
ISBN 978-086315-457-7
Printed in Singapore

Contents

When Mother Troll Took in
the King's Washing

Elsa Beskow

Life for the trolls in the Great Forest was becoming unpleasant, for men were intruding on them more and more. When Father Troll was young, there had not been a single cottage within thirty miles, but now timber had been cut for one cottage after another, and settler after settler had cleared the forest and the earth. The people had become more and more daring as they came closer to the trolls' domain. It would have angered any honest old troll to hear all that cutting and sawing, see the smoke from the charcoal-burners' kilns, and smell the fried bacon and coffee from the cottages. Privately, Troll Mother *liked* the smell of coffee, but still she said "ugh" every time Troll Father mentioned it. At night she would sneak out to get a whiff of coffee and bacon, and to peek through the little cottage windows to see what the people were doing.

Food, too, was becoming scarce for the trolls. In the old days the forest and the mountains had been full of wolves and bears and foxes, and the trolls had feasted every day on bear ham and wolf chops and foxtail soup. Now, though, the forest animals were decidedly thinning out. Traps and snares had been set for them, and Troll Mother herself had been caught in a fox trap, and had nearly lost her tail. This had happened not long ago when she was peeping into a sheepfold looking for something good to eat for breakfast. With dangers like that, no wonder the wild animals gave up and moved away.

If only the people hadn't had dogs it might still have been bearable. Then Troll Father would have been able to get in at the sweet cattle, but that was quite impossible now, with the dogs barking and howling and snapping at his heels and tail. No, it was too much, and eventually most of the trolls had moved north.

At last, only one troll, with his wife and son, was left in Great Mountain, and Troll Father was determined not to go. Wasn't it his very own mountain, where his family had lived for three thousand years? When his wife spoke of moving, he snarled in anger. He became more cross and sullen as time passed, and at last wouldn't set forth from the mountain at all, so that the old woman and the boy had to fend for themselves as best they could.

Then one day an incredible thing happened: the people began to dynamite Troll Father's mountain. A young smith, who had a kiln nearby, had discovered copper in

Great Mountain, and so he and his neighbours decided to mine there. When the first charge of dynamite exploded, Troll Father became so angry that he exploded, too; he really did. He lay like a large stone in all the rubble, and Troll Mother and her son were left alone in the world with no place to turn. They could not stay in the mountain now that the people were dynamiting it. "We must leave and go north into the wilderness," the boy said.

But his mother would not agree to that. She had ideas of her own, which she had mulled over for a long time, even though she had never dared hint of them to Troll Father. The more she had smelled the coffee and the delicious frying bacon fat, and the longer she had stared into the little cottage windows, the more she came to believe that it was certainly much nicer to live the way people did. And at last her old troll brain had come up with a plan.

By the forest lake, two or three miles from Great Mountain, was an abandoned cottage. No one had lived there for at least six years, not since the old man who owned it had died. She and the boy, Drulle, would move there. They would carefully tie up their tails and put on clothes. Troll Mother had snatched quite a few clothes on her nightly visits to the farmhouses.

Best of all, they would boil coffee and fry that delicious bacon, just like people did. First, though, they had to get some of those little round things that were called money — but old Troll Mother knew how to go about that, too. Four miles north, at Stone Hill croft, lived a farm-wife who made a living for herself and her children by taking in washing. Troll Mother had peered for hours at the farm-wife doing her laundry in the wash house, so by now she knew how to do it. And she had watched the farm-wife in the croft accept those round, shiny things called money for what she did, and then later send her children to the village to exchange them for coffee, milk, and bacon. Troll Mother had her wits about her. She had peeped into the market and seen the lovely things and how you behaved there. Her big troll kettle was ideal for washing. With a pinch of troll powder in the water, the wash would soon be white as snow, as easy as that. Trolls knew a thing or two. Life could be very different from sitting in the mountain gnawing on rabbit bones.

Well, the boy troll, who was not used to thinking so much at once, was amazed, and clutched his head with both his big hands in wonder. At last, however, the thought of the fried bacon overcame all else, and when evening came, Troll Mother and her son left their mountain. They carried their troll kettle between them on a pole, and bundled the rest of their belongings on their backs. Then they trotted away to the little cottage by the lake to begin living like men.

Towards evening the next day, someone knocked on the kitchen door of the parsonage. There stood an ugly old woman with a shawl pulled over her eyes and her hands in her apron. "I am a poor woman," she croaked, "and have no money. Would the honourable gentlefolk allow me to do their washing?"

Now it happened, on that very day, that a great stir and to-do was going on at the parsonage. Important visitors were expected, and the parsonage needed dusting and scrubbing, beer needed brewing, and bread baking, and the parson's wife had just realized that she could never, that week, do her big washing. So it was decided that the poor old woman, who was so anxious to work, should take the washing home. The lady herself would decide the price when the wash was returned and she could see if it was fine and white.

Troll Mother went home delighted beyond words. The next morning before sunup, she and her son appeared with an old cart they had found in a shed and tugged the parsonage laundry home to their croft.

With the troll powder, the wash was beautiful, and the parson's wife was very surprised to have it all back in a few days, dry and white as snow. That washerwife was a godsend. And she asked so little money, too. You paid her what you felt like, for the old crone could not count and was deeply grateful for whatever coins she received.

The parson's wife told the country sheriff's wife, and the shopkeeper's wife, and the wives of the more well-to-do farmers about the washerwife in the forest, and soon Troll Mother had as much to do as she could wish. Those were happy days for the trolls. A coffee pot boiled on the fire all day long, and bacon sizzled in the frying pan.

It wasn't hard work, either. They filled the big kettle with water, poured in the troll powder, and lit the fire. The minute the clothes were wet, they turned snow-white, and afterwards they were wrung out and hung to dry. If there was no wind, the old woman just waved her troll apron — one of the few things she had kept from former days — and right away a lovely breeze sprang up and dried the clothes in an hour. The trolls did so well that they bought a horse and cart to fetch the washing, and Drulle bought himself a green necktie with red polka-dots from the country store.

Now it so happened that a king decided to build a castle not far away. His queen was sickly, and he wanted her to recover in the pure forest air. That summer, the queen and her little baby princess, only a few months old, came to live in the castle.

One day the queen's lady-in-waiting visited the parsonage, and talk turned to the old woman and her son, who were so ugly and so shy and so absurdly afraid of dogs, but who washed so quickly and so cheaply that no one would do their own washing anymore.

The lady-in-waiting listened attentively, for she was responsible for the laundry of the whole royal household, for a certain sum of money a year, and she hoped to save a little and put it aside for herself. When the parson's wife assured her that she could entrust the finest and sheerest linen to this strange washerwife, that none would ever be torn, the lady-in-waiting decided that she, too, would use her.

It is easy to imagine how surprised the trolls were when they were called to the king's castle. The troll boy, afraid of the royal hounds, did not want to go, but in the end he set out in the rattling cart, wearing his new necktie and with his cap pulled far down over his black forelock — and succeeded in bringing home the royal laundry without any mishaps at all.

When Troll Mother saw all the baby princess's pretty little clothes, they went to her head. The silken swaddling clothes, the small embroidered vests and nightgowns — she had never in her life seen anything so sweet. She gazed for a long while, and held up the little gowns with her long, crooked forefinger, and then she called the boy to look and admire too, but he did not understand such things.

"Listen, Drulle," Troll Mother said, nudging him. "One day when you marry, you must give your own little mite such small things."

"Fiddlesticks," said the son sullenly. "Now wouldn't that be fine for a little troll child!"

"Troll child!" the mother cried shrilly. "You're not going to marry a troll, are you, now that we're almost human? Oh, no. A fine wife with soft yellow hair is what you will have, and then you will have the sweetest little children with golden curls. 'Hushabye baby, sleep, little baby,'" she crooned, rocking back and forth with the baby clothes in her arms.

"You're dreaming," her son said angrily, kicking the bucket of washing. "Who will have me?"

But once Troll Mother got an idea in her head, it stayed, and she took several of the princess's gowns and hid them in her chest.

"Now see that you divert them when they come to count the washing," she admonished her son as he was leaving to take the laundry back to the castle. "You haven't taken leave of all your troll senses, have you?" She made him repeat a troll rhyme, which she told him to mumble as he waited for the royal staff to count the washing.

It turned out very well. Every week the son collected the king's washing, and every week Troll Mother kept another little piece of clothing, but when the washing was counted, nothing was ever found missing.

Some weeks had passed when the royal nurse announced to the lady-in-waiting that the princess's costly little dresses were mysteriously disappearing. They suspected a castle servant of stealing them, because nothing had ever been lost by the old washerwife.

Their suspicions fell on a young orphan girl named Inga, who mended the linens and sewed the buttons and ribbons onto the princess's clothes. It did not help Inga to protest her innocence. No one else touched the clothes; and when two small garments, which she had taken to her chamber to mend, were discovered there, it seemed to prove that she was the thief. That very day she was sent away from the castle.

Inga trudged despairingly along the highway. She did not know where to go; all she knew was that she wanted to get as far away from the castle as possible, from those who believed her a thief. There was no one in the whole world to whom she could turn — for who would take in a thief?

At last, late one evening, she came to the forest lake and the trolls' small cottage. She walked to the edge of the lake and leaned over the calm, mirrored water. How wonderful it would be to dive down into the cool lake and never be seen again!

Then she felt someone pulling at her skirt. An ugly old woman with a black shawl on her head was standing behind her. The woman's big mouth widened in a smile, and her little eyes gave the girl a friendly wink.

"You should not be out in the cold so late in the evening," she said in a gravelly voice. "Come into the cottage with me."

Inga was afraid of the old crone, but she followed her because it was nice that someone was kind enough to ask her in.

As she entered the croft, she saw Drulle with his black, straggly hair, and realized it was the washerwife of the forest who had taken her in, which made her feel safer. The old woman asked her to stay and help about the house, and Inga accepted gratefully, because she had nowhere else to go. To be sure, she found both the woman and her son peculiar in their ways, but perhaps that happened when you lived alone so long in the forest. Besides, they were very kind to her.

Inga wanted to help with the washing, but she was not allowed to — her hands were much too soft and white, said Troll Mother. But if she would cook a little something for them — the way they cooked down in the valley — the washerwife would be so glad.

So the girl made porridge and gruel, and fried pancakes and baked bread, and all of it delighted the woman and her son. She tidied up the cottage, both her own little room and the kitchen, where the mother and son lived, and at last the cottage began to look quite respectable.

As it happened, as soon as Troll Mother had seen the girl standing so slim and fair by the dark lake side, she had decided that here was just the wife for her son.

She lost no time in confiding this to him. Most of the time the son did not pay much attention to what his mother said, but now, the more he looked at Inga, the more he hoped she was right. He would sit for hours on end in a corner of the kitchen and follow Inga with his eyes as she moved back and forth doing the chores. As for Inga, it was hard to have his brown, brooding gaze fastened on her. He was ugly as a dog that has been kicked too often. Though she could tell he longed for kindness, it really would have been easier to be friendly to a dog than to this boy, who filled her with inexplicable disgust. He was so anxious to please her that she no sooner made a wish than he rushed away to fulfil it, which was very awkward and tiresome.

Inga was thinking about all this one day while walking in the forest. She remembered, too, Troll Mother's odd blinkings and the wry faces she made at times. "It will be hard to stay with them for much longer," she thought, "but where can I go?"

As she made her way along the forest path, she met the queen's young page. He was the last person she wanted to see. When she was banished from the castle as a thief, it had pained her most of all that the young page, who had used to talk to gaily and courteously to her as she sewed in the garden, believed she was a thief. She turned her head away and quickly took another path. But the page ran after her.

"Good morning, Miss Inga. I have looked for you for so long, to tell you that I know you are innocent of what they accused you."

She stopped and regarded him, her eyes full with tears. At last someone believed she was innocent.

"Come with me," he begged. "I will take you to my mother. And in a few years, when I have come into my estate, we will marry."

Inga shook her head. "Your mother could not welcome me as a daughter-in-law," she said. "Your future would be ruined if you married me. But thank you, thank you so much, for believing in me."

The young page tried to keep her from running away and asked her at least to tell him where she lived, but Inga was firm. "You must *not* follow me," she said, and hurried away through the forest.

Now the troll boy, as was his wont, had followed Inga that day, and hiding behind a boulder, had seen her talking to the young page. He was overcome with unhappiness, and shambled off to the cottage, hanging his head.

Troll Mother was there, examining one of the princess's little dresses with great delight; it had the most exquisite lace, thin and fine as a spiderweb. "Look at this one, you," she called to her son. "Won't your blond baby look fine in it?"

The son hissed at her angrily, "Be quiet, Mother. Do you think she could ever like me? Oh, no. He must be straight-backed and slim, and have a green velvet hat with a feather. Look at my black hair and my wide mouth and my big, hairy hands." He was shouting, and in his misery banged his head so hard against the cottage wall that it shook.

"Now, now," said his mother. "Leave it to me. You hurry off to the castle with the washing, and don't forget to divert them when they count it, for this one I am going to keep!" And she tucked the small dress in her chest and banged the lid shut. For a while now, she had not dared keep any of the princess's clothes, having learned of the fuss at the castle when some were found missing, but this one she simply could not resist.

Not long after the boy left, Inga entered the cottage.

"Listen, little Inga," said the woman in a mild voice, cocking her head. "How would it be if you and Drulle married?"

When she saw the frightened look in the girl's eyes, she rushed on, "Come, here, little Inga, and I will show you something." With a sly look she opened the chest. "Have you ever in your life seen anything so lovely? Those are for your little babies when you marry Drulle."

Inga gave a cry of anguish. "But those are the princess's dresses."

"So they are," said the old woman contentedly. "And they are fine enough, I should imagine."

"But Mother," Inga said, "don't you understand that it is stealing to take them?"

"Stealing!" barked the old woman angrily. "People have such strange words. One takes what one can get."

"Have you never learned that it is a sin to steal?" asked Inga in horror.

"I am not going to listen," Troll Mother snapped. She flashed Inga a sly, green-eyed look, snatched the small clothes, and threw them back into the chest. She was so agitated that her tail came loose as she bent over the chest, and Inga saw it plain as day.

Inga sat down on the bench, stiff with fear. The old woman banged the chest shut and stormed out of the door, her tail lashing behind. "You have the coffee ready when I come back," she shouted. "Now I must do the washing!"

But as soon as Troll Mother left, Inga hurried from the croft and ran towards the forest. She had to get away — far, far away from the trolls. She was still trembling with fear at having lived so long with the trolls, and at the thought she ran sobbing through the forest.

She ran right into the young page, who was wandering there sadly, wondering where Inga had gone. This time she did not run from him, but leaned against him, trembling, and murmured something about being so afraid of trolls. He put his hand to his sword at once, and asked, "Where are the trolls?"

"No, no, you must not hurt them," Inga protested. "They have been good to me. They were the only ones who took me in when I was homeless.

Then the page asked her once more to let him take her to his mother, and this time she did not say No. She was far too tired to refuse. And as the young page's mother was a wise and good woman, and saw immediately that Inga needed help, she did not question her. She put Inga to bed and looked after her as if she were her own daughter.

Meantime the troll boy drove on to the king's castle with a scowl on his face as he thought of the young page. When the washing was counted, he completely forgot to mumble the troll rhyme. He did not wake from his brooding until the lady-in-waiting asked repeatedly and sharply, "Where is the princess's christening robe?" Then he realized something was wrong.

"Oh, oh," he said, scratching his head. "I must have forgotten it. I will go home for it."

He drove four miles to the croft, but neither his mother nor Inga were there. He opened the chest and poked around in it. If only he knew which one of all these frilly, lacy garments was missing. To be safe, he decided it was best to take along several things, and he stuffed a number of small vests and linens in his pockets and set out again.

He entered the royal kitchen and held up a small jacket. "Is this the one?" he asked. The housekeeper looked at him in amazement. Stupidly he brought out more of the little clothes. "Is it one of these?"

The housekeeper signalled the cook to fetch the lady-in-waiting. She came in a hurry, but the troll boy noticed nothing until he felt a heavy hand on his shoulder. It was a palace guard who had been summoned to arrest the thief and put him in the tower. Only then did he come to his senses and realize what he had done. Alight with rage, he kicked one guard and hit another with his fist. They both tumbled to the floor, and with a quick jump, he leapt up in his cart and drove away full tilt.

By the time they had collected their wits to follow him, Drulle was out of sight; and when at last the guards reached the little cottage beside the lake, it was empty and deserted. The crooked door was squeaking on its hinges, and some half-dry laundry, which belonged to the wife of the sheriff, was blowing in the wind.

Now the people in the castle realized how unjustly they had accused Inga and driven her away. The queen reproached herself for being cruel, and wanted to search for the girl everywhere. Imagine her joy when her page announced that he knew where Inga was. Immediately, he was ordered to ride out and bring her back; and when Inga learned that the thief had been found, but that both trolls had escaped, she was happy and quickly recovered her health. Joyfully she followed the page to the castle.

The queen received her there with open arms, kissed both her cheeks, and everyone showed kindness and friendliness towards her. The queen wanted to know all her adventures, and after listening to them she said, "I had always hoped to take you back to my court in the city and educate you as my lady-in-waiting, but now perhaps you would rather marry my page?"

Inga had much rather, and the queen appointed her page royal forester, and then built them the handsomest house with a broad view of the small lake in the forest. The trolls' cottage, though, was razed to the ground.

One autumn evening, when Inga had been married a year or so, she was sitting with her husband looking at a tiny little child asleep in her lap. The child was sweet, and Inga smiled happily. Then she suddenly thought she heard a long sigh. She looked up and saw four melancholy troll eyes peering in at her through the window. She gave a startled cry, and her husband ran outside to see if there was anyone there. But he saw no one, and only the sound of the wind answered his calls. He was about to turn indoors when he saw something white on the steps. It was a bundle of laundry, the rest of the princess's dresses.

This was the last time the trolls were seen in the region. Undoubtedly they had followed the other trolls to the forests in the northern wilderness. But Inga thought of Troll Mother and her son sometimes, and in spite of herself, could not help wishing that their life was not too hard.

The Magician's Cape

Anna Wahlenberg

Once a wicked magician built a splendid castle high on a mountain. Between the cliffs in front of the castle he conjured up a garden so wonderful it had no equal. There magnificent flowers glowed, and delicious fruits ripened, and there were the sweetest grapes. The magician would lie on a velvet couch under the branches while beautiful young girls danced for him on the lawn, danced and sang and plucked their guitars.

The songs were merry, but the dancers themselves looked very sad because they hated the ugly evil magician who had taken them from their parents. Yet they trembled for their lives, because as soon as the magician thought one of them did not play or dance well enough, he would open the garden gate and push her into the deep forest outside, which was full of bears and wolves, and where many dancers were lost and never found their way back home again.

Whenever the magician had discarded a girl of whom he was tired, he would put on the fine velvet robes of a distinguished gentleman, dab his lips with honey to make the words come out sweetly, and drip magic dew in his eyes to make them look gentle and sparkling. Then he would don his black flying cape, which he could change into enormous wings, and fly out to find another victim.

If he saw a girl who pleased him, he spread his cape at her feet, just as a noble knight would do to honour a pretty maiden. And if the girl stepped willingly on to it, he would quickly wrap her up in a corner of the cape and fly away with her. Should she ignore him, however, he could not harm her, for he had power only over those who stepped on his cape of their own free will.

During one of his flights, he came to a small village and saw a smith's daughter, Alvida, sitting at a window combing her long yellow hair.

Her face was so serene and her eyes were so clear that everyone liked her, and the magician too was delighted at the sight of her. However, he did not dare approach just then, but watched and waited until he saw her come outside with a basket on her arm and walk towards the forest to pick berries. Then he slipped ahead of her, and where the forest path turned off, he suddenly stepped out and spread his black cape before her.

"Beautiful maiden," he said, "your feet are so small and fine, they ought not to touch the ground. Step on my cape!"

At first Alvida was frightened, but then she laughed. "I am no beautiful maiden. And really, you ought to take better care of your handsome cape. Imagine, dropping it in the middle of the path. It will be covered with mud and pine needles."

She picked up the cape, carefully shook it out, and returned it to the magician. "Now, that's better. Don't do it again, though, for it would be a great pity to ruin such a fine cape." She scolded him with her finger, nodded, and ran lightly into the forest.

But the magician so wanted to take her back to his castle that he followed stealthily, wondering how to catch her.

Then he saw a herd of goats grazing in a dell, and among them an enormous ram with curved horns. If I could make that ram frighten her, he thought, then I could hold out my cape to protect her. She would try to hide behind it and step on to it.

Taking out a magic whistle, the magician blew on it and attracted a swarm of bees and hornets. These stung the ram to a frenzy. It tried to butt the bees with its horns, and when that did not work, it looked around for something else to butt. It caught sight of Alvida and rushed full tilt towards her, exactly as the magician had hoped. In two quick steps, the magician was at Alvida's side holding up his cape as if to protect her from the onrushing ram.

But he miscalculated. Alvida was frightened by the ram, but she did not seek safety behind the magician's cape, and instead ran behind a pine tree, where she and the ram chased each other round and round.

When she tripped over a root, the magician quickly spread his cape, hoping she would fall on it. But she fell to the side, and it was the ram that streaked in and entangled its horns in the magician's cape. The magician knocked it senseless; but when he freed his cape from the sharp horns, much to his annoyance he saw that the cape had a big tear in it.

Alvida saw this, too, and feeling that the accident had happened because the magician had tried to save her from the ram, she felt very sorry and walked towards him. "What a pity that your beautiful cape is torn," she said. "And that I should have been the cause of it. Perhaps I can find a way to mend the tear."

She picked a thorn from a rose bush, and with another thorn pierced the first at the top, and so she made a sewing needle. Then she plucked a thin strand of her yellow hair, and thus she had a thread.

"Give me your cape," she urged. "If I sew it neatly, I don't think you will see the tear, and when you get home someone else can repair it properly." She folded the cape over her knee, and patched the rip as well as she could.

But the magician was reluctant to let her go. "Just let me see if it will do." He held the cape up to the light, and shook his head: she must make a few more stitches.

With her needle in hand, Alvida stood and reached for the cape. At the same moment the magician lowered the cape and dragged it on the ground. Without a thought, Alvida put her foot on the hem, and in a second the magician had wrapped her up in that corner. Full of anguish, Alvida saw the cape turn into a pair of enormous wings, and felt herself being carried aloft.

But more terrible than all was the way the magician's face changed. His eyes became rolling balls of fire, his mouth opened in a grin, and terrible tigerish fangs jutted forth.

"Help, help," Alvida cried in terror.

And as if her cry had been heard, the strand of yellow hair, with which the tear in the cape had been sewn, caught on a high branch of the pine tree. No matter how the magician pulled and tugged, the strand was so strong it did not break; and while he was pulling and tugging, the cape tangled among the leaves and branches. To free it, the magician had to use the arm with which he held Alvida by the waist. Quickly, she slipped from him, caught at a branch lower down, and jumped to the ground.

She ran home as fast as she had ever run in her life, and once she was inside, fell on the floor in fear and exhaustion. It was a long while before she recovered enough to tell her father and mother what had happened.

The magician flew back to his castle so full of rage that everyone within hid for fear of his anger. No one dared speak or even whisper until he had shut himself up in his room.

He lay on the bed and closed his eyes but could not sleep. His room seemed to him unusually light.

"The moon must be shining through the window," he thought, and rolled over.

But the light was still so bright he could not sleep. He rose to close the shutters. When he looked out, he saw that there was no moon in the sky, and turning round, realized that the light was coming from the flying cape, which he had hung over a chair: it came from the seam sewn with Alvida's yellow hair, which shone out as brightly against the black cloth as a good deed shines against an evil one.

"Well, that is easily taken care of," he thought.

With that, he rolled the cape up tightly to that the seam was inside, and climbed into bed again. But he had hardly closed his eyes before the radiance filled the room again. The golden seam was shining right through all the folds of the cape.

Angrily, the magician rushed forward with a knife and cut the seam from the cape, leaving a large hole. Then he threw the golden threads out of the window.

Now I shall be free to sleep, he thought.

But no sooner had he closed his eyes again than once more he sprang up in a rage. The light was there again. He examined the cape and found that the seam was still there, shining brightly.

The magician carried the cape to the deepest, darkest cellar in the mountain, but it was no help. As soon as he lay down on his bed again, brightness filled the room. It shone through walls, floor and ceiling, until he realized that he would never be able to escape its light.

He did not sleep a wink that night, or the next, or the next. As the fourth night approached, he threw his flying cape over his shoulders and flew down to the little village where Alvida lived. He rapped on her window.

"Who is it?" she asked, sitting up in bed startled from sleep.

"It is me," he said. "Open your window so I can talk to you. I will not hurt you."

But Alvida had recognized the voice, and hid silent and shivering under her blanket.

"Come here," he urged. "Your wicked yellow hair, with which you sewed my cape, keeps shining and won't let me sleep. Undo that seam or I will make you suffer."

But he could not frighten Alvida now, for she remembered that trolls and magicians never dare force their way into Christian homes. So Alvida lay still, as if nothing had happened.

The magician began to beg, and beseeched her, "If you undo the seam, I will give you a sack of gold."

Alvida did not move.

"If you cut the seam, you can have a big farm with fields and pastures."

But regardless of the wonderful things he offered, there was no answer. In the end, the magician had to return to his castle with nothing accomplished. As he entered the castle garden, he had an idea. He could not bribe Alvida, but if he could *give* her something, perhaps that would make her grateful and she would agree to cut away the shining seam.

So he bent down the branches of the trees in his garden and picked the most luscious fruits, pulled up the grape vines with their heavy bunches, swept them all in his cape, and flew back to Alvida's window. There he planted the grape vines, arranged them over the wall, fastened them to the windowsill and the roof beams, and hung all the fruit he had picked among the bunches of grapes, so that a beautiful border now framed the small window.

The magician flew back to his castle and went to bed. And the strange thing was that this time when he closed his eyes, the golden thread shone only faintly, and he could go to sleep.

Alvida looked out of her window the next morning, and her eyes fell on a poor old woman sitting by the ditch eating a big juicy pear. The old woman stood and curtsied. "Thank you for the beautiful pear," she said. "It fell from your window to the highway, and fruit that lies on the highway is for anyone to take."

When Alvida saw how handsomely her window had been decorated, she realized that the magician was trying to persuade her to rip out the shining thread.

Alvida did not touch any of the fruit herself. She let it fall, piece by piece, and tired and thirsty travellers came along, picked up a pear or an apple, and blessed the gift. Every evening the vines were bare, but by morning they were full of the most delicious fruit once again.

One night the magician knocked at Alvida's window. "Listen, my girl," he said. "I have given you all the treasures of my garden, because it dims the radiance of your foolish seam. But there must come an end to this. Won't you now cut the shining seam from my cape so that I may finally sleep in peace?"

Alvida did not answer. She thought the seam was all right where it was.

And the magician never did get rid of it. Every night, he — who only wanted to do evil — was obliged to fly away with gifts for the tired and unhappy. And if he ever dared carry off a maiden, no matter how fancifully he decorated Alvida's window, the golden seam shone so blindingly both day and night that the magician did not get a moment's peace until he had taken her home again where she belonged.

The Barrel Bung

Anna Wahlenberg

For nearly five years now, the people of Bolinge parish had suffered from famine. At last even the milk from the cows, which was what they lived on, was gone. The cows had run dry at both the farms and the crofts.

But while life was hard for the parishioners, at the manor house of rich, elderly Lady Skinflint, there was plenty. They called her that because she was so mean and miserly to everyone. She had bought the manor house five years before, and moved there with her tall, ugly daughter, whose face was so ugly it was enough to scare you.

Yes, there was always plenty at the manor house. Even though the old lady and her daughter had only four poor cows, they had hundreds of cheeses and churned big tubs of thick butter to cart off and sell. It was as if all God's blessings had left the farms and crofters' cottages, and gone to the manor house. People shook their heads and said it was not right, yet no one quite understood how it had happened.

At last, when Star, a splendid cow belonging to wife Jonson who lived in one of the crofts in the forest, gave only half a pint of milk, Jerker Jonson, the eldest son, decided that matters had gone far enough, and that he would find out what was happening. That evening when he went to bed, Jerker did not bother to blow out his candle, but instead placed it close to the wood shavings on his workbench, so that the shavings would surely catch fire when the candle burned down. Jerker lay there waiting, pretending to sleep. He knew that if the tomte, or goblin, who looked after the house, was still in the cottage, he would come and blow out the candle. Jerker had almost given up hope and was just reaching out to do it himself, when the little tomte in his grey smock and red tasselled cap tiptoed from one corner of the room and with two fingers pinched the burning wick and snuffed out the flame.

"Good evening," said Jerker, jumping from bed and bowing to the little tomte whom he could see plainly in the moonlight that was shining through the window. "I thought you had moved to the manor house, since all blessings seem to have left us and gone to them."

The tomte looked solemn and stroked his long beard. "It is not my fault," he said.

"Whose is it then?" Jerker asked.

The tomte eyed him doubtfully. Then he stood on tiptoe and whispered in Jerker's ear, "If you can get yourself hired as a farmhand there, and do well enough to be allowed to look in their storeroom, perhaps you will find out what's wrong." And quick as a mouse, he darted back into the corner.

Jerker got up at dawn the next morning. He told his mother he wanted to go out into the world and find work as a farmhand, and he went off with his Sunday clothes tied by a leather strap across his shoulder.

When he reached the village, however, Jerker exchanged all his fine clothes for some soft rye cakes with plenty of butter, and a few fine sausages. He stuffed these into his pockets, for it was sensible to take food when you went to the manor house of Lady Skinflint, where there might not be enough to eat. After this, he set out straight for the manor house and knocked on the kitchen door.

"Come in," a voice squeaked.

Jerker entered. He saw an old manservant who was the only help at the manor house. The servant was so frail and miserable that he could not get work anywhere else, so he had stayed on. He was sitting by the fire eating dinner; that is, a meal of potatoes and well water.

"Do you know if the manor house needs a farmhand?" Jerker asked.

The old servant responded with a loud guffaw. Apparently, he could not imagine anyone wanting to work there.

"They wouldn't want *you*, in any case," he replied. "Even *I* seem expensive to them."

"But suppose you became ill," Jerker said.

"Don't say it. Then I would starve to death."

Jerker pulled forth a sausage and a rye cake and held them up to the old man.

"Oh, no, I must be in paradise," said the manservant, and his eyes were sparkling.

Jerker held the sausage in his right hand and the rye cake in his left. "Go and pretend to be ill," he ordered. "You'll have more to eat if I get the job."

The old man obeyed him at once. He crawled to a corner near the fire, pulled a quilt over his head, made himself comfortable, and began to chew on the sausage and cake. Jerker crept outside and hid near the corner of the house.

He did not have to wait long before he heard a terrible noise. Old Lady Skinflint and her scarecrow daughter had come into the kitchen and were quarrelling with the old man for being idle. They shouted and howled worse than seven dogs fighting eleven cats. Right in the midst of the upheaval, Jerker knocked on the kitchen door a second time.

"Does the gracious lady of the manor house need a farmhand?" he asked as he entered.

"No, get out! Get out of here!" shrieked Lady Skinflint, shaking a poker at him.

But her daughter tugged at her mother's skirt. Now that the old man was ill, they could use a hand for a day or two. And so, one way or another, Jerker was allowed to stay on at the manor house. The first thing Jerker was told to do in his new job was to carry cheese from the storeroom to the larder outside. The cheeses were big and heavy, and there were so many of them that it seemed as if the manor house had a hundred cows instead of just four. But don't think for a moment that Jerker was allowed to set foot inside the storeroom. Oh, no. The daughter brought out every single cheese herself and handed it to him on the front porch. She was so careful about the storeroom door that Jerker did not manage so much as a peep inside.

Suddenly, however, as she handed him one cheese, he pretended to drop it on his foot. Then he began to jump up and down on one leg, howling with pain. Of course the daughter had to come and ask what was hurting him, and in the confusion she left the storeroom door. Jerker himself grabbed it, and leaned against it to steady himself. As he did so, he quickly poked a stick into the lock, then broke it off so that it was securely wedged there. He put his foot down, said he was better now, and carried the cheese away.

When he returned, the old woman and her daughter were both standing there, poking and prodding the lock, both purple in the face from trying to shut the door. Jerker offered to help, but they refused. So the lock had to stay broken until the next day, when Lady Skinflint herself would go to the country store and buy another.

For the rest of the day, the old woman and her daughter took turns guarding the door. They did not leave until evening, when they sent Jerker to the hayloft for the night.

He lay dozing awhile, then he got up and crept down again. Listening intently, he circled the manor house and soon realized that the two women, whom he had believed sound asleep, were in the dining room having their supper. Quick as an eel, he went into the hall, opened the still unlocked storeroom door, and glided in without a sound.

It was still fairly light, but he could see nothing stranger than cheeses and milk buckets on all the shelves.

Suddenly he heard the dining-room door open. Afraid of being discovered, Jerker jumped behind a couple of apple barrels and lay on his stomach on the floor. He had just hidden himself when old Lady Skinflint and her tall ugly daughter came in, holding candles in their hands.

The old woman set her candle down and began to dig in her pocket. Finally she pulled out a big barrel stopper, which is called a bung, and wedged it into a hole in the wall that Jerker had not noticed before. Then she found a milking-stool and sat down on it, with a milk pail between her knees, just under the bung.

Then she began to pat the bung and cry like someone calling cows in for milking. "Come, Boss. Come, Brindle Bell, Come, all you cows."

"Which one will you milk first today?" asked her daughter.

"Oh, I think I'll have the parish clerk's Bean. Come, Bean. Come, Bean, Come, Bean," she clucked.

Jerker watched as a big cow's udder swelled from the bung on the wall. The woman took a firm grip of it and sang:

Cow of gold,
cow of gold,
give as much milk
as the pail will hold.

Creamy white milk streamed from her fingers into the pail until it was full, and Lady Skinflint emptied it into a big tub her daughter had brought in. Then she put the pail between her knees again.

"Which will you have now, then?" asked her daughter.

"Now I think it will be the sheriff's Buttercup," the old woman replied. And once more she began to pat the bung, from which the first udder had disappeared when she stopped singing before. Now she called, "Come, Buttercup. Come, Buttercup. Come, Buttercup."

Another udder appeared, and milk began to pour out as before. The old hag sang along,

Cow of gold,
cow of gold,
give as much milk
as the pail will hold.

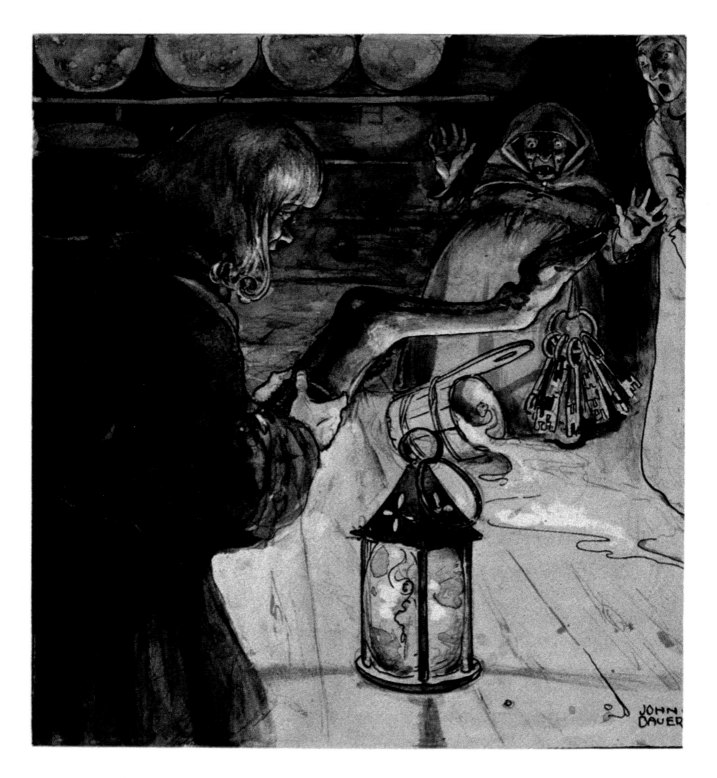

When the pail was full, this milk, too, was poured into the tub, and the daughter asked as before, "Which one will you have now?"

"Well, I think it will be Mother Jonson's Star," the old woman answered, and again began her magic with the bung. "Come, Star. Come, Star, Come, Star," she called.

But when Jerker heard her coaxing the Jonson's own beloved Star, he became quite angry. Before the woman had begun her song, he stuck his head out and cried,

Cow of gold,
cow of gold,
knock the hag out,
knock her cold.

And look! Instead of an udder, a cow's leg shot forth from the bung and kicked the hag solidly. Her daughter came running, and she got a kick, too. Delightedly, Jerker continued to sing,

Cow of gold,
cow of gold,
knock the hag out,
knock her cold.

And the cow's leg kicked, and old Lady Skinflint and her daughter screamed, and whenever they tried to dodge away the cow's leg reached out and gave them an extra wallop.

"You villain, you rogue," cried old Lady Skinflint. "Are you trying to kill us?"

But Jerker paid no attention so the old lady tried another way. "Dear, sweet, good Mr. Crofter Jerker, don't sing anymore, and we will give you anything you want."

"That's more like it," said Jerker, and stopped his singing. The cow's leg became a bung once more, and quickly Jerker took the bung from the wall and held it. "Bring me all the gold you have earned by milking the cows of the village, and I shall temper justice with mercy."

No matter how the old woman and her daughter begged and beseeched, Jerker would not listen until they brought out almost all the gold and silver they had. It filled a sack so big and heavy that Jerker could scarcely lift it.

Then the old hag asked to have the bung back.

"No," said Jerker, putting it in his pocket. "This is mine."

Then he woke the old man servant and asked him to help carry the sack, and all night long they struggled and strained to get it down to the village.

In the morning, Jerker had the church bells rung; and when the villagers came running, wondering what had happened, he opened his sack and all the gold and silver spilled out. Then it was divided fairly among all those whose cows mean old Lady Skinflint had so thievishly milked. The rejoicing went on and on.

When everyone had received his fair share, each gave a tenth part to Jerker, feeling he had earned it well. This was so much that Jerker could afford to buy his own farm, marry the girl he liked, and take the old manservant on as help.

And from then on peace and joy returned to the parish, but not to Lady Skinflint and her daughter, who gradually became poorer and poorer, as they could no longer live by their tricks. As for the bung, this was burned in a big bonfire, and everyone watched to make sure it would never harm them or anyone else in the world ever again.

The Seven Wishes

Alfred Smedberg

I f you had ever seen Olle Niklasson standing by his bundle of firewood in the forest, scratching his fiery, bristly head, you would probably have laughed until you ached. Olle Niklasson looked so different from other boys. He had hair as brown as a juniper bush burnt by the sun, a nose like a potato, and cheeks like two fat mushrooms.

It wouldn't have been so bad if he had simply been ugly, but he was also so lazy he could scarcely bother to stand up again if he fell down, and so foolish he could not tell a squirrel from a crow.

As he ambled about the forest, with his mouth hanging open and his arms hanging down, he might have been taken for a monkey instead of a boy. He was so ugly and so foolish that even the magpies laughed.

Just now, as we said, he was standing in the forest near his bundle of firewood, scratching his head. A seven-year-old child could easily have skipped with that little bunch of twigs, but Olle, who was thirteen years old and strong as a bear, had spent the last hour wondering if he could lift it on his back.

He was standing, fidgeting and fussing, when he saw a viper lying on the ground nearby. The viper was sharply and intently eyeing something small not far away. Olle looked more closely and saw a little frog hopping in starts towards the viper's open mouth. If Olle had not been so foolish, he would have realized that the snake, with its keen eyes, had cast a spell over the frog so that it would hop straight forward, right into the viper's mouth.

"Well, well," said Olle, astonished and wide-eyed. But he was too lazy to pick up a stick and kill the viper. Meantime, the frog hopped closer and closer to the viper's poisonous tongue. Finally, stupid as he was, Olle realized that the frog was terrified. It was trembling all over, and now and then it squeaked faintly. Olle opened his silly eyes wider and stepped nearer.

"Listen, you small short fat thing, don't be so silly. Why don't you run away? Can't you see that the long black one wants to catch you?" It was the longest speech Olle had ever made in all his life, and it was so hard for him to make that he took off his cap and mopped the sweat from his brow.

But the frog kept hopping slowly nearer, until finally it was just one hop away from the snake. The snake never moved its eyes from the frog. The poor little frog was shivering. Then Olle lost his temper and picked up a stick and said, "You stupid little wretch. Do I have to help you?" And with that, he poked the frog with the stick and knocked it aside into the grass, where the snake could not see it.

At once the frog jumped up on to Olle's bundle of firewood, where it sat watching him with beautiful, expressive eyes, as if wishing to thank him.

"Have I got to lift you, too?" Olle said crossly. "Don't you think the firewood is heavy enough already?" But the frog just sat there on the wood gazing at Olle. Its look was so bright, gentle, and friendly that Olle was almost spellbound. Lazy and foolish, he stood there without even the sense to shoo the frog away. Meanwhile, the snake had wriggled off into the grass.

Suddenly the frog laughed, a laugh as clear as silver. It jumped down from the firewood and at that moment became a beautiful fairy girl with rosy cheeks, sky-blue eyes, and curly gold hair.

Olle was so astonished that all he could say was: "Oh."

"Thank you, my friend, for saving my life," the fairy said in a voice as fine as a note from a harp.

"Oh," said Olle again.

"You probably don't realize what you have done for me," said the fairy. "I am not a frog, as you see. I am queen of the fairies. My crystal palace is over there in the small brook that flows through the meadow."

34

"Oh," said Olle, staring at the beautiful little elf.

"You may be wondering," the fairy went on, "why I was a frog just a moment ago, so I will tell you straightaway. Yesterday around noon I committed a great sin. I laughed at a little frog that was hopping towards a big snake which had its mouth open. I did not realize that the snake had charmed the frog so it couldn't escape, and I laughed at it for not jumping away. That was wicked of me, and so I was punished. I was turned into a frog myself for twenty-four hours. There were just ten minutes left when the viper appeared and charmed me, too — put me under a spell. If you had not been there to save me, I would have been swallowed up and dead. Now do you realize what a fine deed you have done?"

"Oh, ho," said Olle, staring harder than ever.

"And now I want to reward you for your goodness," the fairy went on. "I will give you seven wishes, and whatever you wish for will be granted. Only be careful and don't wish foolishly, or you will regret it later. Goodbye."

And with this the fairy floated away through the air towards the path that led to the brook.

"Ho, ho, ho," said Olle, rubbing his elbow. "That was fun. But now, what shall I wish for? Oh, yes, I know. I wish the firewood would run home by itself and carry me on its back."

He had hardly spoken before he was thrown on his stomach across the bundle of firewood. It raced through the forest and sent sticks and twigs, moss and pebbles, flying through the air. Olle was terrified, and had to dig his hands into the branches to hold on. The firewood went like the wind, flying wildly between hillocks and groves. It galloped over stones and tree stumps. Olle was tossed and jerked hither and thither, he lost his cap and his wooden shoes, his face was whipped by bushes and branches, and he himself was bellowing like a cow.

In a few minutes the firewood reached the small croft where Olle lived. It tore through the gate and into the yard. At the threshold, it stopped so abruptly that Olle fell headlong through the door and bumped his head so hard, it gave him a sizeable lump.

"Oh, my," said Olle, getting to his knees.

His mother, who believed the pig had slipped into the croft, came rushing from the kitchen with her broom. Olle could say nothing but "Oh, my," and "Oh, oh," for he was so shaken that he quite forgot about the frog and the snake.

The woman felt so sorry for him that she gave him a bag of almond candy. Now, whenever Olle got hold of something good to eat, he could never stop at enough. So now he sat down on the step and gobbled up all the candy in a wink.

"Yum," he said, licking his lips. "I wish I had a pail full of this candy, and could as eat as much as I wanted."

In a moment, a whole pail of candy was dumped in his lap.

"Oh, my," Olle exclaimed delightedly, and began to grab fistfuls of almond candy from the pail. He ate so much and so quickly it would have made you dizzy to watch him. He stared and chewed and swallowed, then ate some more. He hunched over the pail until, in fifteen minutes, it was empty, and Olle was as fat and round as a sausage.

In a little while Olle was lying on the bed wriggling like an earthworm, with his hands on his stomach, and yelling louder than a pig stuck in a fence.

His mother sent for the doctor, who advised a full bottle of stomach bitters. In an hour, Olle had been so sick that he was as empty as a hunting dog. When he felt well enough to explain what had happened, the wise doctor gave him a sound thrashing with a hazel stick.

A week later Olle's mother sent him out to weed their little carrot patch. Reluctantly Olle went out to do the job, but being lazy, before he began he lay down beside the carrots to rest for a while.

Now it just happened that there was also an enormous cherry tree in the garden, full of the biggest and reddest cherries, but they grew so high up that you could not reach them without climbing the tree. A more sensible boy would have found a ladder to lean against the tree, and that way could be right among the juicy cherries. But Olle was both too silly and too lazy to think of that. So he lay under the tree and got angry with the crows and magpies that flew among the branches, and picked one cherry after another.

"Oh," said Olle, licking his thick lips. "I wish I was sitting up there at the top of the tree."

And just as if a strong wind had lifted him from the ground, in a moment he was flying up into the tree, and there he hung among the topmost branches.

"Oh! Oh!" Olle shouted in delight, and began picking and eating. Now if only he had not been too lazy to close the gate when he entered the garden, everything would have turned out all right. But with the gate open, the pig wandered in and began to scratch its back against the cherry tree. You can imagine what happened next. The tree swayed back and forth with Olle at the top like a magpie on a birch twig in a storm. At last he lost hold and fell down head over heels. Twigs and branches broke as he went, and Olle somersaulted wildly on to the back of the pig.

It is hard to say which if these two cried loudest, Olle or the pig. Certainly, the pig never again dared scratch its back against a cherry tree with a boy in the branches, and for a week Olle went around with cuts on his hands, red scratches on his cheeks, and a swollen nose.

You might suppose Olle would never make a silly wish again, but, like other stupid boys, he didn't remember any of his troubles after they stopped hurting. So it was not more than a few weeks before Olle had another adventure.

On that day, he set out walking to the village. He seldom bothered to walk so far, and when he did, he dragged his feet all the way. He watched a bicyclist pedalling by on the road.

"Oh," said Olle. "I wish I could sit on a bicycle like that and ride all over the countryside."

The very next minute he was astride a bicycle and spurting wildly forward. Where the bicycle had come from, and how Olle got on the seat, he did not know; but he sat there now pedalling and speeding along for all his worth. Olle had never ridden a bicycle before, and he began to shout and yell at the top of his lungs. Nor was the bicycle better behaved, so it raced along frightening both cows and people.

If only the bicycle had kept to the roads, things might have been easier. But the mischievous machine insisted on racing over the countryside, just as Olle had wished, and so it seldom rode on smooth ground.

Olle tried to stop pedalling, but that was quite impossible. Whether he liked it or not, he pedalled, and bumped and jumped along across hills and tufty meadows, through cornfields and potato fields, over fences, ditches, and stone walls. Everywhere people ran from their homes to look at the madly careening cyclist. Olle shouted and thumped, thumped and shouted. "Oh! Oh! Catch me. Stop me!"

The villagers watched angrily as Olle spoiled their crops and ran over their live-stock. He rode pell-mell uncontrollably across corn sheaves and over flower beds, pushed piglets aside, and scared horses so they bolted. Sheep jumped fences, and hens flew cackling on to the roofs of barns.

By now the villagers had come out in force, with sticks and poles, to stop Olle. With the town elders in the lead, farmers and farmhands marched towards Olle in a body. Olle's bicycle lunged towards them like a furious bull, knocked off the sexton's hat, skinned the parish clerk's legs, and gave the richest farmer in the county such a solid poke in the stomach that he tumbled over with his heels in the air.

Olle was so frightened he nearly fainted. He simply could not understand what kind of monster he was riding.

"I wish the wretched thing would break into a hundred pieces," he said.

Immediately the bicycle rolled into a stone wall and was smashed to smithereens. Olle himself somersaulted over the wall and landed in a clump of nettles.

Immediately the villagers rushed forward to beat Olle for the damage he had done. Not only were fields and gardens ravaged, but he had run over and killed three pigs and four hens. But when the farmers saw him looking so frightened and exhausted, they lowered their stick and left him in peace. "Poor lad," they said. "It's a pity. He's so stupid he doesn't know what he's doing. And small wonder, he never even learnt how to read."

Olle limped home, aching all over. He began to think about what the villagers had said. "Is it because I cannot read that I am so stupid?" he wondered. "It would be odd, but perhaps it is the reason I am always getting into trouble. I wish I could read."

Well, if that had been Olle's first wish, he would have acted sensibly and avoided a lot of trouble; for the way the fairy's spell worked, if Olle wished foolishly, he got his wish immediately, but when he wished sensibly, it came to him gradually. So he did not learn how to read wonderfully well at once, but he did get such a burning desire for it that he studied both day and night.

Eventually, Olle could read any book he laid his hands on. And the more he read, the better he understood how foolish he had been, and how lazy, idling away half his life. Now he helped his mother with all kinds of chores, and began to be more dili-gent and industrious.

One day as he was walking in the forest he saw the little fairy queen again. He recognized her immediately, and suddenly remembered his adventure with the frog and the snake, for since he had learnt to read and work, his memory had improved.

"Good day, dear Olle," said the fairy in a mild voice. "You wished foolishly five times, but your sixth wish was a wise one. Now you may have one more wish, but think carefully, for this is the very last one, and after that I will not be able to help you again."

Olle pondered a very long time. Reading and working so much, he had become quite sensible, and that was the reason he was afraid to wish for something silly. He said at last, "I wish to be a good, useful person."

"You couldn't have made a better wish," said the fairy happily. "And therefore I shall grant your wish, but it will come of your own efforts, for what comes other ways isn't worth much. Good-bye!"

The little fairy kept her word. Through study and hard work, Olle became sensible, useful, and good, and everyone like him. And as he became good, he also seemed more handsome, for only the lazy and wicked appear ugly.

Leap the Elk and Little
Princess Cottongrass

Helge Kjellin

Have you ever been in a large forest and seen a strange black tarn hidden deep among the tall trees? It looks bewitched and a little frightening. All is still — fir trees and pines huddle close and silent on all sides. Sometimes the trees bend cautiously and shyly over the water as if they are wondering what may be hidden in the dark depths. There is another forest growing in the water, and it, too, is full of wonder and stillness. Strangest of all, never have the two forests been able to speak to each other.

By the edge of the pool and out in the water are soft tussocks covered with brown bear moss and wooly white cottongrass. All is so quiet — not a sound, not a flutter of life, not a trembling breath — all of nature seems to be holding its breath listening, listening with beating heart: soon, soon.

And then a gentle murmur stirs the crowns of the tall firs, and they lean together and begin to sing softly: *Yes, we have seen him, far, far away, and soon he will be here, he is coming, he is coming.* A murmur sweeps through the forest. Bushes rustle and whisper to each other. The cottongrass blossoms bend and bow back ands forth: *Yes, he is coming, he is coming,* they say, while the still waters begin to murmur: *He is coming, he is coming.* You hear a few twigs breaking far away. They come closer, come together in a solid noise. It grows: there is a crash of snapping bushes, branches, and twigs; a clatter of fast-moving footsteps coming one after another; and you hear a heavy panting. A large elk has thrust itself through the forest to the bank of the pool, where it stops, swings its panting muzzle, and snuffs eagerly. The majestic crown of horns shakes, the elk's nostrils quiver, and then it stands still for a moment. A second later, with gigantic leaps it is off through the swaying tufts, and disappears into the far side of the forest.

That much is true. Now here is a fairy tale about it.

The sun is shining like gold on the meadow of Dream Castle. It is summer, and the grass has a thousand fragrant blossoms. A little girl, rosy and delicate, sits among all the flowers, combing her long, pale yellow hair. It sifts like summer gold through her small fingers. A golden crown is lying in the meadow beside her.

This girl is the princess of Dream Castle, and today she has slipped away from the high, stately chamber where her father, the king, and her mother, the queen, sit on golden chairs, with sceptre and orb, to rule their people. She wishes to be alone and free, and has come to the flowering meadow to play. The meadow has always been her playground.

This princess is small and slim, still a child. She sits there in a gown whiter than white, made of silk and satin and muslin as thin as gauze.

Princess Cottongrass — that is what they call her.

She combs her fair hair with small, thin fingers and smiles at the shining hair strands. An elk snuffs and stalks past. She lifts her eyes.

"Oh, who are you?"

"I am Longled Leap. What do they call you?"

"I am Princess Cottongrass." She lifts the crown from the meadow to show that it is so.

The elk stops to look at the princess long and searchingly, then lowers its head. "You are beautiful, little one."

The princess rises and moves closer. She leans towards the elk's trembling muzzle and strokes it gently. "How big and stately you are. And you have a crown, too. Let me come with you. Let me sit behind your neck, and then carry me out into life."

The elk hesitates. "The world is big and cold, little child, and you are so small. the world is full of evil and wickedness, and it will hurt you."

"No, no. I am young and warm. I have warmth enough for everyone. I am small and good, and want to share the good I have."

"Princess, the forest is dark and the roads are dangerous."

"But you are with me. You are great and strong, and can easily defend us both."

The elk tosses its head and shakes its mighty crown of horns. Its eyes look fiery.

The princess claps her small hands. "Good, good. But you are too tall — bend down so that I can climb up."

Obediently, the elk lies down, and soon the princess is sitting securely on its back. "I am ready, and now you must show me the world."

It rises slowly, afraid of unseating the little one. "Hold on tight to my horns." And it sets off with leaps and bounds.

The princess has never had more fun. There are so many new and beautiful things to see. She has never been beyond the meadow at Dream Castle before, and now they are running over hill and dale, over plains and mountains.

"Where are you taking me?" she asks.

"To Forest Moss," Leap answers. "I live there. No one comes there and it is a long way off."

Evening is coming, and the princess is hungry and sleepy.

"Are you changing your mind already?" teases the elk. "It's too late to turn round. But don't be afraid. Wonderful berries grow in the marsh where I live. You can eat them."

They travel a while, when the forest begins to thin, and the princess looks out over a mile-long marsh, where tufts of sedge come together in soft hollows and hillocks, and where the little stunted bushes on the bank haven't the courage to follow.

"Here we are," says Leap, and bends down so that the princess can dismount. "Now we shall have supper."

Immediately the princess forgets all about sleep and begins to jump lightly from tuft to tuft, just like Leap, to pick the delicious big berries. She and Longleg Leap share them delightedly.

Leap says, "We must hurry on before it gets too dark," and once again Princess Cottongrass climbs on to his broad back. Leap sets off, surefooted, across the marsh, stepping confidently on the tufts as if he knows they will hold him. After all, he was born there.

"Who is that dancing there?" asks the princess.

"They are the elves. But be careful of them. They seem sweet and friendly, but never trust them. Remember what I tell you: don't speak to them, but hold on tight to my horns and pretend you don't notice them."

Yes, the princess promises, she will.

But the elves have already caught sight of them. They come forward and circle around and dance up and down in front of the elk, floating tantalizingly close to the little princess. But remembering what Leap has just told her, she clings to his horns with all her might.

"Who are you, who are you?" ask the elves.

Hundreds of questions are all around, and the princess feels them like the cold breath of the wind, but she does not answer.

Then the tiny elves, in their white veils, become bolder. They tug at her dress and her long yellow hair. Leap snorts and begins to run.

Suddenly the princess realizes that the golden crown on her head is slipping, and she is afraid it will fall off — imagine what Father-king and Mother-queen, who gave it to her, would say — and she forgets what Leap told her and calls to the elves, at the same time letting go one hand to clasp her crown. At that moment the elves have power over her — not altogether, because she still clings to the elk's horns with one hand; but with joyous mocking laughter they snatch the shining crown from her head and float away over the marsh.

"Oh, my crown, my crown," moans Princess Cottongrass.

"Why didn't you obey me?" Leap scolds her. "You have only yourself to blame. Probably you will never get your golden crown back, but you are lucky it was not worse."

Yet the princess cannot imagine anything worse than what has just happened.

Leap walks on, and soon she spies a clump of small trees on an island in the middle of the marsh.

"Here is where I live," says Leap. "This is where we shall sleep."

Soon they are there. The low hill rises above the marsh, and it is dry and delightful among the fir trees and pines.

The princess kisses her dear friend Leap good-night, undresses and hangs her gown neatly on a branch. She lies down and is soon asleep, with the long-legged elk to stand guard over her. It is almost night, and a few small stars are twinkling in the sky.

Next morning the princess is awakened by the soft touch of the elk's muzzle on her forehead. She jumps up quickly, stretches naked in the golden-red morning light, and then collects some dewdrops to drink in her hands. A small chain, with a golden heart on it, is hanging from her neck and catches the sunlight like fire.

"Today I will go bare," she exclaims. "I will carry my dress in front of me and then you will carry me on your back and show me more of the world."

"Yes," says the elk, unable to deny her anything. It had been awake all night watching over the strange, white little girl on the ground, and that morning there had been tears in its eyes. It did not understand why, except it felt autumn approaching and was seized by a longing to do battle and a desire not to be alone anymore.

Suddenly it dashes away into the forest. The fair-haired princess finds it very difficult to hold on. Branches whip her face and shoulders, and the little golden heart dances on its chain.

44

But before long, Leap calms down and slackens his pace. Now they are travelling through a large, strange forest. The long branches of the firs are covered with hanging moss, the tree roots bend like snakes, and large, lichen-covered boulders seem to threaten them from the side of the path. The princess has never seen such a queer place before.

"What is that moving deep in the woods?" she asks. "I think I see long green hair and a pair of white arms waving to me."

"It is the witch of the woods," says Leap. "Answer her politely, but by no means ask her for anything, and whatever you do, hold tight to my horns."

Yes, the princess promises, she will hold on tight.

Now the witch glides closer. She does not want to show herself entirely; she always hides halfway behind a tree. Curiously and slyly she peers at the elk and the girl. The princess scarcely dares look that way, but she can tell that the witch has icy green eyes and a mouth red as blood.

Then the witch begins to slither from tree to tree, following the elk as it runs. She knows Leap well, but is puzzled by the little white one with the golden hair.

Suddenly she calls, "What is your name?"

"I am Princess Cottongrass, of Dream Castle," the girl answers shyly, taking care not to ask the witch's name. Of course, she knows who it is.

"What are you carrying in front of you?" the witch asks.

"It is my finest gown," replies the princess, with a little more courage.

"Oh, let me see it," the witch begs.

Of course she may, and the princess lets go with one hand to show the witch her white dress.

She should never have done so, for in a trice the witch has snatched the dress and disappeared into the forest.

"Why did you let go of my horns?" says Leap. "If you had let go with both hands, you would have had to follow the witch, and probably never have come back."

"But my dress, my dress," sobs Princess Cottongrass.

But after a while she forgets it, and the day passes, and that night the princess sleeps under the fir trees with Leap standing quietly beside her to keep watch.

When she wakes in the morning, the elk is gone. "Leap, Longleg Leap, where are you?" she calls fearfully, and jumps up.

Here he comes, breathing heavily, through the undergrowth. He has been on top of a hill, looking east, sniffing the air, and he has scented something. What? He cannot tell, but his coat is wet and his legs are trembling.

He seems to want to move on, and bends down to let the princess climb on his back. Then they are gone in a rush, galloping east. He hardly hears when she calls to him, and rarely answers. As if in a fever he breaks through the tangled forest at a furious rate.

"Where are we going?" asks Princess Cottongrass.

"To the pool," is the answer. "Deep in the forest is a pool, and that is where I go when autumn is coming. No person has ever been there, but you shall see it."

Abruptly the tree trunks open up, and here is the water, shining brown-black with flecks of greenish gold.

"Hold on tight," Leap warns. "There is danger under the water. Watch your golden heart!"

"Yes. What strange water," says the princess, bending forward to look more closely — but oh, dear, at the moment the chain with the golden heart slips over her head and drops into the pool.

46

"Oh, my heart, the golden heart that my mother gave me the day I was born. Oh, what shall I do?"

She is quite inconsolable. She stares at the water and then begins to wander off over the tussocks to look for her heart.

"Come," says Leap. "It is dangerous for you here. Looking for one thing, you will forget everything else."

But the princess wants to stay. She must find her heart.

"Go, my friend. Let me sit here alone. I know I shall find the heart."

She flings her arms about his bent head, kisses it, and strokes it softly. Then, small and slim and undressed, she goes and sits down on a grassy hillock.

For a long time the elk stands quite still and looks at the small girl. But when she no longer seems to notice that he is there, he turns and disappears with hesitant steps into the forest.

Many years have passed. Still Princess Cottongrass sits and looks wonderingly into the water for her heart. She is no longer a little girl. Instead, a slender plant, crowned with white cotton, stands leaning over the edge of the pool. Now and then the elk returns, stops, and looks at it tenderly. Only he knows that this is the princess from Dream Castle. Perhaps she nods and smiles, for he is an old friend, but she does not want to follow him back; she cannot follow any more, as long as she is under the spell. The spell lies in the pool. Far, far under the water lies a lost heart.

The King's Choice

Anna Wahlenberg

King Helamund was about to set out on a crusade to the Holy Land. So he asked his six councillors to take an oath that, during his absence, they would rule the realm as best they could and that, should he fail to return from the Holy Wars, they would protect his queen and baby son, and hold the throne for the boy. King Helamund, however, had not yet decided which of the six to appoint First Councillor in the land, head of the government. One councillor seemed to him too old, another too young, a third too impetuous, a fourth too dilatory, a fifth too daring, and the sixth too cautious.

One night, as he was deliberating which one to choose, he thought he glimpsed the fold of a woman's dress in the alcove curtains. He sat up in bed and stared as an apparition came slowly towards him.

"Who are you?" he asked in bewilderment.

"I am the fairy of the castle. I have lived in the castle during the reigns of many kings, and I have tried to help them all during their most difficult moments. Most of them have neither seen nor heard me, but you see and hear me. Lay your head on the pillow."

The king's face was fanned softly with a grey veil. A numbness came over him, and he sank down with his eyes closed. A corner of the veil touched his forehead, and he fell asleep and began to dream.

In the dream it seemed to him that he had already set out on the crusade and was far away from the castle, but despite this, he could see everything that was happening in his kingdom. He saw his councillors sitting at the council table. They were quarrelling among themselves and only one of them was detached and quiet, and tried to settle the dispute. Then he saw the six men go down into his treasury and fill their pockets with gold. And again only one of them did not touch the chests, but stood like a guardian before the rest. Then he saw the councillor he had appointed First Councillor of the land ride up with troops of soldiers, announce that King Helamund was dead, and proclaim himself king in his place. King Helamund saw this false king marry his queen and imprison the little prince in a tower, and put in irons the one councillor who had been loyal.

King Helamund was sweating as he dreamt this dream. He wanted to throw himself at his false councillor, and when he awoke, his arms were flailing wildly.

The grey apparition was still standing beside his bed. Quickly the king calmed himself, for he realized that all this was a dream and had not really happened. At the same time, though, he was afraid. Was the strange apparition warning him of what might happen?

And she nodded as if she had read his thoughts. "Yes. By this you see the worth of promises and oaths."

The king clenched his fists in anger. "If only I knew who the First Councillor was, and who the loyal one was," he mumbled. "But I could not see their faces."

"That I cannot tell you," said the fairy of the castle. "But if you do wish to know,

I can help you. Tomorrow, bid your councillors take your golden galley down the river to the jousting grounds on the plain. You yourself ride there through the forest. I will be waiting for you where the river meets the forest."

The fairy waved her veil in farewell and disappeared behind the folds of the alcove curtains.

The next day the king did as he had been told and invited his councillors to sail down the river in his golden galley for a tournament on the plain. He himself rode ahead on horseback, and when he came to the place where the river met the forest, he continued along the shore. He had not been riding long before his horse reared as if frightened. At that moment, the fairy appeared among the tree trunks.

"Tie your horse to that oak," she said, "then come back to me."

Helamund obeyed her. When he returned, the fairy walked towards him, looked at him with her deep-set eyes, and waved her veil gently before his face. She began to sing:

> King so high in all the land
> That equal stands no other,
> Be transformed, assume disguise
> To look a plain woodcutter.

Then the king felt an extraordinary change taking place in him. He grew less tall, but broader and stronger. His shining robes became a poor woodcutter's shirt. His hair and beard hung untrimmed around his face, and in his hand he held an axe instead of a sword.

"What have you done?" he exclaimed, frightened.

"Do not be afraid," she said. "Soon you shall be as before. But now look."

She waved her veil across the grass, and sang:

> Grow little cottage,
> From out of this earth
> A building to serve
> As a poor man's hearth.

And then Helamund saw a small cottage begin to rise from the ground, and in a few moments there stood a miserably small croft with a sagging, moss-covered roof and warped little windows.

"Here is where you will live," said the fairy of the castle. "And in a little while you will have a chance to do your councillors a service. As a reward, ask no more than that in three days, they honour your humble croft by coming to a feasting you are having."

Helamund opened his mouth to question the fairy, but she had already floated away and out over the water, where she melted like a mist.

Soon afterwards, he heard voices and the sound of oars, and saw the golden galley glide into view from behind a point. He was standing there watching it, and listening to his councillors chatting happily, when a sudden windstorm drove across the surface of the water and tossed the galley back and forth so wildly, it looked as if it would flounder.

Without a moment's hesitation, Helamund threw himself into the river, swam towards the galley, boarded it, took the oars from the rowers, and managed to steer the sinking galley to safety.

52

With the fear of death on their faces, the six councillors stepped ashore and thanked the woodcutter. They offered to reward him lavishly: whatever he wanted, let him only mention it and they would grant his wish.

Helamund remembered the words of the fairy. He took off his cap and bowed. "Noble gentlemen," he said. "I am a humble and lowly man, and I don't know if I dare to ask, but in three days there will be a feasting in my cottage among my friends and neighbours. If you could come to my croft then, it would be the greatest honour I could imagine."

The councillors burst out laughing. "Is that all?" they asked.

"Yes, noble gentlemen." Once more Helamund bowed, and invited them all to come to the feasting two hours before sunset.

The councillors were still laughing. They found this woodcutter both silly and naive, but one after another offered his hand and promised to appear at the croft three days later. Then they wrung out their wet clothes, stepped aboard the boat, which the oarsmen had been bailing out, and continued on calmly down the river.

As soon as they were out of sight, Helamund was freed of his woodcutter's clothing, and stood there once more, a tall and distinguished monarch. He went to his horse, jumped in the saddle, and galloped to the jousting field, where he arrived long before the councillors. When they came, they did not say a word about their adventure: they found it humiliating not to have been able to brave the sudden windstorm themselves, and to have had to ask help from a woodcutter. Since they did not mention the adventure, the king also kept silent.

Helamund did not see the fairy for two days, but during the second night he was awakened by someone calling his name. When he opened his eyes, he saw the grey veil again beside his bed.

"Tomorrow, King Helamund, you must hold a great banquet here," said the fairy. "Invite all your noble knights and ladies, and ask your six councillors as well."

"But they have promised to go to the woodcutter in the forest," said the king.

"That is just my reason," said the fairy, and in the next moment she was gone.

Helamund sat wondering, until he understood. The next morning he issued invitations to a banquet, to begin two hours before sunset.

When the time came, the great hall in the castle was filled with noble gentlemen, brave knights, and beautiful ladies. The king entered, accompanied by the queen and the small prince. The king's eyes scanned the assembly eagerly. He was looking for his councillors. And, quite right, there they were. They drew up in a line and saluted him humbly. They had not gone to the woodcutter's cottage.

But when he counted them, he noted that one of the six was missing. It was Ismaril, the one he thought was too young to be First Councillor.

"I do not see the noble councillor Ismaril," said the king.

The steward of the household approached. "Your Majesty, the noble councillor Ismaril sends word that he cannot attend because he has already accepted an invitation elsewhere."

The king drew himself up and frowned as if he were very angry. "And does anyone know what highborn person's company Ismaril prefers to that of his king?"

The five councillors looked questioningly at each other, as if they did not know what to do. However, being secretly jealous of Ismaril, they did not want to miss an opportunity of throwing him deeper into disgrace. So they went to the king, told him of their adventure with the galley, and of the woodcutter, and of the absurd feasting they had promised to attend. Then they all bowed at once.

The king called several servants to him. "Go out into the forest near the river," he commanded. "Find Councillor Ismaril and bring him to me immediately."

The servants left and the banquet began. No more than an hour had passed when they returned with the missing councillor, whom they had found wandering in the forest vainly attempting to find the woodcutter's croft. Ismaril held his head high and his back straight, and with a fearless look, walked up the great hall to the king, who sat quietly observing him.

"So," said the king. "You disdain my banquet for supper with a woodcutter."

Ismaril looked him straight in the eye. "I had promised it," he said.

The king was silent for a moment.

"Then you hold the invitation of a common woodcutter more than your King's summons."

"I had promised," the councillor said.

The king raised his head. "Do you mean that a promise to the lowliest of my subjects is more to you than my own grace and favour?"

Ismaril also raised his head. "Yes."

The king rose. "What punishment does he deserve?" he asked the company.

But the guests only mumbled and whispered among themselves, averting their eyes.

"You do not answer," said the king. "Then I shall give him the punishment I myself believe he deserves."

He stepped from the throne, walked towards Ismaril, and embraced him tenderly. Then he picked up the little prince and placed him in his councillor's arms.

"Herewith I appoint you, Ismaril, First Councillor of the realm. Having found one who values his word to the most lowly above all graces and gifts, I know I can safely place in his hands my land, my life, and that which is most precious to me."

The Four Big Trolls and Little Peter Pastureman

Cyrus Granér

All this happened long, long ago, when there were only trolls in the dark mountains and the big dusky forests. Each crevice had its old troll living in a cave or hollow under the snakelike roots of the giant trees. Some trolls lived alone; others had a wife and child. There were big trolls and little trolls, and naturally the big trolls thought they were superior to the little trolls.

The four biggest trolls counted themselves most important of all: Bull-Bull-Bulsery-Bull, who lived in the north; Drull-Drull-Drulsery-Drull, who had settled in the east; Klampe-Lampe from the south; and Trampe-Rampe, who liked wandering but said his home was in the west.

Many long miles separated the trolls from each other, but given the way trolls can walk, it wasn't as far to them. Twelve miles to a step was nothing for a big troll, and in half a day any of them could visit the others. Their paths did not cross often, however, because they did not get along very well together. Each wanted to be the most important big troll, and looked down upon the others.

Bull-Bull-Bulsery-Bull lived in Bunner Mountain, and he was as cosy there as a troll could wish. Just in front of his mountain was a lake, big enough for a bathing pool and a fishpond. He was very proud of his lake, Bull was, for he had made it himself. One day he had thrown a strong troll rope around an acre of land, harnessed up his two troll oxen, and pulled the land away. Then he arranged with old Whitebeard, who was master of Snowfall Mountain, to supply him with water all the year round. And old Whitebeard filled his lake with water clear as crystal and cool as the morning wind on High Mountain.

Drull lived well, too. His den was in Steep Mountain, splendid in a thousand ways. He had big deep chambers in there, and on top he had placed a large boulder. From here he could stand and look out over the still, dreamlike, mighty forests.

Klampe-Lampe had dug himself a large hole under seven immense spruce trees. It was warm and pleasant there, and most of the time Klampe-Lampe stayed at home guarding the thousand-year-old fire on his hearth.

Trampe-Rampe was seldom so still. He ranged far and wide over the mountains and would go racing by when you least expected to see him. You would hear his storm song, then the next moment he was sweeping by with a Hi and a Ho.

The little trolls were so numerous it was quite impossible to keep track of them. And yet we must not forget to mention little Peter Pastureman.

Peter Pastureman was small even next to a little troll, and he hardly reached the waist of a big one, but he was a real thunderclap of a boy. He worked for the four biggest trolls: he drove Bull's oxen and herded Drull's goats, caught Klampe's unruly rams, and rode Trampe's fast horses. None of this was easy to do, yet Peter Pastureman never wanted to be more than a farmhand. He had a birchbark horn and a reed whistle to blow on, and they resounded over bog and forest, and he was gay and merry, rain or shine.

We must also remember an old troll witch, who was wiser than anyone under the stars. Whenever the trolls wanted to do anything important, and were not sure how to go about it, they always asked her advice. Her name was Uggle-Guggle, and she lived in an old cottage in the densest part of the wild forest.

Now, as we said, the big trolls were not friends, and if any one of them could play a trick on another, he was delighted. He would go about chuckling to himself, thinking it wonderful to be so shrewd and cunning, until the other had found a way to trick him in turn, whereupon his joy turned to anger and he hissed like nineteen north winds.

Peace, more or less, had reigned for a while among the four big trolls when something happened to make them even worse enemies than ever.

One day their king, their good old troll king in Seven Mile Mountain, king of all the world's trolls and tomtes, entered the dark gorge in Black Mountain, and its door closed behind him forever. Never again would they be able to look at him, never touch his hand, never hear wise and beautiful words from his lips. He had ruled for three thousand years, and had been revered as no troll king ever was before. But now the trolls had to find a new king.

There were many who would have liked nothing better than to be his successor. It was finer than sun and moon to be king of all the big and little trolls, and tomtes and sprites; to live in Seven Mile Mountain, which had seven hundred magnificent halls and chambers; to own all those oxen with gilded horns, goats with silver hair, horses with golden manes, and so many other wonderful things. So now the four big trolls dreamt day and night about becoming king.

Bull believed he was cut out to be a king. Drull knew none could deserve the honour more than he. Klampe-Lampe let it be known that he would be the most logical choice even if you scoured the troll world five hundred times. While Trampe-Rampe would have been willing to wager his big nose that, as king, he could surpass all before him.

These days, when they met, the four biggest trolls would not even look at one another. Each was so furious with the rest, he would have liked to grind them to powder, for each imagined that, but for the other three, *he* would naturally become the new king. The longer the troll council debated whom to choose, the angrier the four became and the harder they considered how to win the throne in Seven Mile Mountain.

The big day arrived, and the troll council still had not come to a decision. They all went home and thought for seven more days, but it didn't help. They thought about it for seven days longer and still could not decide. So they had to go to Uggle-Guggle, the troll witch who was wiser than anyone under the stars, and ask her advice.

When Bull learned of this, he thought it would be sensible to be in the old woman's good graces, and decided to pay her a call. With his walking stick in hand, he took the road that led to the densest part of the wild forest. He walked along carefully, keeping an eye open, for naturally he did not want anyone to know what he was doing. At last he arrived at the cottage and knocked on the door.

The old witch received him. "A distinguished visitor," she said.

"Yes," said Bull. "I was passing through the neighbourhood and wanted to see how you were getting on all on your own here."

They began to talk and finally Bull brought up the subject of being king. "Help me in this," he said, "you who are wiser than anyone under the stars, and I shall give you the best golden cow in Seven Mile Mountain, as sure as my name is Bull."

At that moment there came a heavy knock on the door.

"Oh, dear, Mother Uggle-Guggle," cried Bull, "you must hide me, for no one must know I have been here."

The old woman pushed him up to the attic, and then went to open the door.

It was Drull. He had had exactly the same idea as Bull.

"A distinguished visitor," said the witch.

"Yes, indeed," said Drull. "I was just passing by and thought it would be nice to see if you were well, old Mother."

They talked of this and that, and at last Drull brought up what was on his mind. "Help me to Seven Mile Mountain," he said, "and you shall receive the best golden cow there is, as sure as my name is Drull."

But matters turned out no better for Drull than for Bull. Before the witch had time to answer, a loud clap sounded on the door. Someone else wanted to come in.

Drull, frightened at being discovered, begged the witch to hide him. The old woman lifted the cellar door and down he crept. Then she went to open the cottage door.

This time it was Klampe-Lampe who had also had the idea of talking to Uggle-Guggle, and was delighted with himself for being so cunning.

"A distinguished visitor," said the witch.

"Yes," said Klampe-Lampe. "The weather was so fine that I thought I would take a little stroll around the countryside, and when I passed I thought it would be nice to call and see how you were these days, dear Mother."

Then he talked for a while about different things, of this and that, and at last he offered, "If you will help me to the throne in Seven Mile Mountain, I shall give you its biggest and most magnificent cow to keep forever."

But Klampe-Lampe learned no more than Bull or Drull about what the witch thought of his offer, for once again the door shook with a heavy knock.

"I must hide," cried Klampe-Lampe. "You realize what it would mean if anyone saw me here!"

The old witch pushed him into her large empty oven and shut the door with a mighty bang.

"I wonder if perhaps it isn't Trampe-Rampe thundering out there," mumbled Uggle-Guggle to herself. "Wouldn't it be strange if he, too, had decided to look in on me just now?"

It *was* Trampe-Rampe.

"A distinguished visitor," said the witch.

"Yes," said Trampe-Rampe. "I have been out on a long walk again, and was beginning to feel tired and wanted a rest a while before I set off again. But since I am here,
I will mention a certain matter which is very important, and get your advice — you
who are wiser than anyone under the stars."

So Bulsery-Bull, Drulsery-Drull, and Klampe-Lampe had to lie there and listen
to Trampe-Rampe make up to the old crone and promise her gold and a life of
splendour if only she would put in a good word for him.

How strange! He did not receive his advice either, for just then came a fresh
banging at the door. Eager voices were heard outside. Messengers from the troll people had come to consult the witch. By the time they entered, Trampe-Rampe had

disappeared; Uggle-Guggle had hidden him out in a shed in the back, and there he waited until the coast was clear.

The messengers explained to the witch why they had come. "As you know," they said, "our good old troll king is gone. And now all the big and small trolls and tomtes and goblins and sprites in the world need a new king. The throne is waiting for him in Seven Mile Mountain. But we don't know whom to choose, so we ask your help. Who shall be king of the trolls and lord of Seven Mile Mountain?"

Uggle-Guggle, the witch in the wild forest who was wiser than anyone under the stars, hesitated with her answer. She sat down in a dark corner of her cottage, opened her big book of wisdom, put glasses on her nose, and began to mumble some very mysterious words. No one dared interrupt her, and a few minutes of solemn silence passed, broken only by the old crone's murmurs.

At last she rose. All were eagerly awaiting what she would say — all the messengers in the cottage, Bull up in the attic, Drull in the cellar, Klampe-Lampe in the oven, and Trampe-Rampe out in the shed. They pricked up their ears so as not to miss a word.

"So speaks Uggle-Guggle," she began, "and this I have read in the book of wisdom. What I know I know, and what I know is my secret. Many have turned their eyes to the throne on Seven Mile Mountain, and many would like to be king of the trolls. One is up there, and one is down there, one is in there and one is out there, and there are still other ones, too, big and small, trolls and tomtes. Still, what I know I know, and what I know is my secret, and no one will become lord and master of big and small trolls, of tomtes and sprites and goblins, who cannot always keep his head. The throne in Seven Mile Mountain will be occupied in seven days by a new king."

And with this the messengers had to be content. Everyone — big and small trolls, tomtes, and goblins — wondered who it was who could always keep his head.

The four big trolls were not having a pleasant time in their hiding places. In the oven, Klampe-Lampe's legs fell asleep, he was so terribly uncomfortable, but he did not dare even wiggle a toe. Once he took a deep breath — otherwise he would have suffocated — and some flour tickled his nose. He thought he was going to have to sneeze. He fought it as hard as he could, pinching his nose with his fingers.

In the attic, Bull, too, was suffering. The floorboards squeaked at the slightest step, and he feared that any minute they would break under his great weight. Drull, in the dark cellar, had bumped against the barrels and buttertubs, and now he did not dare move lest they tumble down and everyone hear. The only one who was still feeling light-hearted was Trampe-Rampe. He did not know the other big trolls were there, and so clumped in gaily through the back door to talk again to the witch and try to get more information from her.

But just then Klampe-Lampe found it impossible to hold back his sneeze any longer. Had you offered him all the treasure in Seven Mile Mountain and the troll kingdom to boot, he would still have sneezed. He simply had to. So he sneezed as if he had a giant trumpet at his nose. He also kicked out with both legs, and they were not so asleep that they did not push open the oven door, and out he came.

The excitement was tremendous. Already frightened by the blast from Klampe-Lampe's nose, both Bull and Drull completely lost their heads. Bull leapt in the air and the floorboards gave way, and he crashed downstairs into the arms of Trampe-Rampe. Drull, too, jumped, and the barrels and buttertubs boomed and clattered around him. Fearing the cottage itself was tumbling down, he flung open the cellar door and raced upstairs.

So there they stood, all four, and gaped at each other with something less than mild-ness in their eyes. None of them said a word, but slunk home as fast as they could go.

There they sat down to think. They understood that they were getting in each other's way, and that it was hard not to. And that no one would become king of the trolls in Seven Mile Mountain unless he could always keep his head. That was what the crone Uggle-Guggle had said. But to each one the most important thing seemed to be how he could get rid of the other three competitors.

Over at Steep Mountain, Drulsery-Drull paced his chamber like a caged bear, and thought and thought. Finally he climbed up on his big boulder to look around and caught sight of Bull, who was pulling a net from his fishpond. Drull was so angry that he lost his head again. He grabbed his boulder with his two great hands and threw it with all his might towards Bunner Mountain to put an end to his rival with one blow. "I'll show you, you Bunner Mountain fool," he muttered between his teeth.

The boulder flew through the air, and not a bad shot at that. It missed the troll but it did land in the fishpond with a splash that echoed seventeen miles around and was heard underground, too. All the water spilled out as if it wished to escape; it thundered, roared, and boomed out, swallowing everything in its way. It spread and spread until the whole valley, where thousands of trolls and tomtes lived, was in danger of being flooded. The trolls and tomtes were beside themselves with fear, and rushed out to see what had happened. Bull scratched his head and stamped his foot in anger; his splendid bathing pool and fishpond had been ruined, but there was nothing he could do about it. Again everyone lost their heads.

The danger was at its greatest when Peter Pastureman came strolling along the road driving Bull's oxen back from pasture. He realized in a second what had happened, and in the next second knew exactly what was to be done. He told all the trolls to go home and get spades and pickaxes, and then dig a ditch to release the water. A thousand troll arms soon accomplished it, and the floodwaters poured into the ditch and soon were flowing harmlessly out to sea.

"No one else would ever have thought of that," said the trolls. "He is a real thunderclap of a boy, our Pastureman, even if he is so small."

By now, however, Bulsery-Bull had discovered who had played the trick on him. He had recognized the boulder. That boulder he had last seen perched high on Drull's mountain.

"You will pay for this, you Steep Mountain fool," he snorted, and he found himself a boulder even bigger than Drull's. He flung it furiously and watched with wicked joy as it curved through the air. It landed so hard on Steep Mountain that it started a landslide on one slope, and the rest of the mountain nearly followed it.

Drull barely escaped with his life, and now sat among the ruins of his home not knowing what to do. It was terribly cold in there. All the icy winds of the slopes were playing hide-and-seek through the thousand cracks and holes that had been opened by the landslide. In addition, Drulsery-Drull had a toothache. It was not just a little toothache, but one such as no troll had ever had since trolls began. Poor Drull began

64

to howl like eleven hundred wolves until trolls for miles around hurried over to find out what was the matter. But Drull would not tell them; he only cried and yelled and kicked. They begged him to be quiet, but in vain. That night no one within fifty miles slept a wink.

The next morning Peter Pastureman went to Steep Mountain to take Drull's goats to graze. When he saw what was the matter, he took his scissors, sheared the whole herd, and wrapped some of the soft, fine hair around Drull's head, so the ache went away. Then with the rest of the hair he filled the cracks and crevices in the mountain so that the winds stayed outside. When all this was done, he blew a jolly tune on his reed pipe and led the goats, leaping and jumping in their shorn coats, up to their mountain pasture.

"Drull would never have thought of that," said the trolls. "And none of us, either. But Peter Pastureman always knows what to do, one way or another."

Peace had hardly been restored before the trolls heard loud shouts from the south, and saw enormous clouds of smoke billowing up. This time it was Trampe-Rampe, up to his tricks. He had been wandering about as usual when he caught sight of Klampe-Lampe hauling logs for his thousand-year-old fire. He remembered the unlucky sneeze in the witch's cottage, and his anger got the better of him. He decided to pay back Klampe-Lampe. He knew that the fire that was always burning was Klampe-Lampe's dearest possession, and so he was going to extinguish it for good. He approached the fire and blew with all the breath in his lungs, but things did not turn out quite as he had hoped.

The fire began to burn more fiercely and so he blew a second time, even harder than before, so hard that all the sparks and burning logs were blown from the hearth, and the whole forest caught fire. The blaze spread as if it had wings, and every moment the danger increased.

All the trolls rushed towards the fire and ran here and there, scared out of their wits. Klampe-Lampe himself scampered off in a panic. But look, once again Peter Pastureman came to the rescue.

Peter Pastureman was grazing Klampe-Lampe's big herd not far off when he saw smoke. He went to look, then like a whirlwind turned back again, gathered his very best horses, harnessed them to a giant plough, and ploughed a wide furrow all around the burning part of the forest — so wide that the fire could not jump it. And so the fire burnt itself out, and the rest of the forest was saved.

Everyone, big and little trolls, tomtes and goblins, went to shake Peter Pastureman's hand. "A real thunderclap of a boy you are," they shouted. "Who else would have thought of that?"

Peter Pastureman patted the horses, blew a gay tune on his birchbark horn, and took the herd back to graze again.

It was not long before Klampe-Lampe discovered who had tricked him. Trampe-

Rampe had been seen running away. Now Klampe-Lampe could think only of revenge. He went to High Mountain, where he knew Trampe-Rampe often passed, and where they met almost immediately. They attacked each other with thunder and noise until High Mountain shook from top to bottom, and the earth trembled. The trolls ran from their caves and caverns, believing the world was cracking open. And what a terrible sight — to see two of the biggest trolls slugging away at each other like savage forest wolves! They rolled around like great balls, kicking up stones and tree roots, and spitting and hissing like dragons. What possessed the old trolls? Not even a king in Seven Mile Mountain could have stopped them.

Attempts to separate them were in vain. An old man and woman who lived in a big gorge on High Mountain, were the most troubled of all. They were used to the wild roaring of the winter winds that fought on the mountainside, but never to a tumult such as this. The old man shouted to them to spare his mountain, but Klampe-Lampe and Trampe-Rampe, in the thick of the fight, neither heard nor cared. They fought all that day and the next, too, without a moment's pause and without either of them winning or losing. How long the fight might have gone on is difficult to say, had not Peter Pastureman come along and found a way to end it.

Peter hurried away to old Whitebeard of Snowfall Mountain and whispered in his ear, his eyes shining with mischief.

The old man nodded, and Peter left with a big bundle under his arm. It was Whitebeard's biggest troll sack, it contained a million times a million snowflakes, and it was used only once every hundred years.

Peter Pastureman came to High Mountain and untied the bundle. At once, the snowflakes, delighted to be free, whirled out into the eyes of Klampe-Lampe and Trampe-Rampe, who were still rolling around, hitting each other. Snowflakes came in hundreds and hundreds, in thousands and thousands. Soon the two trolls were blinded. They could not see a thing, their eyes were covered with snowflakes, and they had to stop fighting. They had been so preoccupied that they had not noticed a great crowd of spectators gathering. As they emerged from the clouds of snow, they looked around, shamefaced. Both Klampe-Lampe and Trampe-Rampe knew their reputation was in shreds, and without a word they ran away and hid.

The old man and woman of High Mountain took Peter Pastureman's hand and thanked him. "Little Pastureman," they said, "you have more sense than anyone north or south, east or west. You have helped us out of many dangers, and you certainly do keep your head."

A murmur went through the crowd of trolls. That was exactly what Uggle-Guggle had said, she who was wiser than anyone under the stars: "No one will become the king of the trolls and master of Seven Mile Mountain and lord of the big and small trolls, tomtes, and goblins who cannot always keep his head."

Had seven days passed since the troll messengers visited the cottage in the densest part of the wild forest? The days were carefully counted, and it was so.

Once again High Mountain was in an uproar, but this time it was a happy noise. Little Peter was hoisted on the shoulders of the crowd in triumph, and a long row of dancing, singing trolls wove down to Seven Mile Mountain, where Peter was solemnly placed on the throne. Thousands and thousands of trolls proclaimed him king over mountain and valley, forest and lake.

Thus Peter Pastureman became king of all the trolls. He lived a long and happy life, and it was said of him, "Our king always keeps his head."

And to this day, the water from Bulsery-Bull's lake flows down that mountainside and around the stone that Drulsery-Drull threw in anger. Even today there is a river all the way to the sea where the trolls dug their ditch. Steep Mountain still looks lop-sided from the boulder that split it. And hardly a bush grows where Klampe-Lampe's fire burned the forest, while on the top of High Mountain the snow from White-beard's troll sack never melts.

The Troll Ride

Anna Wahlenberg

Peder Lars, the young son of a farmer, came riding along the highway. His heart was gay. He was bound for the city to buy a new jacket because that evening he was going a-courting and wanted to look his best. And he felt rather sure that he would not be turned down. However proud and rich Lisa was, and even though Peder Lars was the poorest of all her admirers, she had looked at him kindly. His spokeman had extracted a promise that he and his father might come to her at six that afternoon to state their intentions.

Peder Lars rode across fields through a long deep forest, then he emerged from the forest on to a green meadow. Suddenly he saw something that seemed to be moving in a ditch. He drew nearer, and realized it was a strange-looking woman, crawling along.

She lifted her head and stared at him. He had never before seen anything as ugly and evil-looking as her face. Her small peppercorn eyes were almost hidden in matted hair. Her nose looked like a carrot, and her lips were brown as bread crust.

"Will you do me a good turn?" she asked. "I shall reward you for your trouble."

"What is it?" asked Peder Lars.

The woman said that she had hurt her leg wandering in the forest and had limped this far because in the next wood, near a path that climbed a hill, there grew seven pine trees. A little resin from each of these pines rubbed into her wound would make the pain go away immediately. But before she got very far from the forest she had collapsed, and so was lying here helpless in the ditch. She badly needed someone to collect resin from the wood for her. She would see that he was well rewarded for his trouble. Already, five people had accepted a gold coin for saying they would help, but they had probably enjoyed themselves with the money and taken another road home, because she had not seen any of them again, although she had been lying in the ditch since early morning. She held up a brightly shining gold coin before Peder Lars and said she would give it to him if he would fetch the resin.

Peder Lars stepped back. "Who are you that look so evil and have so many gold coins?"

She moaned, and rubbed her leg. "Oh, how it hurts! And my mother is walking in the forest looking for me, and calling me. Listen, can you hear?"

"No, I don't hear anything," said Peder Lars. But then the woman grabbed the mane of his horse, pulled herself up, and put her hand like a trumpet to his ear. Now he heard someone singing deep in the forest:

Where are you, daughter, sweet and fair?
I'm looking for you everywhere.

Peder Lars could not help laughing, because he did not think that "sweet and fair" really suited the ugly one by his side. "Sweet and fair," he repeated, chuckling.

The woman sank rapidly back into the ditch again. But she kept her head over the edge, and her small peppercorn eyes shot fiery glances.

"You laugh like all the rest," she hissed, "and hate me! But I will give you money, as much money as you want, if only you will get me that pine resin." And she rattled the gold coins in her fist.

Peder Lars stared at her. Then he knocked her hand so that all the gold coins fell into the ditch.

"No, thank you," he said. "You are a troll, and I don't want to have anything to do with a troll." And he cracked his whip and continued his journey.

He rode into the city, bought himself a gay jacket, and turned homewards again. When he came to the hill that the woman had mentioned, he could not help looking around for the seven pine trees. There they stood in a row, murmuring softly. At that moment he heard someone singing far, far away:

Where are you, daughter, sweet and fair?
I'm looking for you everywhere.

He looked up the pine trunks to see if there really was any resin to be found. But it would have been impossible to find it without looking carefully, now that the afternoon light was fading.

No, I must hurry, he thought, or I'll reach Lisa late, and that might cost me dearly, proud and particular as she is. And so he rode on.

He had gone only a little farther when his horse stopped by itself and pricked up its ears, listening. Once again he heard the song:

Where are you, daughter, sweet and fair?
I'm looking for you everywhere.

If only I had time to gather some of that resin, he thought, and turned around. But after a minute he changed his mind. "It's madness," he said to himself. "What do I care about an ugly old troll woman?" And so he turned homewards again.

It did not take long before the horse stopped again and once more he heard the song:

Where are you, daughter, sweet and fair?
I'm looking for you everywhere.

I can't bear it, thought Peder Lars. If I don't get the resin, I'm afraid I will never stop hearing that song. And so he galloped back to the pine trees.

He examined the trunks and branches, and did at last succeed in gathering resin from each of the seven trees. By now it was almost dark, and he began to gallop along the road. He came to the ditch and saw the troll woman still sitting there.

"Here you are, you ugly old hag," he shouted, throwing the resin into her lap. "And I hope I never see you again, for you have probably cost me my sweetheart's hand."

He spurred his horse on without waiting to hear whether she would thank him or not. He was angry and anxious, sure that he would be too late. And then what would Lisa's father say? Peder Lars knew he wasn't too happy to have a pauper for a son-in-law. And Lisa herself? Her pride might be hurt.

Suddenly he heard the tramp of horses' hooves nearby, and from round a bend in the road a rider approached him. It was his brother. He looked a sight, and his horse was all in a lather.

"You'll be late, you'll be late!" his brother called. And as the two of them galloped on together, he told Peder Lars that he and their old father and the spokesman had been waiting by Lisa's farm-gate for Peder Lars to come, when suddenly the rich miller Jonas, who owned half the village, had pulled up in his carriage. He, too, was going to ask for the beautiful Lisa's hand. When miller Jonas heard that Peder Lars was expected at six o'clock, he was not at all dismayed. If Peder Lars was turned down, he said, then he was ready to take his place. And so there he sat now, waiting. By the time Peder Lars and his brother met on the road it was a quarter to six and they had several miles to go.

"Good-bye," Peder Lars called, urging his horse to the utmost and streaking along the forest path at breakneck speed. It was so dark that he could hardly see the road before him. Branches tore at his handsome new jacket, and scratched his forehead until it bled, but he paid no attention. All Peder Lars could think of was that the beautiful Lisa might give her hand to the rich miller Jonas so as to punish him for being late. That was what you got for having anything to do with trolls.

Soon his horse began to pant and stumble and trip, and Peder Lars was afraid it might collapse under him. The horse went slower and slower, no matter how he urged it forward.

Then he felt the reins stiffen and go taut in his hands. The horse lifted its head, and its hooves began to fly over the ground. Something seemed to have brought it back to life, and it went so fast that Peder Lars' cape was billowing behind.

Peder Lars turned round in the saddle. It seemed to him that someone was sitting behind him on the horse's back. No one was there, though, and yet he imagined he saw what looked like a grey bundle slip down over the horse's rump.

The ride became wilder and wilder. Peder Lars no longer felt in control of the reins; now the horse no longer followed the road, but turned in among bushes and undergrowth. It jumped hillocks and streams, and every time Peder Lars cast a look behind, he dimly glimpsed a grey bundle sliding farther back on the horse. And every time he looked ahead, he felt more and more sure that someone was sitting behind him.

They had reached open fields now, and the cape was flying straight up over his head, stretched as trim as a sail. The horse flew like a bird and its hooves barely touched ground. At the first fork in the road, Peder Lars met his spokesman, who had run out to find him and urge him to hurry.

"You are too late, Peder Lars!" shouted the spokesman. "Only five minutes are left."

72

"We'll see," Peder Lars called, and was gone in a wink.

A little further on he met his old father, who shook his head sadly. "You will never get there. You have only a minute left."

"We'll see," Peder Lars called, and disappeared so fast that the old man did not even see him go.

At the farmer's house everyone was waiting. Beautiful Lisa, her arm leaning on the window-sill, was listening for the beat of hooves, while her father and the miller rubbed their hands contentedly.

"Now," said her father looking at the clock on the wall. "There is only half a minute to go. And if he were going to come on time, we would have heard his horse on the bridge by now. Lisa, you may as well give the miller your hand right away, for you would never be satisfied with a suitor who kept you waiting."

"I will wait until six o'clock," Lisa said. She stood there with beating heart. For though she was so proud that she would rather have made herself unhappy for the rest of her life than be kept waiting a single second by a suitor, it would be desperately hard to lose Peder Lars.

The clock began to chime.

"Too late!" cried the miller.

The strong beat of hooves was heard on the bridge just then, and Lisa's eyes shone with joy.

"Listen, he is coming!" she exclaimed.

"Too late, though," said her father.

But just as the clock was ready to chime for the sixth time, the door was flung open and there stood Peder Lars, dripping wet, his hair tousled, and his new jacked dusty and torn. Somehow he looked jaunty and dashing all the same. Lisa ran to him and put her hand in his, so firmly and confidently that he knew she was giving it to him for life.

The miller and the farmer could only gape. They could not understand how Peder Lars had managed to arrive on time, and no one else understood either.

But this was not the last time people would marvel at Peder Lars. From then on, regardless of how late he set out on any journey, he would always arrive on time, and no one ever saw him anxious to get started. Whether he rode on horseback or in a carriage, he was calm and assured. And he could well afford to be, for he always felt he had someone with him, someone who held the bridle and reins in such a way that all his adventures always finished well. But who this was he never could discover, no matter how many times he thought he glimpsed a grey bundle slip down the rump of his horse or off the edge of his carriage the moment he turned his head. Yet inside himself Peder Lars knew who it was that sat behind him.

He had not asked any reward for what he had done for the troll in the ditch, but for all that, it had been an honest troll, and a reward he certainly did receive.

The Trolls and the Youngest Tomte

Alfred Smedberg

In a storehouse on a small farm at the edge of a woods lived three tomtes: Tjarfa, Torgus, and Tjovik. They were only about ten inches tall and were of an old tomte family that had lived on the farm for more than nine hundred years. The farm had changed owners many times. Old people had gone away and new ones had come, but the tomte family had faithfully remained, and the honour of being the tomte who looked after the farm passed from father to son.

Now it was Christmas Eve, and a feast was being held in the shed that was the storehouse. Old grandfather tomte, Tjarfa Jorikson, had his five-hundredth birthday on Christmas Eve, so his birthday and Christmas were to be celebrated together this year. Grandfather Tjarfa was brisk and active despite his age, and had recently handed down his authority to Torgus Tjarfson, who was three hundred years old and in the prime of life. The old one had retired, and lived between a couple of flour barrels in a corner of the shed.

The youngest tomte, Tjovik Torgusson, was a boy of only one hundred years. He did not even have a tomte beard yet, and he scarcely reached his father's shoulder.

The little shed was situated prettily between hilly pastureland with beautiful leafy trees and a dense, dark forest.

In the forest was steep, craggy Fozhall Mountain. Two trolls, Jompa and Skimpa, lived there. Jompa was troll king of the mountain and Skimpa was his wife. They had lived there long before people came to the region, and were four thousand years old.

The tomtes and the trolls had always been bitter enemies. The trolls were large, strong, evil, and stupid; the tomtes were as small as dolls, but kind and very intelligent. The trolls wanted to hurt the people on the farm, which is why tomte tomtes hated them. They were always fighting. Sometimes the tomtes won, sometimes the trolls. It could not be otherwise, since it was a battle between strength and intelligence.

Be that as it may, a party was being held in the storehouse. All the tomtes in the region had been invited, and they were all in high spirits. The storehouse was well stocked with apples, loaves of wort bread, ham, and sausage, all spread out on a small table that was really an upturned sugar-box. The farm people knew well that the tomtes were careful with all things, never wasting so much as a spoonful of flour.

"Now, Grandfather, tell us stories about Skimpa and Jompa," said Tjovik, climbing up into the old tomte's lap and stroking his long white beard.

"Well, my son," said the old tomte happily. "Sit still and you shall hear about how it used to be."

All the tomtes made themselves comfortable. Some lay on the floor, hands under chins; others sat and dangled their legs from anchovy tins.

Old Tjarfa began: "I shall tell how it was eight hundred years ago, when my grandfather Tarja Torgusson was in his prime, and of the things that happened up there on Foxhall Mountain. Christianity had just been introduced into the country, and the Christians had begun to build their church out there on the plain. The trolls would not stand for that, naturally, so every night they tore down what had been built the day before."

"But the church *was* built, wasn't it?" said little Tjovik.

"It was indeed, and it was Grandfather Tarja who helped built it. You see, he filled a bag with ashes and climbed a tree growing on the mountain. When the trolls came out of the mountain at night to throw boulders at the church, he threw ashes in their eyes."

"And they could not see the church!" cried the delighted tomtes.

"They could not. You may imagine there was an outcry from the trolls, who were throwing their boulders but never hitting the mark."

"Poor Jompa," giggled the boy tomte.

"And so the church was finished," continued old Tjarfa. "The bishop blessed it, and after that the trolls could not damage it. But they were all the wilder in the forest. At that time there were wolves and bears, and the trolls encouraged them to attack the farm animals. Grandfather always had to fly back and forth like a shuttlecock to help the farm folk."

"Did the trolls every catch him?" asked Tjovik.

"Oh yes. Many times they took him into the mountain, but he always knew how to trick them and escape. Sometimes he came out sooty and scratched, but other times he brought out more gold than he could carry."

"Do the trolls have gold in the mountain?" asked Tjovik, surprised.

The other tomtes laughed until their beards shook. "It's clear you are just a child, little Tjovik," they said. "Or else you would know that Foxhall Mountain is full of rings and bracelets and other gold and jewels."

"Really?" exclaimed the boy gnome. "Then shouldn't we go and get some of the treasure? The poor people around here need a few luxuries to brighten their lives."

"No, my little boy," said the father crossly. "The gold you get from trolls is never a blessing. It causes pride, laziness, greed, strife, fighting, and hatred. My grandfather taught me this early, and for that reason my father and I and all the tomtes here have left the mountain gold untouched."

"It must be hard to find," mused Tjovik.

"Well, on a night like this it is quite easy," replied the old grandfather. "On Christmas Eve the trolls bring out all their treasure to count it, and they are so eager and excited that they don't see or hear a thing."

"But can anyone get into the mountain?" asked Tjovik.

"On Christmas Eve the mountain doors swing open by themselves," was the reply. "But woe to anyone who is still there when the churchbells ring for matins. Then the trolls both see and hear, and you are trapped."

"Did your father ever have trouble with them, Grandfather?"

"Jovik Tarjason, I should say so! Once he was within a hairsbreadth of losing his life. That time he rode an ox out of the mountain."

"What happened, dear Grandfather? Tell us, tell us."

"Well, you see, Skimpa had stolen the ox from the farm. My father was furious,

76

of course, and he crept into the mountain. It was easy, for the troll woman had forgotten to shut the door. Jompa was standing there with an axe raised over the head of the ox, ready to kill it. Well, Father was bold. He climbed up the ox's tail, pricked its back with a pin, the ox jumped, it knocked over both Skimpa and Jompa, and they fell to the floor with their feet in the air. Then the ox tore out of the mountain door with Father on its back."

The tomtes laughed so hard that two of them fell off the anchovy tin.

"And you, Grandfather. Have you ever been inside the mountain?"

"Many times, but I have never taken anything from the trolls except what they had stolen from our farm people. Once I barely escaped with my life. I lost my red tasselled cap and my wooden shoes, and came home black as a chimney-sweep."

"Why were you black, Grandfather?"

"I had to go out by way of the chimney because all the doors were locked."

"My brother had the same bad luck a few years ago," said another tomte.

"What happened to him?" Tjovik asked.

"He was trying to find a young shepherdess whom the trolls had carried away, and he was in the mountain when the cock crowed and all the doors shut with a bang. There was nothing for him to do but throw himself into the mountain spring and go underground with the stream. The brook that flows through the farm has its source in the mountain, you know. Poor man, he was soaked to the skin when he came home."

The young tomte listened to all this with the greatest interest. He would very much have liked to snatch a bracelet or a golden chain from the trolls to give to Anna Lisa, the farmer's oldest daughter, who was soon to be married. She was good to everyone, and Tjovik wished her the very best of fortune.

The tomtes sat and listened to old Tjarfa for a long time, until at last they all became sleepy. Then the guests trooped away to their own storerooms, Grandfather fell asleep on an old mitten in a corner, and Torgus and Tjovik lay down on a catskin between a couple of sugar-boxes.

But the young tomte could not go to sleep. He was wondering how he could fetch Anna Lisa a treasure from the mountain, just one. Surely there could be no harm in that. Surely it was only when you received too much gold that you became wicked. At last he sat up, put his cap on his head and his wooden shoes on his feet, picked up his little stick, and set out for the forest.

The night was dark and silent. Not a star winked from heaven and not a gleam of light shone from any of the cottage windows. Everything slept in a deep, quiet, midnight sleep, and only the drawn-out howl of a fox could now and then be heard from the forest. The tomte boy trotted along quickly. He was not afraid of the dark, and did not care about the fox. When you have legs only three inches long, you cannot go very fast, so although the little tomte took five steps for every one a human would have taken, he did make progress after all. In an hour he was at the foot of Foxhall Mountain.

My, how craggy and steep and high it rose! Not a glimmer of light to be seen from any of the mountain's cracks and crevices, but from deep inside there came a tinkling, clanking sound, as if someone were rattling and jingling gold and silver coins.

"You just wait," said Tjovik, and began to climb the mountain.

It was slow going, but he managed it somehow. Sometimes he slipped a little, but then he took fresh hold and climbed higher and higher. Breathless and hot and sweaty, he climbed from crag to crag, rock to rock, and swung himself up one ledge after another until he was halfway up the mountainside.

An owl hooted from a nearby grove, but Tjovik would not let himself be scared. He would climb until he found an opening. At last he saw a faint light through a small crack in the rocks. He poked his little stick into the opening and twisted it. The door must have been well greased, for it opened slowly and soundlessly on its hinges.

Now the little tomte entered a vast hall with walls and a ceiling of rugged black stone. He saw the bones of big cattle here and there on the floor, and rusty weapons hung on the walls. It was dismal and gloomy; he walked on.

He came to a second door, which seemed to be made of copper. It opened as easily as the first, and now Tjovik stepped into another hall. Silver coins were heaped against the walls, but not a creature was in sight. Surely there is enough money here to buy a watch for the good farmer, he thought. But wait! What is that tinkling and jingling on the other side of that silver door? I wonder what they are doing in there.

He padded silently to the silver door, opened it, and what did he see? There was an open chest in the middle of the floor, and beside it sat two terrible trolls, jingling and rattling gold rings, bracelets, pearls, and precious stones. They were so busy counting the treasure in their chest that they neither saw nor heard Tjovik enter.

On the far side of the hall was a well where water rushed up from the rock and earth below. An old cracked wooden shoe was in the well, tied to the wall with a string to keep it from being washed away.

"Skimpa must have put that wooden shoe in the well to make the wood swell," Tjovik said to himself. "I could always sail away from here in that if the doors are closed."

He approached the chest quietly and carefully. But it was so high he could not reach the top. He stretched and stretched on tiptoe, as far as he could, and then what do you think happened?

Jompa and Skimpa sneezed, both at the same time. My goodness, how it echoed through the mountain! The breeze was so strong that the little tomte flew into the air like a feather, and landed headfirst right in the middle of all the gold in the chest. It's all over now, thought Tjovik, holding tightly to his stick to defend himself from the trolls.

But those stupid trolls had not seen him. They kept counting and counting. Tjovik looked around at all the gold and treasure. He picked out a chain, just long enough to hand around someone's neck, and tried to climb to the edge of the chest and jump to the floor.

That was when all the churchbells began to chime, calling the congregations to matins. Both trolls jumped up and stuck their fingers in their ears. The mountain doors were closed and locked, and the lid of the chest fell down on the gold, and on the little tomte boy.

Poor Tjovik sat there like a mouse in a mousetrap. But he was not one to lose courage easily. Now if only I can trick the trolls into opening the chest again, I can

get away, I am sure of it, he thought. And he put his mouth to the keyhole and began
to squeak like a mouse.

"There's a rat in the chest," cried the troll woman.

"Let it stay till next Christmas, for all I care," said the old man.

"It will gnaw a hole through the chest," the woman replied.

"You might be right," her husband admitted.

And so they opened the chest again and saw the little tomte sitting near the edge.

"My, what a funny looking little rat," said the troll, and laughed until his belly
shook. "What kind of a snippet are you?"

"I am Tjovik Torgusson, a tomte from the farm," Tjovik answered fearlessly.

"Ha, ha, ha! Hi, hi, hi! Ho, ho, ho!" laughed the troll, and took Tjovik between his thumb and forefinger. "He will make a fine dessert after the Christmas ham. Have you a frying-pan ready, Mother?"

"You can't fry me before I've washed the dirt off my fingers," said Tjovik.

"Just hold your tongue, you," warned the troll. "You'll be washed all right, and you can be sure of that." And he put the boy on the brim of the well and poured water all over him.

"That won't do," Tjovik cried. "You had better get a scrub brush and some soap."

"You're a fussy little man," grumbled the troll, but he loosened his grip and went to fetch a scrubbing brush.

Instantly, the tomte jumped into the wooden shoe, opened his knife, and cut off the string that anchored the shoe to the wall. Heigh-ho! Right away the wooden shoe began to follow the stream down the mountain wall. Jompa and Skimpa howled loud enough to break your eardrums, but the little tomte just waved his pointed red cape and called "Hurrah!"

The rapids carried him and the wooden shoe down through an underground channel and out again into the brook that ran by the farm. There Tjovik jumped ashore and made his way home. But he had lost the golden chain; he had dropped it when the troll dashed water over him.

It was a close thing whether Tjovik would get a good thrashing from both his father and grandfather for this foolish adventure. But he escaped because he had never done anything wrong before. He had to promise never again to look for treasure, except for that which can be earned through honest work. And this is a promise he has never broken.

The Ring

Helena Nyblom

Once upon a time a young prince went riding out in the moonlight. The air was so light he felt that he was flying. The sky was deep blue, with a big white moon floating among small, curly clouds. Far away over the mountains, lightning flashed silently. The prince rode quickly, and in the moonlight his shadow was so large it looked like a giant unearthly rider.

When the prince reached his castle, he dismounted and gave his horse to a groom, but he was reluctant to go in. With his riding crop in hand, he walked to the sea and began to stroll slowly along the sandy shore. He was not thinking of anything in particular, it was a pleasant and easy walk, and he drew deep breaths of the cool night air. Suddenly, while he was walking, he struck his riding-crop into the sand and felt the tip catch on something. What was it? A ring!

A ring, thought the prince, and held it up in the moonlight. Who could have lost a ring here by the shore? It must have been one of the ladies-in-waiting. And so the prince tucked the ring in his breast pocket. It was a small ring, slender as a thread, with several little blue stones set to look like a forget-me-not.

The court assembled in the great hall after supper, and the prince put his hand in his breast pocket and said, "Could any of you ladies by chance have lost a ring?"

Immediately all the ladies looked at their hands. They had numerous precious diamond, emerald, and sapphire rings, and now they peered anxiously from finger to finger to see if any of their magnificent rings were missing. But they were all still there.

"What does your ring look like?" a beautiful lady dared to ask.

The prince held up the ring.

When the ladies saw it, they all put on superior and disdainful expressions. Certainly none of them would claim such a ring as that. It was nothing, a mere trinket, and so little it seemed made for a child's hand.

But now the ladies had something to talk about, and for the rest of the evening they busily compared their beautiful rings, passing them from hand to hand and exclaiming over their cost. The prince rose and strolled to the balcony, where he stood gazing at the moonlight.

Later, he went to his chamber, undressed, and got into bed. He set the little ring on a table near him. Just as he was about to fall asleep, he heard a strange noise, a clicking and whirring as if a small insect were darting among the glasses on the table.

When the prince opened his eyes, he was surprised to see that it was the little ring rattling around, as if an unseen hand had set it in motion.

Quickly he lit a candle. Then the ring became still. But as soon as he blew out the candle, the ring began to dance again. It was strange and eerie. The prince put the ring in a drawer, yet he could hear it skittering all night long, and hardly slept at all. Of course he could have thrown the ring away, but for some reason, that seemed to him quite out of the question. He did not wish to part with the ring at all, and the next night, too, he brought it to his chamber.

Hardly had he snuffed out the candle than the ring began to dance again, and this time it did not just bounce about the table, but jumped to his breast and bounced just as quickly there.

"What can it mean?" said the prince, and sat up in bed. He caught the ring, jumped out of bed, and put it in a small jewel box, which he locked. As he did so, holding the ring between his fingers, it seemed to him that it quivered and trembled, just as if it were alive.

The prince was silent and serious all the next day. He brooded and wondered. What kind of magic ring had he come upon with his riding crop? That evening, he placed the ring on the table beside his bed as before. He was so tired that he fell asleep at once, but he had not slept long before he was awakened by something brushing his face, and instantly he realized it was the ring running back and forth over his forehead, dancing down his cheeks, and spinning along his lips.

"Now I understand," he exclaimed, and jumped up. "I must find the owner of the ring."

Dawn had just begun to break over the sea when he went to the stable, saddled his horse, and thundered out across the drawbridge. He rode all day without seeing anyone, but towards evening he arrived at a large castle, beautifully situated in a green meadow surrounded by tall trees. Ivy and roses climbed the walls, and high in an arched window the lady of the castle was standing and looking over the countryside. She was a widow, but still a young and handsome woman, who ruled her large estates with a firm hand. When she saw the prince approaching, she dispatched a servant to greet him and welcome him to the castle.

The prince accepted her invitation and gladly went in. The noble lady received him in the friendliest fashion. He was given a splendid chamber, and when he came to dinner he found that the large banquet hall had been lit with candles and torches. The table was laid with silver and gold. Servants in festive dress passed around delicious dishes, and the lady herself looked as distinguished as a queen in red velvet and ermine. She talked gaily, and seemed highly amused by all the prince had to say. He did not explain why he had ridden alone into the world, but now and then he cast a quick glance at the lady's hands. Could she have lost the ring?

But as it happened, this noble lady had very large, very red, and very worn hands.

Her carriage and walk were distinguished and imposing, so you could not doubt that she was of noble birth, but when you caught sight of her big hands and lumpy fingers, you thought instinctively, These are the hands of a cook.

She wore many costly rings on her fingers, yet they seemed badly out of place and only showed up her rough hands all the more At the end of dinner, she peeled an apple for the prince, and looking sharply at her ring-bedecked fingers he asked, "You have so many exquisite rings, my lady. I suppose you could easily lose one bathing or picking flowers?"

"I always take my rings off before I swim in the lake," she laughed. "And I never pick flowers myself. The maids do it for me."

The prince was silent a moment, then he brought forth the little ring and showed it to her. "What do you think of this ring?" he asked.

"That little thing," she said, trying to put it on her little finger. "It doesn't go over the first joint of this finger. It seems to belong to a child. A poor child. Where did you get it, your highness?"

"That I can't tell you," the prince answered, and hid the ring in his breast pocket.

The lady's keen black eyes looked searchingly at him for a moment, then she began to talk of other things. And the next morning before dawn the prince rode from the castle.

His eyes were on the horizon. A child, he thought. A child — a poor child. But where are you?

He rode through forests and valleys, across meadows and fields, and when the sun was high he came to a large manor house set among waving wheatfields and beautiful flower gardens. Even at a distance he could see a number of people in a large courtyard. The sound of violins and trumpets reached his ears, and as he came nearer he realized it was a wedding.

The bride and groom were standing on the front steps. The bride had a crown of bright ribbons and flowers on her head, and the groom had a silver-buttoned coat, a glossy black hat, and a happy smile. In the courtyard, a hundred young boys and girls were dancing merrily together. The prince reined in his horse on a small hill not far from the manor house and began to watch the dancing. When the dancers stopped and sat down to rest, on benches under the large linden trees that spread their branches over the yard, he rode nearer.

All eyes turned towards the strange rider who had appeared so unexpectedly. The prince held up his little ring. He called, "Is there any girl here who has lost a ring?"

The girls flew to him like doves to look at the ring. "I have lost a ring!" "And I!" "And I!" several cried, crowding close to the prince.

But before long — "No, the ring I lost didn't look like that one," said one girl after another, until they all began to babble and chatter, laugh and giggle, and the music started up again. They hurried back to dance, while the prince rode sorrowfully away.

He rode on until evening when, feeling tired, he slowed his horse to ride along the bank of a river that cut through the meadows. Then he caught sight of a woman dressed in black, walking with downcast eyes as though looking for something among the stones by the road. As the prince drew nearer, he saw that the woman was very beautiful, but that the big black eyes in her pale face were full of pain and suffering. He was very sorry for her.

"What are you looking for, dear one?" he asked. "Have you lost something precious to you?"

The woman's face became even more melancholy than before. She raised her eyes and her lips trembled. In a quavering voice, wringing her hands, she said, "I have lost all I ever had in life: my husband, my estate, my fortune. I had only one thing left, a ring that was a gift from my late husband. I had hoped to sell it well, but now I have lost it and I don't know how or where. And so my last hope is gone. All that is left for me to do is beg my daily bread."

The prince's heart was beating eagerly. Could she be speaking of the ring he was carrying at his breast? Yet all who had seen it had said that it was worthless.

Slowly he held up the ring, and asked, "Could it possibly be *this* ring?"

She gave him a sad smile. "My ring was set with a large, costly diamond. That little one there is nothing but a cheap toy."

Then the prince opened his purse, full of gold coins, and let them rain into the bereaved woman's arms. "Here. Here is enough to provide for the present at least," he said gently. "This gold may help you." And before the woman had had time to thank him, he rode off.

He rode for days and nights without encountering anyone who recognized the ring. Always he carried it in his breast pocket, and though it no longer danced as it had during the first nights, he could still feel it tugging at him, as if sobbing quietly. The prince heard the small, sorrowful throbbing at his breast over the beating of his own heart, and every day he loved the ring more and more.

One morning he came to a swiftly running river. On the opposite bank was a tall mountain, wrapped in the blue veil of early morning mist. All over its slopes sparkled what looked like little gold fires, but they were really broom bushes in flower, so attractive that the prince could not help feeling happy. He wanted to go to them and look more closely, but that would not be easy, for there was no bridge over the river.

I suppose I must swim across then, thought the prince, and he and his horse plunged into the rapids. The prince hardly noticed as water sprayed high above him and his horse was almost pulled downstream by the current. His long futile search had made him so dejected that he enjoyed having to struggle with all his might to get to the far bank. At last he stood there, tired and out of breath, with his horse panting and snorting beside him. The mountain rose before him.

The prince could not climb the slope on horseback, so he let the horse graze on a green meadow, and struggled on foot up a narrow mountain path that wound through a forest towards the summit.

It was a hot day, and the shade of the trees in the cool forest felt good to him. Everything was still. The sun cast golden flecks over the forest floor, which was smoothed by last year's leaves covering the knotted tree roots along the path. The climbing was not easy, though. And why do I go to so much trouble? thought the prince. What for? His heart was beating so violently that he could hear it, and he could also hear the heartthrob of the little ring, pulsing more than it had for a long time.

He paused a moment, then climbed on.

He thought he heard the sound of rippling water, and all of a sudden he realized how thirsty he was. Now at least he knew what he wanted: he wanted to get to the spring and drink and drink. The sound of the bubbling water came even stronger, and then he saw something flash white under the leaves of the chestnuts. Two steps more, and he was standing by a fresh mountain spring that was gushing out from a rock wall into a little pool. Then he stood stock still; he was not alone.

At the spring was a girl, one hand on her hip, watching as the water filled a pail she had set beneath it; another empty pail was in the grass nearby. The girl's legs were bare, she was dressed in a short grey skirt and white blouse, and her hair hung down her back in two blond braids. The prince could not see her face, but when the pail was full, she turned in his direction. Her blue eyes looked surprised for a moment, but then she bowed her head in greeting, and put the second pail under the water-fall. When it, too, was full, she turned and hooked both pails to a yoke that lay in the grass. The prince smiled at her but she did not smile in return. Her face looked so quiet and serious that suddenly the prince, too, became serious.

"Forgive me," he said, "but may I have a drink of water? I am so thirsty."

"What will you drink from?" asked the girl. Her voice was soft and beautiful; it sounded like music. "I know," she said with a quick smile. "Come here. I will help you."

The prince went to the spring, and the girl put her hands together to make a small drinking cup. The water gushed into them and in a second they were full.

"Hurry and drink," she called, laughing merrily.

The prince emptied the little cup in a moment. With water still dripping from his mouth, he said, "More. Give me one more cup of water."

The girl closed her hands again, and they were filled by the spring. But this time when the prince bent to drink, he noticed a curious change in the girl's face. She blushed, and her eyes, that before had looked as blue as a summer sky, now seemed almost black. She snatched the chain from the prince's neck and seized the ring, which had fallen from his breast pocket when he bent to drink.

"My ring," she said tremulously. "Where did you find my ring?" She put it on the little finger of her left hand, and it went on as smoothly as if it had come home. "My ring!" she repeated, and looked at the prince with tears in her eyes.

She sat on the grass under the low branches of the chestnuts, and turned the ring slowly around her finger with as much tenderness as if it had been a living thing.

"Why do you love your ring so much?" asked the prince, seating himself beside her.

She looked up at him. "My mother gave it to me on the day she died," she said. "I was only a little girl, but she told me, 'It will always help you in misfortune, and if you are ever in need, throw it into the sea. It will know how to find your saviour.'"

"And it has found him," said the prince, smiling and taking the girl's hands in his. "It called and beckoned me, and has not given me a moment's peace until I found you here in the forest. But tell me, why are you here? How did you get here? What is your misfortune?"

The girl looked around anxiously, and whispered, "I live here with an old moun-tain troll, who makes me work like a slave." And she told him the sad tale of her life.

She had been born in a castle high among the mountains, and would have become a fine and noble princess, but her mother had died when she was a child; and when she was fifteen, a duke from another country captured the castle, murdered her father, and carried her away. Then she had lived in a tower of the foreign duke's palace and was given the best of everything: costly gowns and delicacies, and numerous servants to wait on her. But she was never allowed to leave the palace. Only from a window in her chamber could she see the outside world of flowering meadows, green woods, and the river that wound like a ribbon of silver through the valley. One day the duke came to her room and told her that in three months she would marry his son.

The girl looked at the prince with sad eyes. "It was the greatest misfortune and shame that could ever have befallen me. The duke's son was big and coarse as a giant, his face was red, and he was almost always drunk. I would rather have died than become his wife."

However, the girl had pretended that she would very much like to be married to the duke's son. But first, she said, she wanted to make him a gift of a braided rope for the anchor of his sailing ship, and when that was finished she would happily become his bride. And so she began to braid a rope of the strongest hemp she could find, and soon it was so long it reached from her window all the way down to the valley.

On the evening before the wedding, she locked herself in her little tower chamber, tied the rope to the window, and climbed down. When she reached the ground, she ran as fast as she could to hide in the forest. There she crept into a dense thicket and fell into a deep sleep.

Next morning she was awakened by a tickling on her forehead. When she opened her eyes she saw a terrifying face looking down at her. It was the troll of the mountain, who had been taking his morning walk through the forest, and he was poking her with a blade of grass. A long red tongue lolled from his mouth, and he had great furry black hands like a bear.

"I was so frightened," said the girl, "that I hardly dared breathe."

The troll had laughed horribly and said, "What luck to find you, little sweet one. I want someone to care for me, cook my food, carry my water and my wood, and be my own companion." And so the troll caught her by the hair and carried her to his cave on the mountaintop. It was a deep black cave, and even on the hottest summer day it was cold as a cellar, and heavy drops of water trickled from the stones.

"Now I have served the mountain troll for three years," sighed the girl. "And every summer he tells me, 'Next Christmas, when you are a little fatter, I will eat you.'

"So I hardly dare eat, and I have not thought of anything but how to escape. One spring day I ran all the way down the mountainside to the river, hoping to cross to the other side. But there was no bridge, only the rapids and spray. So I took off my ring and threw it in the water and called out as my mother taught me,

Ring, ring, pulse and spring
And my knight to me bring,
A knight so good, a knight so brave,
To rescue me, a helpless slave.

"The ring disappeared into the water. But now," finished the girl, smiling, "the ring has found the knight who will help and save me." And she kissed the ring.

"You kiss the ring," said the prince. "Do you think you could rather kiss me?"

"Do you think so?" she asked, and then with a smile flung her arms around his neck and kissed him.

That moment they heard a strange, thundering sound.

"It is the troll of the mountain," the girl cried, and jumped up. "Quick! Quick! We must run as fast as we can."

And quickly, quickly they sped down the mountainside to where the prince's horse was grazing quietly by the river. Quickly the prince swung into the saddle, lifted the princess in front of him, and plunged into the water. Waves splashed over their heads, the horse panted and snorted and kicked in the river, and the mountain troll in the forest howled and bellowed like a pack of hungry wolves.

The prince and the girl rode for days and nights through forest and plain, across rivers and brooks, past groves and hedges. The horse never tired until they reached the prince's castle. They arrived there one moonlit night, and rode slowly along the seashore, the princess wrapped up in the prince's big cape.

She lifted a corner of the cape and looked down at the sand. "How strange," she said, with a smile on her face. "Looking at the shadow, one would think there was only one rider on the horse."

The Old Troll of Big Mountain

Anna Wahlenberg

Once there lived a poor crofter and his wife who had nothing more in this world than their little cottage, two goats, and a boy-child of five whose name was Olle.

The crofter and his wife worked far away from their cottage every day, so they had a paddock for the goats to graze in. They gave Olle a bread roll and a mug of milk, then they locked the door behind them and put the key under the doorstep.

One night when they came home, both goats were gone. Someone on the highway said he had seen the evil old troll of Big Mountain dragging them away.

You can imagine their distress! Now the crofter and his wife had even less to live on than before, and instead of goat's milk, Olle got nothing but water in his mug. But worst of all, no one could be sure that the evil old troll would not come back, put Olle in a sack, and carry him away up the mountain. The troll was known to have stolen children before, though no one knew what he did with them because none ever came back.

Every day before they left home, the crofter and his wife warned Olle never to sit by the window; for who could tell, the old troll might pass by and catch sight of the boy. If the troll ever knocked on the door, they told Olle, shout "Father, Father," exactly as if his father were at home, because that would surely scare the old troll and send him away.

So that Olle would recognize the troll, his parents described him carefully. He was terribly ugly, had real bushes for eyebrows, a mouth that reached from ear to ear, a nose as thick as a turnip, and instead of a left hand, a wolf's paw.

Yes, Olle would keep a lookout and defend himself, he promised them, and he began to make some weapons. He hammered a nail into a log and it became a lance. He ground an old knife, meant for splitting kindling, against a stone, and it became a sword. That old troll had better watch out, or he would be sorry.

One day as Olle was busy polishing his lance and his sword, he heard someone groping at the door. Olle looked out of the window and saw a man with a sack on his back crouching on his knees and poking his hand under the doorstep. It was none other than the evil old troll who had come to take Olle away, but Olle did not know it.

"What are you looking for?" asked Olle.

Of course, the troll was looking for the key so he could come and steal Olle, but naturally he did not want to say so. "I've lost a coin," he said instead. "It rolled right under your step. Will you come out and help me look for it?"

"No," said Olle. "Father and Mother have locked me in so that I will be safe from a wicked old troll."

The troll looked at Olle out of the corner of his eye. He wondered if the boy had any idea who he was. "Well, I don't look like an old troll, do I?" he said to test him.

"Oh, no. I'm not afraid of *you*. And I am not afraid of the old troll either, for if he comes here, he'll regret it. I have a lance and sword in here, you know. Look!"

The old troll peered through the windowpane, but pretended that he could not see anything. Then he asked Olle where the key was, so that he could unlock the door and come in and see better.

"Oh, yes," said Olle. "The key is under the first broken step on the right side."

Indeed, there it was. Quickly the old troll unlocked the door and stalked in. And to tell the truth, Olle was glad to have company. Proudly and eagerly he showed the old troll how finely he had ground his sword and what a wonderful lance a nail in a log makes. He was even rather wishing the old troll would come, so that he could pay him back for stealing their goats.

"I believe I know where he hides his goats," said the old troll. "If you come with me a little way into the woods, you might find them."

That was a good idea, thought Olle. Imagine, if he could bring home the stolen goats.

"Well, shall we go then?" said the troll.

"Yes," said Olle.

Olle wanted to bring along something to eat, because the troll's pastures were probably a long way off. So he broke his bread into pieces and put them in his pocket. He offered the old troll a piece, but the troll immediately said No. The reason for this was that trolls can never harm anyone from whom they have accepted something. If the troll took the bread now, he would not be able to stuff Olle into his sack. And that, of course, would never do.

When Olle was ready he reached for the old troll's hand, expecting to be led to where the goats were. But the troll pushed his hand away.

"You must take my right hand," said the troll. "I have hurt the left one." He showed Olle his left hand, which was bandaged with a thick cloth.

Olle felt sorry for him. "Oh, my. You poor man. Let me blow on it, that will make it better," he said.

But that didn't help. His only thought was to leave without being seen. It would have been quicker, of course, to stuff Olle into the sack right away, but as he was walking along so willingly, that saved the trouble of carrying him.

And so they walked hand in hand, Olle with his lance and sword ready under his arm, in case they met the evil old troll.

After they had gone a little way into the forest, Olle was tired and sat down on a stone. He began to eat his bread, for he was hungry, too.

The old troll eyed him. He wondered if this wasn't the moment to put the boy in the sack. Besides, it annoyed him that Olle was not afraid of him. That wasn't right. It would have been better to put him in the sack kicking and yelling the way all the other children did. And so he decided to scare Olle.

"Olle," he said, "suppose *I* were the old troll."

"Oh, no," Olle said, looking at him. "You don't look like him at all. He has bushes for eyebrows, and you haven't. He has a mouth that goes from ear to ear, and you haven't. And he has a wolf's paw instead of a left hand, and you haven't. So don't think you can fool me."

"How *do* I look, then?" asked the old troll.

"Like any other old man, of course," Olle reassured him.

That sounded so funny to the troll's ears that he let out a loud guffaw. And in the same moment Olle threw a piece of bread into his open mouth.

"That's for being so good to me, not like an old troll at all."

"Oho, oho, oho," the old troll coughed with all his might. But however much he coughed, the bread did not come up; it slid further and further down his throat, until he swallowed it.

Now a strange thing happened. The old troll could not treat Olle the way he had intended to. Now that he had accepted something from Olle, he could not wish him ill.

"So you think I look like a man," said the troll. "It's the first time anybody ever said that to me. But if I look like a man, I had better act like one. Listen!"

He stood up and pulled a small pipe from his pocket and began to play it.

Olle listened. He thought he heard someone answering from the forest. Then the old troll blew once more, and again Olle pricked up his ears. Now he could hear footsteps, some light and some heavy, running across the twigs and moss.

The old troll blew one more time.

Something white appeared among the tree trunks, and Olle saw his parents' goats, Pearl and Flower, running towards him. They recognized him, and pushed and butted him. Olle was so excited that he shouted for sheer joy, and jumped from one leg to the other.

But there were more steps. Behind Pearl and Flower came hundreds of little kids, tripping about, tiny and delicate, just like tufts of white wool beside the bigger goats.

"But whose are these other goats?" asked Olle, looking at the old troll.

"Troll ways are different from man's ways, and goats have many kids when they stay with the old troll on Big Mountain," he replied, and patted Olle on the head. "But run along now. You must be home before your mother and father return."

Olle nodded, but before he had time to say a word, the troll had hurried in among the fir trees, because trolls do not like to be thanked.

Olle stood quite still for a moment, wondering where he had gone, but then he patted the goats again and they all set off for home.

On the way Olle met some people. They stopped, amazed at the sight of a small boy leading two goats and so many, many kids. They followed Olle to his cottage, and as the herd was let into the paddock, they stood gaping, a ring of wide eyes around the fence.

Just then Olle's father and mother arrived. When they saw their boy in the midst of all the goats, they were so surprised they had to sit down on a stone. Then Olle told his story and they wrung their hands and groaned. Who could have gathered all those goats? It sounded like magic. It couldn't have been the old troll, could it?

"No, it wasn't," said Olle. "He had big eyebrows, but they weren't real bushes. And he had a big mouth, too, but it didn't go from ear to ear. And he certainly didn't have a wolf's paw for a left hand. His left hand was all bandaged because he had hurt himself."

"Gracious!" exclaimed the crofter and his wife and all the others around the fence. "It *was* the old troll. He always wraps a cloth round his paw so as not to be recognized when he is passing the cottages."

Olle sat down and looked around at all the worried faces. He still could not understand. "Well then, maybe even bad old trolls are good sometimes," he said at last.

And no one who saw all those goats could doubt it, though no one there would ever have believed it before.

The Elf King's Ball

Anna Wahlenberg

Just after the sun had gone down, as twilight was falling softly over the valley, a little elf suddenly put her head out of the door of the stone cairn where she lived with her parents and sisters, to see whether the moon had risen; for when it had travelled halfway across the heavens she was going to a grand ball down in the valley by the shore. The Elf King who was giving it had invited all the families of elves for twelve miles around, and his Queen having been dead for some time, everyone thought that he meant to choose a new one from among the assembled maidens.

Of course his choice would fall on the best dancer; and the little elf felt her heart beat fast when she thought of the stately, handsome king, and remembered that he had once thrown her a kiss when she danced before him.

But as she stood gazing from the open door, a puff of wind found its way into the cairn with such force that the fire flared up fiercely on the hearth, while the veils which her sister had just ironed out were wafted almost up to the ceiling.

"What a terrible draught," said her mother, who was busy polishing the silver crowns. "I am sure that the veils will be torn." The little elf shut the door in a great fright, and went back to her veil, which was not quite ready; but after smoothing and straightening it for a few minutes she stole softly to the door again, to see whether the moon was yet in sight.

No, not a sign, and back she went to her work until she could not resist another peep; and there it was just rising over the wood.

"There it is, there it is," she cried, clapping her hands, and opening the door ever so much wider to see it shine above the tree-tops. Then all at once she heard her sisters shriek, "The veil, the veil!" and rushed in to see them all bending over the hearth, where it lay a blackened, shrivelled web, having been blown into the fire by a strong gust of wind while no one was near enough to save it.

"Well," said her mother, "that serves you right. You should not have stood there gaping at the moon. Now you cannot go to the ball." The poor little elf's heart seemed to stop beating for a minute. Then plucking up her courage she ran as fast as she could to ask some of her neighbours if one of them would stay at home and lend her a veil. But they all shook their heads at once.

"Do you think we are so stupid?" they said. "Are we likely to stay at home when we have such a fine invitation? No, indeed; we intend to go and try to please the Elf King, and see who will be his Queen."

Next she went to the spiders who were sitting in the corner of a bush, and asked gently: "Dear kind ladies, will you spin a veil for me? I will give you pearls from my casket and diamonds from my crown." But the soldiers hardly stirred as they replied, "You silly creature! Do you take us for conjurors?" and then crept further into their webs to sleep in peace.

So the elf returned to the cairn, and combed the long hair which reached to her feet (not one of the whole elfin family had hair like hers); then she carefully spread it out just like a veil, put on her silver crown, and went shyly to her mother. "Could she not dance thus?" she asked. "Surely her hair would take the place of a veil!" And big tears stood in her eyes, for this was her last hope.

Alas, all the elves burst into shrieks of laughter. Who had ever heard of an elf going to a ball without a veil? She might as well have no dress on! And away they floated out of the cairn.

The unlucky little victim could only stand in the doorway and watch them pass out of sight accompanied by a whole troop of their neighbours, with veils waving above the long grass, and silver crowns glittering in the moonlight.

Then putting her hands before her face she cried bitterly. It was dreadful to be left at home alone, she who had danced so beautifully before the King. She would have soared as if on white wings, drooped like a wave on the beach, shimmered like a moonbeam; and there, there was the moon which she had longed to see. But of what use was its light now? Still, unhappy as she was, she could not help seeing how it seemed to turn the whole valley into a great shining ballroom and entice her willing feet hither.

Yes; she would dance away this dreadful sorrow. And spreading her golden hair round her, on she went over moss and brushwood, stones and hillocks, until she reached the mill where the brook ran gaily over the pebbles, with the miller's red house close by.

A pear-tree shaded one half of the gable window, but a flood of moonlight streamed through the other, which was partly open; and the little elf wondered what was inside.

She knew how to ride on moonbeams, so swinging herself up, she accompanied them into the room, where the miller's pretty daughter lay asleep with her cheek upon her hand.

Over a chair hung a blue skirt with yellow ribbons, a white bodice, and a pink neckerchief. Two neat red shoes stood side by side under the bed, while on the chest lay a heavy bridal crown, for tomorrow was her wedding day.

But the little elf's eyes rested most eagerly on the transparent white veil lying folded on the table, and in half a second she had lifted it and thrown it over her head.

Could she dance in it? Yes; it was bigger than hers, and fell in heavier folds, but that did not matter. Perhaps it would look more beautiful still.

Now she could go to the ball! But as she gaily flitted towards the open window, the miller's daughter suddenly woke, raised herself, and with one bound left her bed and closed it; while the poor little elf, shrinking back in fright, managed somehow to get entangled in the curtain.

"Are you going to steal my veil?" cried the maiden. "Give it to me this moment or else you shall not go out." But the elf only wrapped herself more closely in the curtain, holding the veil fast on her head. Then clasping her hands, she piteously begged for the loan of it, and related the whole story of how her own had been burnt, and how the Elf King had once thrown her a kiss when she danced before him.

He would be certain to choose her for his Queen if she could only dance at the ball that night. "Oh, might she not have it, just for a little while?"

"No, indeed," was the reply; "I shall want it myself tomorrow."

"You shall have it back before then." "Torn and dirty, I suppose. Thank you. I want to look nice on my wedding day." "It will be far more beautiful than it is now," and big tears were very near the elf's eyes again.

But the miller's daughter would not give way. Who ever heard of lending a wedding veil before it had been worn? She was not such a fool; and, stamping her foot on the ground, she cried, "Give it to me or I will take it myself!"

And the veil slowly fell to the ground as the elf floated out of the window, which opened of its own accord to let her pass, her long shimmering hair giving her so close a resemblance to the moonbeams that she could hardly be distinguished from them.

As the miller's daughter stood watching, her eyes shaded by her hand, she felt a sharp pang of remorse on seeing her sink among the willows which grew beside the streamlet hiding her face with her hands, while her silver crown shook with the violence of her sobs.

Now she realized the sadness of letting an opportunity of doing good to others slip by, and that thoughts such as these would steal away all her bridal happiness. She could not be so unkind, and hastily pushing the window further open she threw out her lovely veil, and called loudly:

"Take it, but I must have it again before daybreak." The elf was there in a twinkling, seized the veil, and flew over the wide plain like some soft white cloud.

Determined to see what would happen, the miller's daughter slipped on her shoes, threw a cloak over her shoulders, and sprang out of the window, following the cloud until she reached the valley beyond the alder-trees which lay near the shore.

There a sight met her eyes which seemed to chain her to the ground as if by magic, for the whole valley was full of hovering elves, with the King in their midst, seated on a throne formed of a large white lily. His face, surrounded by long flowing hair, beamed with beauty and light, his mantle of silver tissue was fastened with shining clasps, and a golden sceptre was in his hand; but though he watched each movement of the elfin maidens who glided before him, his eyes rested most frequently on the tiny figure robed in a bridal veil.

How the little white cloud seemed to rise and fall like some crested wave, now spreading itself out as though possessed of wings, now flying rapidly past with the speed of a rushing whirlwind.

At length the King raised his sceptre, and the dance ceased as he stepped down from the lily, which bowed itself to the ground. His long mantle flowing behind him, he approached the little elf, took her hand, and led her to his throne, while the lily bent its head once more as they seated themselves upon it.

Now all the elves joined hands to form a close ring round them, bowing low meanwhile; then widening it as far as their slender white arms could reach they bowed again, and thus greeted their King and Queen.

At that moment the moon became hidden by a cloud and she saw nothing more, for when it shone out afresh they had vanished, doubtless to celebrate the betrothal feast inside the King's palace. So she went home to lie down, and sleep like a happy child with her cheek upon her hand, until the sun stood high in the heavens and her mother came to dress her for her bridal.

The red shoes and the pretty dress were soon put on, her hair was combed and plaited. But where was the veil? What had become of it?

All at once the maiden remembered what had happened in the night. The elf must have forgotten to bring it back. Yet she dared not utter a word. It was always unlucky to speak ill of the fairy people.

High and low they sought in vain. The horses prances and neighed at the door, the guests crowded both parlour and kitchen, but nowhere could it be found.

Suddenly she rushed to the window, which she had shut on coming in; and as the elf had not been able to open it, there hung the veil on the ledge outside! But, alas, it was sadly bedraggled and damp from the night dew. Indeed it was just like some limp rag.

"You wicked, careless girl," cried her mother. "How *could* you leave your beautiful veil out there?"

Well, she must wear it at any rate, so she mounted her white horse and rode to church, feeling as if her heart would break under such a load of disgrace.

The bridegroom came to meet her beside the churchyard wall, saying "God bless you" as he took her hand, then suddenly started back as though some strange sight met his eyes.

"Now he is ashamed of me," she thought, turning red and pale by turns; but he only came nearer and touched her veil, with the words "How beautiful!" while the whole company echoed his words in tones of surprise.

Still she thought they were jesting, until she raised the veil herself and found that the little elf had kept her word, for it was indeed more beautiful than before.

Dewdrops had turned into shimmering pearls and precious stones, and surely no bride was ever dressed in more costly array than the miller's daughter as she passed through the doorway and up the aisle of the venerable church.

The Boy who was Never Afraid

Alfred Smedberg

Once there lived a poor crofter with eight hungry children and only one cow, so it is easy to see why his children often had to make do with little. Yet the cow, Lily White, was a great blessing to the crofter, for she was the best cow in the whole country. She gave as much milk as the finest manor-house cow, which was lucky, considering all those children. She was big and handsome, and clever, too. She understood everything the children chattered about, and they chattered night and day.

Words cannot tell how kind and devoted the children were to their cow as they petted and fussed over her. Lily White was just a cow on a croft, yet she was happy as a wasp in a jam jar. In summertime she grazed in a large pasture by the manor house, but when the sun went down she always managed to come home by herself, because she was so clever.

But one evening a sad thing happened. Lily White did not return as usual. The crofter spent half the night looking for her, then he came home alone and tired.

At daybreak the next morning, he and his wife and the elder children went to look for their cow in the pasture. They walked from one end to the other without finding her. At last, in a far corner of the field, they found Lily White's hoofprints in the soft earth. But beside them were others, made by big, clumsy feet. The crofter was frightened, for he realized at once whose footprints those were. It was none other than the big troll in Hulta Wood.

Now it was not difficult to guess where Lily White had gone. The troll had come down to the pasture from his caves in the granite mountain and led the cow away with him. The troll must have known that Lily White was the finest milk cow in the whole country.

No wonder, now, the crofter's little home was full of sorrow and dismay. The children cried, and their father and mother were so worried they scarcely said a word. It was out of the question to try to get the cow back, for up to now no one had ever dared enter the terrible mountain caves where the trolls lived.

There were not only trolls to be frightened of in the deep haunted forest; there were three other creatures, too, nearly as dangerous. One was the green-haired witch of Hulta Wood. Then there was the bellowing watchdog of the forest; and the third was a bear, the shaggy king of the forest.

Now it happened that among the crofter's children was one small red-cheeked boy named Nisse. There was no one like him in seven parishes. It was strange: he wasn't afraid of anything in the world, no matter how dangerous it was.

The reason Nisse was not afraid was that he was so goodhearted and friendly towards every living thing that not even the fiercest animal had reason to harm him. So he wasn't afraid of wolves or bears or witches, or the trolls in fearsome Hulta Wood.

As soon as Nisse learned what had happened to Lily White, he immediately decided to walk to the troll caves and bring her back. His mother and father let him go, for they knew that Nisse, who was so good to everyone, had nothing to fear.

He took a stick in his hand and put a slice of buttered bread in his pocket, and set out. Soon he arrived at the forest. It was not easy for him to cross the ravines and boulders, the fallen trees and brooks and marshes; but Nisse was small and thin and quick. He went through the brushwood and groves like an eel.

After a while he caught sight of a witch sitting on a ledge combing her tousled green hair. It was the quick-footed witch of Hulta Wood, and her hair fell all the way down to her hips.

"What are you doing here in my forest?" she called, as Nisse came walking along.

"I'm looking for our cow, dear lady. The trolls have stolen her," replied Nisse without stopping.

"Now wait a minute, you," the witch screamed, and she jumped down from the ledge to grab his collar.

But at that moment her long hair caught in the spreading branches of a fir tree, and she was left hanging, the tips of her toes just above the ground, and she could not get free.

She began to kick and twist and shout as loud as she could. Anyone else would have laughed and said it served her right, but Nisse was not like that.

"Tch, tch, little Mother," he said in a friendly voice. "I'll help you."

So he climbed up the tree, pulled and loosened the thick tufts of hair, and at last managed to free the witch from the heavy branches.

"You're an odd one, to help someone who wants to hurt you," said the witch, surprised. "I intended to give you a thrashing, but now I might help you instead."

"That would be good of you, little Mother," said Nisse.

"You'll never be able to get past all the dangerous animals in the forest unless you know their language," said the witch. "But I will give you a magic herb. If you put it in your ear, you will understand everything they say while you are in the forest."

Nisse thanked the witch, did as she told him, and walked on. After he had gone some way, he came to the great angry watchdog of the forest. It limped towards him on three legs, and made a fierce face.

"Poor little doggy," said Nisse, full of confidence and sympathy. "Have you hurt yourself? Can I help you?"

The dog had been ready to jump on the boy, but was so surprised by his kindness that it sat down on its hind legs just like a well-behaved dog. "You're not like other people, are you?" it said.

"Perhaps not," said the boy. "Let me see your paw, little Father."

The dog gave him its forepaw, and Nisse saw there was a big thorn in it. He pulled the thorn out, put a little wet moss on the wound, and tied it together neatly with grass.

"That feels better," said the watchdog, standing on all fours. "I had intended to bite your ears, but I don't want to now. Where are you going?"

"Our cow is lost," Nisse replied. "I am going to the troll caves to find her."

"My, my!" said the watchdog with a pitying look. "That is not an easy errand, for those trolls are not to be trifled with. But since you were kind enough to cure my foot, I'll go with you and show you the way. Perhaps I can help you."

The watchdog did as it had promised. It leapt ahead, and the boy scampered after it, and then they went deep, deep into the forest. They had run for several hours when they caught sight of the bear lumbering through a peat bog, sniffing for cranberries.

"You had better go round," said the watchdog, "for he attacks people and cattle."

"Well, I like the way he looks, even if he is big and shaggy," said the boy, and kept on walking.

Just then the bear saw him. It rose on its hind legs, let out a terrible growl, and padded towards him.

"My, what a great rough voice you have," said the boy, putting out his small hand in greeting. "You would make a fine bass in a church choir."

"Uff," grunted the bear, stepping closer.

"Yes, a very loud voice," continued the boy. "But you seem very friendly, anyway, holding up both paws to greet me."

The bear was just about to gobble Nisse up, when the green-haired witch jumped out from the trees. She had followed Nisse at a distance to see what was going to happen to him in the troll caves.

"Don't touch that boy," she cried to the bear. "He is not like other people."

"It's none of your business," roared the bear, and opened its jaws wider.

Then the witch of the wood picked up a knotted fir stump and flung it into the bear's wide-open mouth. The stump stuck between its jaws so that it could neither growl nor bite.

"Ugh," said the boy. "That was a mean thing to do to old Father here, who was so friendly and wanted to greet me with both his paws. But wait, let's see if I can't help you out of this."

He found a long wooden stick and began poking it into the bear's mouth. The bear sat still, panting, and after much picking and prodding, Nisse at last managed to loosen the stump.

"That was well done," grunted the bear contentedly. "I can see you are a boy with pluck and nerve. I was going to swallow you in one gulp, but now you are safe from me for the rest of your life. What are you doing here in the forest?"

"I am looking for our cow. The trolls stole her," Nisse replied.

"Humph, you are a daring boy to set out on an errand like *that*," said the bear. "If you can outwit the trolls in Hulta Wood, you are cleverer than you look. I think I'll follow you and perhaps I may be of help."

They all set off again. The dog padded first in line, the bear lumbered along at the back, and the green-haired witch of the wood went on ahead to see how the adventure would turn out for the boy.

They arrived at the trolls' mountain caves as the sky began to darken. The entrance was covered by mighty boulders, but there was a small opening just about big enough for a bird dog to squeeze through.

"Nisse can crawl in there," said the bear. And it added, "If the troll attacks you, just call 'Bear, come in,' and then the trolls will have a *real* fight on their hands, I can promise you."

"I don't think it will be necessary," said Nisse. "But thank you just the same."

And so he crawled through the narrow opening. He entered a cave as big as a barn. The old troll was sitting by a fire, munching on a bone. He looked awful, with an enormous nose, hairy arms, and yellow-green cat's eyes. And there in one corner of the cave was Lily White, chewing on some rough thistles the troll had picked for her in the forest.

"Why, look, a little urchin!" exclaimed the troll, and grabbing Nisse around the waist he lifted him to the table. "Where do you come from?"

"Dear friend troll," said Nisse politely. "I have come to fetch our cow, who seems to have wandered into your cave."

"Don't be so foolish," clucked the troll. "Oh, no, my little fellow. I needed milk, you see, and so did my old woman. And you yourself will make a fine little chop for our dinner. As soon as Mother returns, she'll put the pan on the fire."

"Oh, you're joking," said Nisse. "You wouldn't be so cruel to a little boy who never did you any harm."

"What nonsense!" cried the troll. "Of course I'll fry you. Aren't you frightened?"

"No, I'm not afraid of you," said Nisse boldly. "I know you're not as bad as you pretend."

"I've never seen the likes of you in my life," growled the troll. "Mother, Mother, come here quick and light the fire."

A troll woman rushed out of a grotto and started rubbing flint and steel together to make a fire.

"It's good of you, Little Mother, to make a fire to warm your old man," said Nisse happily. "But now I think it's time for Lily White and me to go home."

But then the old troll caught hold of Nisse and prepared to fling him into the frying pan.

Now most creatures, it is true, can be won over by friendliness, kindness, and generosity, but only force helps with a troll. Nisse realized this now, and so he called, "Bear, come in! Bear, come in!"

You should have seen what happened next. The bear tossed the boulders at the entrance, left and right, with its great paws. Sparks flew in the air. Then the bear rushed into the cave, and behind it came the witch of the woods and the watchdog.

The bear caught the troll firmly by the neck, and flung him on to the floor. The dog dug its teeth into the troll woman's leather jacket, until she fell down with a splash right into the waterpail by the fire. Meanwhile, the witch of the woods went over to Lily White and loosened the rope with which she was tied.

Nisse lost no time in climbing on Lily White's back. He held tight to her long horns and called, "Thank you all for helping me. Don't be too hard on the trolls." Then he urged Lily White on: "Hurry, dear Lily White! Hurry, dear cow!"

And with the boy on her back and her tail in the air, Lily White set off. Nisse waved his cap in the air and shouted, "Hurrah!" They galloped over tree trunks and stones, through forest and meadow, and were both safe and sound back at the croft by the time the sun came up.

The rejoicing was great at the croft. But back in the cave the trolls were so frightened by the fact that their own forest friends had helped Nisse — just because he was kind and trusting — that they never dared show their noses in the manor-house pasture again.

The Magpie with Salt on her Tail

Anna Wahlenberg

Once there was a boy who was always wishing for things. One time he would wish very hard for a little horse to ride, another time he would wish for a sled or a boat, or even just a cheap clasp knife. But his father had died and his mother was a poor woman who made brooms for a living, so none of his wishes ever came true.

One day when he was busy wishing like this, he was given some good advice by a wise old man. The old man told him to go to the woods, sprinkle a pinch of salt on the tail of a magpie, and then he would get whatever he wished for. But he had to wish quickly, while the salt was still on the bird's tail, or else it would be no use.

From that day on the boy always went about with salt in his trouser pockets. He would set out early in the morning and come home late at night, and he saw many magpies, but he never could get close to any of them. Then one day he found a magpie that was friendlier than the rest. She let him come so close that he could almost touch her, but then as soon as he stretched out his hand with the pinch of salt, off she flew and sat in the nearest tree laughing at him. She teased him like this all day, and when evening came the boy was so tired he threw himself down under a pine tree and closed his eyes and tried to sleep. But he could still hear the magpie hopping about in the undergrowth, and finally he heard someone call his name. "Olle! Olle!" The boy looked up and saw that it was the teasing magpie.

"What's this?" he exclaimed. "Can you talk?"

"Yes, really I am an enchanted princess and you shall indeed have your wish if you will help me. Get me a really fine clasp knife to clean my beak and claws, and I shall sit so still that you can sprinkle salt on my tail."

Well, the boy thought that was fair, and the next day he went picking berries, which he sold, and this he did until he had earned enough money to go to the city and buy a really fine knife. Then he went straight back to the forest to find the magpie, and opened the blade so that it would shine in her eyes.

Immediately she came hopping up. She looked at the knife, first with one eye and then with the other.

"Rubbish," the magpie said. "That is no knife for a fine princess like myself. It doesn't even have a gold handle." And she flew up into the trees again.

Olle felt so sad that tears filled his eyes. "I'll try to get you one with a gold handle then," he said.

"No, thank you. I don't want a knife any more. But you can give me a beautiful sled instead. That would really be fun, to go sleigh-riding this winter."

So Olle began to whittle breadboards and wooden spoons with his new knife, and did it so well that they were a delight to look at. He sold them quickly in the city, not even waiting long enough to carve a little boat for himself. In six months he had earned enough money to buy a splendid sled, and so he went back to the magpie in the woods.

"Here is the sled," he called out boldly, for he was sure she would like this beautiful sled.

Down she flew from her tree, and perched on the seat and began to peck at the iron runners. She laughed loudly. "Did you think this would do for such a fine person as myself?" she said, as she flew on to a branch overhead. "No, it should have been made of silk and silver."

Olle almost cried in frustration. "I will try to get you a better one," he said.

"No, no," squeaked the magpie. "Now I want a carriage and horses, or else there will be no sprinkling of salt."

Poor Olle left with a heavy heart, but he had not given up hope. Whatever the cost, he would get the magpie her carriage with horses.

He took the sled to a hill where the local gentry used to go sleigh-riding, and there he hired it out to everyone who would pay well. He found many customers, for really the sled was the best to be had for miles around. Olle did not ride even once himself. Whenever he wasn't busy with the sled, he carved more beautiful things in wood with his clasp knife.

At last he had saved up enough to buy a horse. He trained the horse and taught it to do tricks, and showed it for money until he could afford to buy another horse, which he also taught tricks; and soon he was able to buy an elegant little carriage with wheels that had silver spokes and an apron that had silver clasps. He braided the horses' manes and put cockades on their ears and gave them silver bits, and then he drove off into the woods to the magpie.

She was sitting on a branch, just as lively and skittish as ever.

"Well, this *is* something," she said, when she caught sight of the glittering silver.

She flew down to inspect the carriage, both from above and below, pecked the horses' backs to find out if they were young and fresh, and then she cocked her head.

"I don't like open carriages," she said. "I prefer to ride in a closed one. And the horses should have been white, not brown."

"Oh, me, oh, my," sighed Olle, and sat down on a stone to think. A fussier woman than that magpie could not very well be imagined, but of course she was a princess.

"Well," said the magpie. "I can see you are no judge of horses and carriages. So now, if you want me to help you, you must give me a castle. It must be at the foot of a hill by a lake, and there must be no fewer than a hundred rooms, and a park and garden too."

Olle sighed deeply. It was a lot to ask. But then he remembered he had his horses and the carriage, and began to drive around the town. Everyone wanted to hire him out, for even if the magpie had not liked the horse and carriage, certainly it was the finest the townspeople had ever seen. Soon Olle earned enough money to buy another horse and carriage, and then another and another. At last Olle had his own stable and was making money hand over fist.

After that it was not difficult to build the castle, and within a few years it was ready, built of shining white marble, with flags waving from the towers. Olle went out into the woods to fetch the magpie and take her to the castle.

She tripped after him, hopping from room to room, looking into the kitchen and the pantry to see that everything was there. When she had seen it all, she perched on the banquet table in the great hall.

"Oh, well," said she, "it would all do but for one thing that is missing. That is, three chests full of gold, without which I cannot maintain my court."

"For shame!" cried Olle, who had grown bigger now and was able to speak up.

"Otherwise there will be no salt sprinkled on my tail," said the magpie. And she flew out the window and was gone.

Olle had already achieved so much that he did not want to stop now, and besides, he had learned how to make money. So he worked hard for five more years, until there were three enormous chests filled with gold coins on the floor of the banquet hall.

He went to the forest to bring the magpie to the castle the second time. As soon as she entered the hall, she flew to the three chests, perched on the middle one, and eyed the gold coins.

"Yes," she said. "That should do. You may sprinkle some salt on my tail."

The solemn moment had arrived at last. With a beaming smile, Olle put his hand in his trouser pocket and brought forth a pinch of salt. The magpie sat quite still, and he sprinkled the glittering crystals on her tailfeathers.

"Well, what is your wish?" asked the magpie.

Indeed, what should he wish? Olle had been so busy working that he had completely forgotten what it was he had wanted to wish for.

"One, two ..." said the magpie.

"Just a moment, just a moment. Let me think."

But for the life of him, Olle could not think of what he wanted to have.

"Three," said the magpie, and with a flip of her tail feathers, flew up so suddenly that the salt fell off. Then she sat in a window and laughed at Olle, until the hall echoed.

"You — you make me so angry!" Olle shouted. "Now I know what I want. I'll buy myself a gun and shoot you."

"That would not be nice, little Olle," said the magpie. "To shoot me after I have granted all your wishes, so that you have nothing more to wish for? Don't you already have a clasp knife and a sled and horses and a carriage and a castle and money, and all this without your having to say a word?"

Olle stood there with his mouth and his eyes wide open. It was true. He already had everything he could wish for, and he had never even noticed.

"Well, I declare," he exclaimed, clapping his hands in astonishment. "I worked so hard just to be able to sprinkle salt on your tail feathers, and it was all quite unnecessary."

"Yes, how do you explain that?" laughed the magpie louder than ever before, and lifted her wings and was gone.

But Olle did not bother to try to explain it. He just settled down in his castle, and there he lived well all his days.

The Changelings

Helena Nyblom

O nce there lived a king and queen who had no children, although they wished for one so much. At last, one summer, the queen gave birth to a daughter, and the king and queen were indescribably happy. The little princess, a beautiful child, was christened Bianca Maria. Her eyes were big and blue, her little mouth turned up sweetly, and her skin was as delicate as the petal of a flower. Naturally, she must have the noblest lady in the land as her governess.

And so the countess of the realm and Mistress of the Robes, Esmeralda, was entrusted with watching over the princess. At night two nurses slept by the cradle, one on each side, and in the daytime Countess Esmeralda looked after the royal infant. All this was very right and proper, for Countess Esmeralda was enormously aristocratic, though she was not at all suited to be a governess in any other way. She was very old, and always sleepy. Time and again she would nod off, although she always said she was only resting her eyes.

At night the princess slept in a big bed chamber; during the day her cradle was carried to an acacia grove near the palace. There a fountain splashed, and tall rose bushes grew all around. The tall acacias dropped their white flowers on the princess's coverlet; the air was mild and fresh; and white pigeons flew from their cote to look at the sleeping child. "She is so sweet," they said, tripping silently around the cradle. "As white and soft as a dove."

But one day something terrible happened.

Behind the castle, in a black forest on the mountain, a troll and his wife lived in a cave. Now this troll wife had also just given birth to a little girl — a small, swarthy baby with keen eyes and matted hair. One day the old troll went to the palace fountain to fetch some water. He padded along quietly — so quietly that no one would hear him. Countess Esmeralda was fast asleep in her big easy chair by the cradle, and the pigeons were tripping over the gravel cooing, "Isn't she lovely? Isn't she as white and soft as a dove?"

The troll crept cautiously up to the cradle and looked through the silk curtains at the sleeping child. Then he went home and told his wife, "Now I have seen the child that I would have liked to have. White and soft as a dove, with the sweetest little mouth."

"You couldn't be the father of that child," said the troll wife, showing all her green teeth. "A big troll begets a little troll, and must be satisfied with that."

But all the time now the old troll was thinking about the little princess, until finally it was too much for him. "Mother," he said, "let's steal the royal baby. It would be easy. The old crone who watches her is always snoring. We can take the princess and put our troll midge in her place."

At first his wife did not want to agree at all. She was only an ugly old troll, yet she loved her own child. However, her troll husband never left her in peace, until at last she was so tired of his nagging day and night that she pulled the baby troll from its cradle, wrapped it in a rag, and said, "Go along, take your child. But I warn you, don't come back empty-handed."

The old troll ran to the acacia grove as fast as he could. There was the golden cradle. The pigeons were tripping around, the acacias were dropping flowers, and Countess Esmeralda was snoring softly in her deep chair.

In a trice the troll had ripped off the cradle curtains, snatched the princess, put his troll baby in her place, and then run faster than a hare up the mountain with his precious bundle.

The countess awoke and noticed nothing. She believed the princess was asleep. After a while, the queen came into the grove. She liked to walk there in the mornings and see her baby. Imagine her horror when she leaned over the cradle and found, not dearest Bianca Maria, but a little troll bundle staring up at her with small, evil black eyes. She cried out, nearly fainting, "What is this? Where is my child? This is not my child. This is not the little princess!"

Countess Esmeralda started in terror. "Not Your Majesty's child?" she said. "Who else's child could it be? No one has been here, not a soul. I have been here wide-awake the whole time." Countess Esmeralda did not mean to lie, for really she didn't know how often she fell asleep.

The king and all his court were summoned, and the royal physician was asked for his advice. "A strange case, a very strange case," he said. "I believe it is what is called —" and he mentioned a long Latin name which no one understood. "But it is probably a thing that will pass," he added, and prescribed sweet milk baths. They were to lay the baby on a bed of violets, and then surely it would not be long before she looked the way she did before.

The finest cows were bought and the child was bathed in their warm, creamy milk. The cradle was filled with violets, which smelled heavenly, but the queen did not find her child at all changed. Black she was and black she stayed. Well, not really black, but brown as a hazelnut, with coal-black eyes and hair. All the court, however, said she looked perfectly sweet and enchanting, until finally the queen, too, thought the same. Still, every time she actually saw her, she would sigh and think, "This is not my angelic little Bianca Maria."

In the meantime, the old troll had run home with the little princess to his cave.

"Isn't she sweet?" he asked, opening the shawl he had wrapped her in.

His troll wife threw him a scornful look. "Such a miserable washed-out little thing! She looks like a leek, pale and thin. But you wanted her, and now you have to put up with her."

They laid the baby in the troll child's cradle, but the pillows and mattress were stuffed with coarse straw, into which a thistle or two had also found its way. When Bianca Maria felt this hard and prickly bed, she began to cry bitterly.

"Why is she crying?" the troll wife asked.

But her husband had already run down to a peat bog. There he gathered cotton-grass, and then, on the mountainside, he picked wild thyme. With these he stuffed a new mattress for the cradle, and when once again everything was soft and fragrant around the little one, she stopped crying immediately and fell quietly asleep.

In the castle the troll princess grew up into a very strange child. We call her the troll princess because she had no other name. Troll children are not baptized. They arrive in the world and their father simply spits on their neck and says, "Out with you into the world, you little cribble-crabble." And that's all there is to it.

But the queen could not bring herself to call the changeling Bianca Maria; she only called her Black Eye, for the troll baby had a pair of flashing black eyes.

"Where did our daughter get her strange black eyes?" asked the king, staring at the queen.

"Yes, who can explain it?" she said, and sighed. "When she was born she had eyes as blue as yours and mine."

Nor was little Black Eye easy to manage. She gave them all trouble, the king and the queen and the whole court. When she didn't get what she wanted, she lay on the floor on her back and kicked her feet in the air and screamed until they had to close the windows to keep her from being heard outside. If she had a new dress, she found it funny to pour soup all over it, or else to pierce it with a poker and make a big hole. Then she looked out of the corner of her eye at the queen to see how angry she would get.

She behaved worst, however, to the old countess Esmeralda. She could not stand the countess, and would sprinkle sand in her hair when she fell asleep in her chair, or hide her shoes in a bush where the old lady could not find them. Sometimes she hid, too, and had a wonderful time of it when the countess woke from a little nap and could not find her. She would creep behind bush after bush for hours on end while the Mistress of the Robes tottered about with her cane, trembling and out of breath from looking for her so frantically.

For a while the king spanked the troll child when she was naughty, but then she became so furious and looked like such a little wild beast, purple in the face and shrieking horribly, that even the king was frightened. From then on he did not beat her any more. Surprisingly the king had something of a soft spot for this obstinate child, which she soon enough took advantage of.

She was not more than eight years old when one day at the dinner table, after listening to something the king had said, she pulled his beard playfully and said, "Is that so, old Father King? I suppose some might think so." The queen became quite red and looked at her husband in alarm. But the king put his arm around the girl's waist and laughed, "You are the worst little troll child in the whole world."

Among the trolls up in the mountain, Bianca Maria was also eight years old. She was tall and thin for her age, and had beautiful yellow hair. She obeyed the trolls in everything for she believed they were her parents, although she often felt in her heart that she did not love them as much as she should. To the old troll, she was still the very sweetest thing imaginable.

"Such white fingers," he would say. "And such silky skin and such wonderful yellow hair." He became affected when he talked with her: he would cock his head, kiss her finger, and squeak like a little rat.

"Don't be silly, you ugly old scamp," his wife said, and smacked his hand hard. She had no soft spot for the king's daughter. Indeed, it annoyed her when Bianca Maria was always so mild and obliging, and said Yes to everything you asked her to do.

One day the troll wife called to the girl angrily, "Yes this and Yes that, you always say Yes. Can't you say No, you wretch?" But Bianca Maria did not mind. She went quietly about her work, and said nothing in the face of scolding.

Even as a little child she was given work to do. She went on bare feet deep into the forest to a bubbling well to fetch water for the kitchen. The well never ran dry, winter or summer; and in the forest, birches rustled in such a friendly way, and the pine trees murmured so courteously that Bianca Maria made all the trees her friends.

And how she loved all the forest animals! Little squirrels darted up with their tails in the air to stare at her. "Out so early?" they said, sitting on their hind legs. "Do you by chance have some nuts or something good in your pocket?" And Bianca Maria had always brought nuts or acorns, which the squirrels ate from her hand.

She knew every bird in the forest, and could have told you immediately if it was a chaffinch or a siskin chirping in the branches. She stood still and listened to the song of the thrushes, the quiet cooing of the wood pigeons.

It was not only forest animals that Bianca liked; she was as good and friendly to such unpleasant ones as the big toads that waddled into the mountain cave. Bianca knew the old troll woman would kill any toad she caught sight of, so she hurried to pick them up and carry them away to safety. They were heavy and wet, and unpleasant to touch, but Bianca Maria would take each one carefully between her small fingers and whisper, "Poor thing. You can't help it if you are ugly and clumsy. But don't come in here, or they will kill you with a broomstick." And she set the toad down in the grass. She did not even mind rats. She saved grain in an old earthenware jug which she put on the floor behind her bed, and at night the rats came running, and squeaked, "Now we are having a party! Now we are having a party!"

One day the old woman caught two wood pigeons. She killed them and plucked their feathers and put them in a pot. Bianca stood by and wept. The troll wife became very angry. "Well I never!" she cried. "To set up a howl over a couple of miserable pigeons. You will never be a big daring troll child. I cannot understand where you came from."

Of course, the troll woman knew very well, but the old troll had strictly forbidden her, by the slightest word or sign, ever to let Bianca know she was the daughter of a King.

Years passed, and before long the two girls were each seventeen years old. The troll princess had become strangely handsome. She was not tall, but she was slim and comely. Her skin was not as dark as it had been as a baby; her hair was raven black and fell in waves and curls about her face. And she had a pair of big black eyes that probably would have been beautiful had they ever expressed a little friendliness and kindness, but instead they stared crossly at everyone. When she was angry, her eyes flamed so, people were afraid to look at them. And when she was pleased, they seemed to express ridicule and scorn. She appeared to look down on everyone, and the older she grew, the meaner she became. She boxed the servants' ears and stuck pins into her maid when she was being dressed. If old Esmeralda dared to scold her, she would reply, "Why should I listen to you? You're too old. Sit still and go to sleep in your chair and leave me alone. I am going to do exactly as I like."

And so she had all her own way. Sometimes she did not want to get up, so spent the whole day with a blanket pulled around her ears. If someone tiptoed into her room to see if she was awake, she would shout, "Get out of here and leave me alone!"

Sometimes she rose before sunrise, while the mist still covered the meadows and the morning star was still in the sky. Then she walked to the stable, woke the groom by pulling his hair, and made him saddle the wildest horse. She rode out alone. "I don't want a lout like you at my heels," she told the groom as she swung into the saddle. She neither trotted or cantered, but galloped so fast she swept through the forest like a whirlwind. As she rode, she hallooed and shouted so loudly that all the hares and foxes and deer and squirrels fled before her.

One day the troll princess came home so wet and red in the face from her headstrong ride that the king asked her earnestly to be more careful. At this she became so angry that she cracked a large mirror with the handle of her riding crop. The broken glass rained down like icicles, and the king paled and left the room. Neither he nor the queen could manage her, and they decided to marry her off as soon as possible. "Perhaps she will be a better wife than a daughter," said the king, though the queen herself did not see much hope for it.

So they chose a bridegroom for her, the noblest and handsomest young duke in the realm. Of course, he was enormously flattered to take the king's only daughter to wife, and it wouldn't have done for him to ask questions. So he bowed deeply and said, "My most humble thanks." Besides, the princess liked the young duke. She found him handsome, and she was so sweet and mild in his presence that he thought she was an angel. In time, preparations began for the wedding.

It was not long, however, before she began to show her true character. The young duke was amazed. He had never expected to see a princess slap her servants and cuff the ears of her ladies-in-waiting, and one day she even stuck out her tongue at old Countess Esmeralda in front of him. "Princess!" he said with dismay in his voice, and his eyes flashed angrily.

But Black Eye turned on him and cried, "Princess and princess! As if a princess is not permitted to do as she likes. You can't expect me always to go on tiptoe for that old scarecrow. And don't pull a long face. Remember, I am of better birth than you."

Eventually she became more and more capricious before her young betrothed. Sometimes she turned her back on him, and said, "Go away! I can't bear the sound of your voice." At other times she found a thousand faults with him, or his coat or doublet. If they went riding together, it amused her to gallop so fast that he could not possibly keep up. She would wait for him at the castle gate and laugh as he returned: "Poor boy, haven't you ever been on the back of a horse before?"

120

The next day butter wouldn't melt in her mouth and there were not enough beautiful and kind things she could say to him. "Little sweetheart, darling, handsome, charming duke's child!" she would murmur, and flash her black eyes at him. "You are like a honeycomb and I could eat you up." And she would open her mouth as if she wanted to bite him.

The young duke became more and more nervous about his royal bride-to-be. He would have liked to run away, but his father would not permit it. "Even if she were the meanest old troll witch," the father said, "it is a rare honour to be chosen as the bridegroom of the princess. She is, after all, the king's daughter."

By now Bianca had also grown into a young maiden, and one day the old troll said to his wife, "It is time to present our daughter at the troll court. I am very proud of her and want all the trolls to see what a beautiful daughter we have."

"If only they don't notice that you stole her, for she looks no more like you or me than a wood pigeon resembles a toad."

But the old troll was firm, and one midsummer evening they went with Bianca deep into the forest to a big mountain cave, where the king of the trolls lived and was holding a great ball. The sun had just set as they came to the troll king's mountain cave. The ball was so crowded and smelled so pungently of trolls that Bianca, standing at the entrance, stepped back. But she had been seen already. The troll woman gave her a shove and said, "Don't be coy now. Show a little troll sense."

And so Bianca entered the hall. The king and queen sat on thrones at the back of the cave. They were decked out with so much glitter and gold that they could hardly move. The queen looked a little like a large toad, and the king was as old and wizened as some strange wind-bent tree, and he had a long and magnificent tail decorated with gold tassels and precious stones. Their only son, the crown prince of the trolls, stood next to the throne. He was thin and spindly. When he saw Bianca, he smiled and showed two rows of pointed yellow teeth.

Trolls of all sizes and shapes stood along the walls. Some were furry as bear cubs, others pale and miserable looking, and some had the bulging eyes of a fish. There were trolls transparent as green glass; others that had no heads but spoke from their stomachs; but all of them were in high spirits. They laughed and shouted and made as much noise as a cat-fight at night, and then the music began.

The musicians could not be seen — that would not have been considered elegant — but you could hear them just the same. Trumpets blew and drums rolled, and the shrill notes of the flutes rang through the air like the pangs of a toothache. It was absolutely magnificent.

At first the trolls danced rather quietly, but it was not long before they all began to jump up and down, do somersaults, or wiggle as wildly as any snake. They thumped about in such a jumble that Bianca could hardly tell one troll from another.

Suddenly the crown prince came towards her, bowed deeply, and asked her to dance. He began to jump and leap like a grasshopper, flapping his big troll ears and grinning to show his teeth. Bianca turned cold with fear. The mountain cave became warmer and warmer, and soon she felt so dizzy she sank to the floor in a faint.

"Wake up!" shouted her troll mother, splashing water on her face. "Think how happy you will be. The crown prince has approved of you and if you become his bride, one day you will be queen of all the trolls in the forest."

She was quite right. The crown prince of the trolls had fallen head over heels in love with Bianca, and before the summer was out their wedding was set to take place.

You can imagine how sad this made Bianca. She was not an assuming girl, with fancy notions about herself, but to be the wife of the troll crown prince! Imagine living in a horrible cave with such a misshapen monster; it was too terrible to think of, and from that day on Bianca only thought and thought of ways to get away. She did not know where she could go, but she knew that she must escape.

The troll princess felt the same way. She was tired of her fiancé, the duke, and he was more afraid of her than ever. When he had introduced her to his noble parents, she had behaved so badly and yawned so loudly at table, then danced so wildly in the evening, kicking her legs in the air and letting out shrill hunting calls, that the duke and duchess were very angry. She herself was so bored with them that she decided then and there never to marry into this noble family that stared at her whenever she moved and was embarrassed by her every whim. She, too, wanted to go out into the wide world and discover new and exciting things far from the king and queen and the royal court.

Her wedding day was set for the middle of August, the same day that Bianca was to become the bride of the troll prince. Early that morning, when the grass was still covered with dew, both girls slipped into the forest. By chance, they passed each other in a certain grove of hazel bushes, yet they did not meet. Bianca had heard something rustle in the grove, and thought, It is a fox sneaking through. The troll princess had stood still and listened as Bianca made her way through the brush, and thought, It is a wood pigeon fluttering there. And thus they missed each other.

Bianca followed the road until she came to the acacias in the palace garden where the trolls had stolen her. The queen was standing by the fountain watching the splashing water, but her thoughts were far away. She was remembering her dear, sweet little Bianca Maria, and what a happy mother she had been then.

Suddenly, before the queen stood a girl so like herself at seventeen that she uttered a cry of surprise and Bianca realized almost at the same time that this was her own mother holding open her arms to her.

"My own Bianca Maria," said the queen.

Bianca threw herself into the queen's arms and for the first time knew what it was like to be hugged to a mother's heart. Then she told the queen of her life among the trolls, and the queen realized what had happened. But they could no longer ask old Countess Esmeralda about it, for she slept deeply now, too deeply for snoring — she was dead. Yet neither the king nor anyone else could doubt that Bianca was the queen's own daughter. She resembled the queen down to her fingertips and delicate ears.

In the forest the troll girl came to the cave of the old troll. The old troll mother was chopping wood. It was hard, green wood, and Troll Mother swore terribly as she chopped. Standing there, the troll girl burst out laughing. "That's right," she called. "That's how things ought to be: when you don't like something, say so."

The troll mother looked up and caught sight of the girl. Immediately she realized it was her own daughter. "My own wild baby!" she cried, holding out her arms. And lovingly the troll mother began to rumple the girl's hair. "See here," she said suddenly. "Here is the twisted little curl no human being can comb straight. Isn't it so?" And the girl laughed, for she remembered all the trouble they had gone to at the palace to try to comb the one little twisted tuft of hair that lay hidden under all the rest. "Let me kiss you, my chick," said the troll mother, giving her daughter a hearty smack.

So it came about that the young duke took Bianca as his bride at the same time as the troll girl married the troll prince, so that she would one day be queen of all the trolls. Both weddings were celebrated with great magnificence.

That evening as Bianca and her bridegroom, followed by their retinue, rode through the forest to the duke's castle, they saw a large fire burning deep among the trees. Smoke and sparks whirled into the night sky, and wild cries and shouts rent the air. They rode on, out into open countryside, and behind them the fire slowly died away and the sparks disappeared. But high above in the sky, millions of stars shone on, never to be extinguished. At the castle, the duke lifted his young bride from the saddle and walked hand in hand with her towards their life together.

Stalo and Kauras

P. A. Lindholm

On Big Mountain, where snowdrifts pile six feet high and never melt, lived a cruel, evil giant named Stalo. No one dared approach Stalo's cave, or fish in the lake at the foot of Big Mountain, without first putting a reindeer steak or two, or a big cheese, on a stone table the giant had built near the lake. Every spring and autumn the Lapp people had to place a whole reindeer there, or else things would not go well with them for the rest of the year. Stalo would kill their reindeer, or send wolves to hunt and destroy them. It was said that Stalo ruled all the wild beasts of the forest.

When Stalo was angry, a rumbling and roaring could be heard from the mountain, as if the giant were amusing himself by flinging rocks and boulders. Then everyone fled, for they knew that Stalo wanted to kill and eat some human being.

Now there also lived in the neighbourhood a courageous and quick-witted Lapp boy named Kauras. One day Kauras decided to put an end to the troublesome giant. So he went to fish in the lake without first putting a gift on Stalo's table. Down the mountain stormed the giant, who was so big Kauras could have fitted into his pocket, and whose one eye was nearly as big as Kauras's head.

"Go away! Go away!" Stalo shouted, threatening Kauras with his enormous fists. But Kauras sat quietly where he was, by the shore, and smiled at the furious giant.

"Calm yourself, Father," he said. "I will leave as soon as I have caught all the fish I can carry."

"Go immediately, or I will kill you," roared the giant.

Kauras burst out laughing. "You are going to kill me, Father? My, that wouldn't do at all." And he laughed even louder.

Stalo was astonished, and asked Kauras if he wanted to fight him.

"No," Kauras replied. "I don't want to squeeze you to death, but we can match strengths another way."

Stalo agreed eagerly and urged Kaurus to suggest something.

"Let's see who can make the largest hole in a fir tree with his head," said Kauras.

"Agreed," said Stalo. He made a running start and banged his head into the nearest tree, so that fir cones rained over him, yet there was no hole in the tree trunk.

"Are you so weak, Father, that you can't even butt the bark off?" asked Kauras.

"Once more," said the giant, and threw himself so heavily at the fir tree that it

126

trembled as if shaken by a thunderstorm. A little bark came loose, but the giant had knocked himself out, and lay on the ground with a bleeding head.

As he lay there, Kauras hurriedly stripped the bark off another fir tree, and cut a hole in the trunk, so large he could easily put his head inside. Then he wrapped the bark back over the hole, and returned to Stalo.

The giant awoke at last, but was unwilling to try another butting contest.

"What a weakling you are," said Kauras. "Look, let me show you how to do it, Father Stalo." And Kauras leapt against the tree where he had made the hole, and his head went in up to his ears.

Then Stalo was afraid and wanted to go home.

"Oh no, Father Stalo," said Kauras. "Wait. We must settle the prize. You will have to pay because you lost the contest."

"Yes, all right, you may fish free here, Kaurus," Stalo replied.

"That is not enough for me," said Kaurus. "You must give back all the cheeses and reindeer you have taken from the Lapps each spring and autumn."

"I've eaten them long ago."

"Then you must pay for them."

"I have no money with me."

"Then I will come home with you."

"Do you dare to?"

"What should I be afraid of? You, who can hardly butt the bark from a fir tree?"

Stalo was silent, and let Kauras accompany him home.

There the giant's wife brought out great dishes of meat and fish. Stalo ate heaped platefuls — Kauras had never seen anyone eat half as much — and when at last the giant had finished, he lay down to sleep without saying a word about repaying the Lapps.

And Kauras pretended that he, too, had nothing more on his mind than a good nap after dinner. The woman showed him a bed in the next room.

Kauras entered the room and closed the door behind him. He realized that the giant planned to kill him during the night, so that he would not have to settle his debts with the Lapps. So now Kauras looked around for a hiding-place. He took a birch log, laid it on the bed, covered it with the blanket, and he himself crept under the bed.

Around midnight, the giant entered the room with an axe. Silently he approached the bed and gave the birch log a powerful blow with his axe, sure that Kauras was lying there.

In the morning Kauras got up and went to Stalo. The giant's one eye opened wide in astonishment. "How did you sleep?" he asked.

"Fairly well," Kauras replied. "But there must be fleas in the bed, because I felt one bite me in the night."

The giant exchanged glances with his wife, then began to pour silver coins into a big sack for Kauras.

"I would like you to carry the sack to the lake for me," said Kauras. "I'm still a little sleepy. Then we will take away the table and the Lapps may come and go without making offerings. If you say No, I will have to challenge you again and then it will go even worse for you."

Stalo believed that Kauras was so terribly strong that he did not dare contradict him. He promised to move away from Big Mountain and never return, and he kept his word. No one ever saw or heard of him after that morning.

And Kauras became rich and important, famous all over Lapland for outwitting the terrible giant Stalo.

The Field of Jewels

Anna Wahlenberg

There once was a young man named Inge who was very poor indeed, for his brother, being bigger and stronger, took everything when their father died except one field, which fell to his share.

This field was so full of stones that there was hardly room for a blade of grass to spring up between them, to say nothing of an ear of corn, so he was obliged to work for a farmer in the village in order to get enough to eat.

Maja, the farmer's daughter, was very pretty. Her cheeks were plump and rosy, and she could make such nice sausages that Inge fell over head and ears in love with her, and at last grew bold enough to ask her father whether she might be his wife.

The farmer opened his eyes in surprise.

"Are you mad?" he said. "Where are you going to live? What will you have to eat? No, indeed; come again when you have gathered a crop off your field, and built a house fit to live in."

Poor Inge looked very sad as he turned away, but towards evening he went down to his field and began to loosen the stones, for he had to work so hard all day that this was his only spare time.

He often sighed on reflecting that it would take at least ten years to finish his task, and felt inclined to throw down the pickaxe and have a nap on a heap of hay close by; but the thought of Maja and her nice sausages cheered him up again, and then he worked with a will.

Suddenly he thought he saw something move at the edge of the ditch, and found that a young giantess was staring hard at him between the boughs of a juniper-tree.

She was a very extraordinary-looking creature, with a mouth like the opening of a great cavern, and eyes like two plates full of milk with a suet dumpling in the middle, while her yellowish-green hair hung in a thick tangle over her ears, just as though it had not been combed for a week! At first Inge felt rather frightened, but he went on with his work, pretending not to see her, for he knew that giants still lived in the mountains, and had often seen traces of them at the edge of the wood.

"Good evening," she said. "Do you expect to find a great treasure there, as you are digging so late?"

Inge had heard that giants are generally stupid, and thought he would find out whether this was true, so he replied:

"Of course. This field is full of jewels which I am going to dig up and sell in the town."

The giantess lifted a stone from the ground, turning it from side to side, while she looked more stupid than ever.

"This is only a common grey stone," she said.

"Oh, that's all you know about it," replied Inge, raising his head. "Why, it's a beautiful blue amethyst! The whole field is shining with them. But you don't understand, so please put it down again." The giantess obeyed, but she could not take her eyes off it, and then said suddenly:

"Now I see that it is blue."

"Indeed," replied Inge.

"Will you give me some stones, as you have so many?"

"I should just think so! I could get ten marks each in the town for those that are no bigger than a pea."

"May I have some if I help you to dig them up?"

Inge chuckled as he replied:

"Well, you may have one, but you will have to do a lot of work first."

"You shall see what I can do"; and she raised herself to her full height, looking just like a beanstalk on two legs; then stooping, she filled her apron with stones which she had thrown on the heap where Inge had thrown his. On she worked the whole night long, and when day began to break and she was forced to go, quite a quarter of the field had been cleared.

Inge hunted through the heap very carefully, as though afraid of parting with something valuable, and at last gave her a stone as big as a child's head, saying: "There, that's really too much too good; you don't deserve it, and mind you take care of it."

The giantess was so pleased that she actually kissed the great lump of stone, and with three huge leaps was back at the mountain again. On reaching her room she took the pin from her neckerchief, and, boring a hole in the stone, hung it round her neck by a cord, just as most girls wear a locket on a ribbon.

After this she felt very proud of herself, especially as she was going with her parents to a great feast given by the King of the giants, who lived in a palace in a high mountain ten miles away, which could only be reached by an underground passage.

She did not say a word to them about her wonderful jewel; this was to be a surprise for the whole party, and so indeed it was! When she took off her neckerchief in the great hall before all the assembled guests, and showed them the lump of stone on her white neck, a loud murmur of surprise arose, and everybody asked at once what sort of an ornament that could be.

"Bless me, child," cried her mother, the old giantess, "you have hung a common stone round your neck."

The daughter smiled scornfully as she related what had happened, and how the field glistened with beautiful amethysts; though giants, as a rule, did not understand how valuable they were.

"H'm," said her Royal Highness the giant-queen, peering through a piece of mountain crystal which served her as an eye-glass; "I really do think that it has a blue shade."

Both the giant princesses hurried up to look more closely.

"To be sure it has," they cried. "We are almost blinded, it is so bright!" And they put their hands before their eyes to shield them.

Then the other guests wanted to see it, and the young giantess received all sorts of compliments and attentions; indeed, before the feast came to an end she was betrothed to a young giant who owned two large mountains and five hills.

The next evening Inge went to his field again, where he delved and dug, wondering all the time whether anyone was coming to help him, until at last he saw some big, round eyes like plates peeping between the branches of the juniper-tree.

They belonged to the two giant princesses, who had never thought about anything but the field of jewels since hearing of it, and had now come to see for themselves.

"Good evening," they cried, as he turned to look at them. "May we help you?"

"If you like," replied Inge carelessly, for he did not want them to know how pleased he was.

"But we don't want to work for nothing. Will you give us some stones for earrings?"

Inge rubbed his hands together.

"Well," he said at last, "that is far too much, but I won't be hard on you this time."

Oh! How the princesses went to work; filled their skirts with stones, and then emptied them, backwards and forwards, till morning dawned, and three parts of the field looked as if they had just been ploughed.

Inge gave each of them two large pieces of stone, and quite overjoyed, they hurried home to bore holes in them and send all the court ladies crazy with envy at their good fortune.

When Inge reached his field on the third evening he set to work as usual, though he could not help looking round to see whether anyone was coming to help him.

All at once he saw a very tall figure standing against a birch-tree, none other than the giant-king himself, looking so grand in his grey mantle and everyday iron crown that Inge felt obliged to bow as low as he possibly could.

"Good evening," said the King, "you are very industrious, but I really don't think you need be. See," and spreading his mantle on the ground he heaped it so full of

133

stones that there was not one left in the field. When he had emptied them on the stone-heap he said to Inge:

"If you are willing I will buy every one of them. I want to build a new throne. My old one is made of diamonds, and I like amethysts far better."

Inge's eyes twinkled as he looked at him, and asked:

"Are you rich enough to buy all those?"

The giant-king gave a loud laugh which sounded like a peal of thunder.

"Yes," he said, "I have twenty rooms full of silver, ten of gold, and five of precious stones; why, I can give you ten barrels of gold without missing them."

This was not a bad bargain. Inge was only too delighted, and made a second bow as low as the first, whereupon the giant-king stamped on the ground so hard that it shook like an earthquake.

Two giants ran up, and he commanded them to fetch the ten barrels of gold as fast as they could, and also bring some sacks for the precious stones.

Very soon they returned with other giants who rolled the barrels along, then filling the sacks with stones threw them over their shoulders and started homewards, the king walking at the head of the procession, while his face beamed just like a full moon, for he was going to have a finer throne than any other king in the world.

Inge stuffed his pockets full of gold, hid the barrels in the ground, and as day was breaking went off to look at the farmer and begged him to come and look at his field.

Of course he came, while Maja tripped behind, and both stood stock-still in surprise when they saw how beautiful it looked.

Then the farmer shook his head, as he said:

"But you haven't built the house yet!" "Here is money enough for the house and the stable and the barn and the pig-sty," Inge returned, pulling the gold pieces out of his pockets and letting them fall carelessly on the ground. "If that is not enough I have plenty more."

How the farmer and Maja stared! They could hardly believe their eyes, but it was all true, and before long Inge had built a house finer than the King's palace, where he and Maja lived happily to the end of their lives, while they ate sausages morning, noon and night.

Dag and Daga, and the Flying Troll of Sky Mountain

Harald Östenson

When the parents of Dag and Daga died, the children believed, as every one did, that they would never stop grieving. But after a while the worst of their sorrow went away, for there was plenty of spirit in these two children who had been left by themselves so suddenly in their little forest cottage. They tended their goats, which gave them plenty of milk, and picked mushrooms and berries, which the boy Dag sometimes exchanged for a little flour.

The girl Daga cooked porridge and baked bread as her mother had done, although she was very young. Dag was as skilful with a bow and arrow as his father had once been, and since in those days no one worried about poachers, he was able to get all the wild game they needed.

Some days Dag would return with a hare or grouse, and once or twice he even brought home a deer, so they did not go hungry.

The brother and sister lived like this year after year, helping each other in every way they could.

But one day Dag stayed out hunting unusually long, and Daga waited up for him all evening and all night, and still he did not return. The next morning she went out to look for him. She knew the direction he had set off in, but that was all.

About midday she came on a bank of wild roses. Suddenly she gave a happy shout. Dag must be in there among the roses, for she could see the feather of his cap, which she herself had sewn on, sticking out of the bushes. She ran up, full of hope. But when she came nearer, she saw that the cap was hanging all by itself on a high branch.

A little farther on, she caught sight of his bow and arrows, but there was no sign of her brother. And the wild roses grew so thick, it was quite impossible for her to get any nearer to his things.

"How could he have got in there?" Daga wondered, after she had tried in vain to break through the thicket. "I couldn't get in there without an axe to cut down these bushes."

So she went home for an axe, and when at last she held her brother's belongings in her hands, night had fallen.

The next morning Daga rose early. First she put food in a bundle, then she let the goats out to graze. They would have to look after themselves as best they could, while she took a walking stick in hand to look for Dag. She walked to their nearest neighbours, a long way, and when she finally reached them they could not help her.

"If he has run into mischief, you who are only a girl won't be able to find him and help," they said. "You should leave him to his fate and come and work for us. We could give you food and lodgings, and there wouldn't be any danger. If you go out to find him, you will probably be lost, too."

Of course Daga realized it might be dangerous, but she could not leave her brother to his fate. So she said goodbye and went her way.

She walked through great forests and over high mountains, and was often so tired that her legs collapsed under her. Then she would rest awhile and trudge on. She spent many nights on beds of moss under sheltering fir trees, and was terrified that wild animals would come and eat her up, but they never did.

And do you know why? Because Daga was never as alone as she thought she was. If she had looked really carefully behind her, she would have seen someone following. It was a tiny old man with a wrinkled face who had followed her when she left the cottage in the woods. He was the tomte of their little cottage, as you may have guessed; and when she fell asleep on the forest floor, he kept watch beside her. If a wolf or any wild beast approached, he stared at it hard until it ran away.

One day, after Daga had walked several hours, she sat down to rest on a moss-covered stone. Around her, the forest was fresh with dew. The chaffinches in the tops of the pine trees were singing happily, and would have made her happy if she had not felt so sad.

Suddenly she heard the sound of dogs barking, and soon a handsome prince in splendid hunting costume walked towards her.

When he saw her he stood still, looking at her for a moment, then he called his attendants, who had by now caught up with him. "Look! A beautiful princess," he exclaimed. "She will be my bride. Hurry back to the castle and fetch a sedan chair and bring her there."

Hearing this, Daga fell on her knees before the prince and pleaded: "Let me go, my lord. I must find my brother, who has been stolen away. I cannot be your bride, for I am not a princess but only the daughter of a poor hunter."

The prince only answered, "Please come. My servants will find your brother for you."

And in a little while a sedan chair arrived, and Daga had to agree to the prince's request, whether she liked it or not.

She was escorted into a chamber at the palace, and by the prince's command, ladies-in-waiting dressed her in a magnificent white gown. Then the prince placed a crown of gold on her head and golden bands on her arms.

"These are welcoming gifts," he said. "You may keep them even if you do not become my bride." So saying, he led her into a large hall crowded with noblemen and ladies. All evening she sat by his side, and he was as courteous and attentive to her as if she had been a real princess.

But as Daga returned to her bedchamber after the banquet, she overheard two valets talking in a dark corridor.

"Can you imagine it, seven of us have to go to look for a hunter who is supposed to have disappeared in the forest," said one.

"Yes," replied the other. "But don't worry. You'll be gone a few days, have a good time, and then you can come back and say you couldn't find him."

"Well, how could we find him, anyway? The trolls have probably caught him. There seem to be so many trolls these last few years."

You may imagine how Daga felt when she heard this.

As soon as she reached her chamber, she quickly gathered her belongings together, tied them in a little bundle, and slipped from the castle so quietly that no one saw or heard her. It was night, but she could not have slept peacefully in a beautiful bedchamber knowing that no one was doing anything to find her brother.

She still wore the white gown and had the golden crown on her head as she walked sadly under the dark pine trees. The little tomte from the forest cottage followed behind. He had been welcomed by the palace tomte, who had given him a velvet suit and pointed shoes, but when Daga left the castle, he, too, had to go.

It grew darker and darker. Then Daga caught sight of two monstrous trolls on the ground between the trees. They had round eyes shining like fireflies, and enormous hands that seemed ready to clutch whatever came close. Daga was terrified, but she did not return to the safety of the palace.

The trolls came closer, then they stopped. They must have seen something behind her, something that frightened them.

At daybreak, Daga sat down to rest. By now she was far from the castle, hidden by dense undergrowth, and was sure no one could find her and make her go back. So at last she stopped to take off her golden crown, the golden rings, and the white gown. She put them all in her bundle, and wore her old clothes again.

She walked all day until, towards evening, she met an ugly little girl. It was hard to tell whether she was a troll or a girl, but she looked a little like a girl. As always when she met someone, Daga spoke of her lost brother and asked advice about how to find him.

"Give me a gown fit for a princess," said the ugly girl, "then I'll tell you who caught your brother." And she looked disdainfully at Daga's plain dress.

"But I _can_ give you a princess's gown," said Daga, and she took out the white dress the prince had given her.

It was plain that the little girl had been taken by surprise. She wanted to go back on her promise, but she could not. "The Flying Troll of Sky Mountain caught your brother," she burst out angrily. "And if you go to Sky Mountain, you, too, will be caught." Then she snatched the gown and ran off.

"The Flying Troll of Sky Mountain," Daga said to herself, and after that, all she could think of was how to get to Sky Mountain.

For seven weeks she wandered until at last the mountain loomed ahead of her, high as the sky, steep and awesome. At the summit could be seen the turrets and battlements of a dark, gloomy castle.

For three long days Daga walked around the foot of the mountain, trying to find a place to begin climbing. But the mountain rose as sheer as a wall, and it looked impossible to climb.

In the evening of the third day she met a hunchbacked dwarf. "Good evening, little Father," she said. "Can you tell me where to begin climbing the mountain?"

"Certainly," said the dwarf with a mocking laugh, "if you'll just give me two heavy gold rings for my trouble." And he laughed again.

"Here you are," said Daga, pulling forth the arm rings the prince had given her.

Abruptly the dwarf stopped laughing, and seemed both surprised and angry. But he had to keep his promise, so he took the girl to a place where a crevice ran zigzag all the way up the mountainside.

"If you are strong and agile and don't get dizzy, you can probably go up here," he said. "I expect, however, that you'll fall and break your neck." And he went on his way.

As soon as the sun rose the next morning, Daga began to climb the mountain. It was difficult, dangerous, and tiring, because she could only put her feet on little ledges and outcrops, and had to hang on with her hands. Here and there, however, the crevice became deeper and levelled out horizontally, so she could sit and rest, or even lie down for a little while. If she had been the least bit careless then, she would have fallen into the abyss, so she tried not to look down and not to become dizzy. She climbed for nine days until at last she was on top of the mountain.

The path that led to the troll castle wound among jagged, craggy rocks overhung with boulders which seemed ready to fall at any moment. She was trudging along this path when suddenly she heard a loud shout.

Her brother's head thrust up from among the rocks. His face was pale, but he was clearly still alive. He had caught sight of her.

"Run, dear sister! Run!" he called.

"I have not walked a hundred miles through the forest and climbed a sky-high mountain to run away just when I find you," his sister answered. "I have come to help you."

"You cannot," said her brother. "All that awaits you here is terrible imprisonment. The troll flew with me here, and wanted me to hammer gold for him like a slave. When I neither could nor would, he cast a spell on me. My whole body is caught in this stone. All I can do is move my head a little."

Daga covered her face with her hands and wept bitterly, but after a while she hurried on towards the castle.

Inside the castle, sitting on a high golden throne, was the terrible Flying Troll. All

142

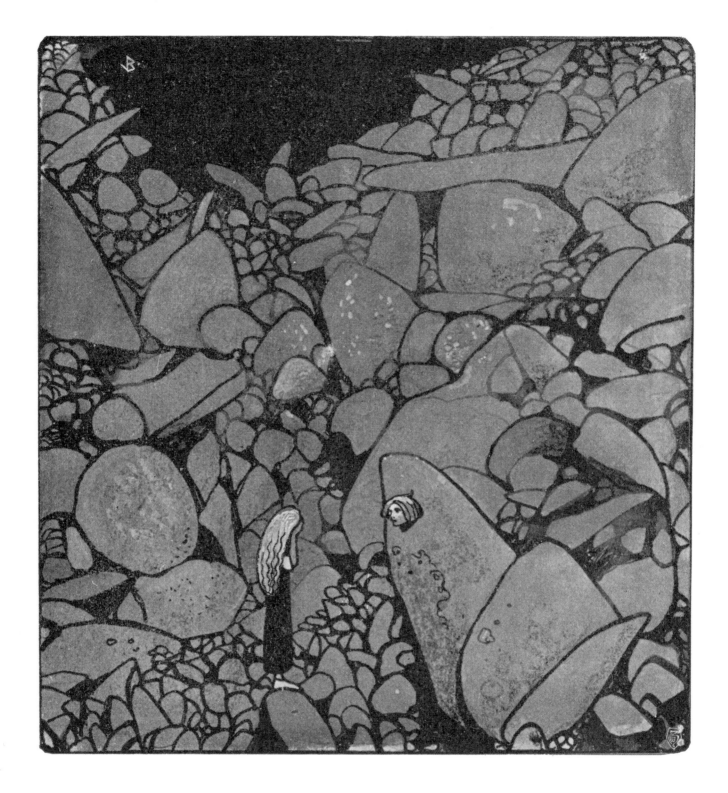

around him, goblins and sprites were busy hammering and forging gold. When Daga entered, they were so surprised, they all dropped what they had in their hands.

"Please, Flying Troll," said Daga, "don't keep my brother in that rock any longer. Let him come home with me."

"Did you really believe that if you climbed all the way up here I would free him

just because you asked me?" said the troll, "If so, you are too foolish for words. But if, before I count three, you give me a solid gold crown fit for a queen, you and your brother may leave in peace. If you don't give it to me, I'll throw you higher than you can see, and then let you fall to the ground in front of your brother's nose."

When the troll had finished speaking, he and the goblins began to laugh so uproariously that you could have thrown half an ox into their ugly mouths. The troll began to count, and as he said "two" Daga brought forth the golden crown and threw it into his black claw of a hand.

You can imagine how baffled the trolls and goblins looked. But the Flying Troll had to keep his word, no matter how angry he was, and soon Dag and Daga were happily on their way home.

But the merry prince of the castle had not forgotten the forest girl. The lady-in-waiting who had escorted Daga to her bedchamber had told him what Daga had overheard, and then he understood why she had left him. First he punished his false valets, then he himself set out to look for Daga.

At last he found her, long after she and her brother had returned to their little cottage in the forest. Daga could not now refuse when the prince asked her to be his bride, and he learned all she had done for her brother and what a faithful and courageous sister she had been.

So Daga and the prince married and were very happy together, and Daga had lost nothing by leaving the safety of the palace to save her brother from the trolls.

Linda-Gold and the Old King

Anna Wahlenberg

Long, long ago there lived an old king who was rather eccentric. People said he was odd because he had had many sorrows, poor old king. His queen and children had died, and he himself said his heart had been torn apart. Who had done that and how it happened, he never told; but it was someone with claws, he said, and since then he imagined that everyone had claws on his hands.

No one was allowed to come nearer than two arms' lengths to the king. His valets were not allowed to touch him, and his dining-room steward had to place his food at the very edge of the table. The king had not shaken anyone's hand for many, many years. If people were careless enough not to remember about the two arms' lengths, and came an inch closer, the king had them put in irons for a week to refresh their memory.

In all other ways, the old king was a good king. He governed his subjects well and justly. Everyone was devoted to him, and the only thing his people regretted was that he had not found a new queen, or appointed anyone prince or princess to inherit the realm. When they asked him about this, however, he always said, "Show me someone who does not have claws, and I will let that person be my heir."

But no one ever appeared who, in the king's mind, did not have claws. The claws might be under the fingernails, or curled in the palm, but they were always there, he believed.

Now one day it happened that the old king was walking alone in the forest. He grew tired and sat down to rest on the moss and listen to the birds singing in the trees. Suddenly a small girl rushed up the path, her hair streaming behind. And when the king looked up, he saw in the trees a shaggy grey beast with flashing eyes and a grinning red mouth. It was a wolf, who wanted the little girl for breakfast. The old king rose and drew his sword, and straightaway the wolf turned in fear and ran back into the forest.

When the wolf had gone, the little girl began to weep and tremble. "Now you must walk home with me, too," she said, "or else the wolf will chase me again."

"Must I?" asked the king, who was not accustomed to taking orders.

"Yes. And my mother will give you a loaf of white bread for your trouble. My name is Linda-Gold, and my father is the miller on the other side of the forest."

What she said was right, the king decided. He couldn't very well let her be killed by the wolf, and so he was obliged to accompany her.

"You go first," he said. "I will follow behind you."

But the little girl did not dare walk first. "May I hold your hand?" she asked, and moved closer to him.

The king started, and looked closely at the little hand raised to his. "No, I am sure you have claws, too, though you are so small," he said.

Linda-Gold's eyes filled with tears, and she hid her hands behind her back. "My father says that, when all I have done is forgotten to cut my nails." She felt ashamed and looked at the ground. But then she asked if she might at least take hold of his mantle, and the king agreed to that. He simply could not make himself tell her to keep two arms' lengths away, for she was only a small child who would not understand.

So she skipped along beside him and told him of her cottage and all her toys. She had so many beautiful things she wanted to show him. There was a cow made of pine cones, with match sticks for legs; a boat made from an old wooden shoe, with burdock leaves for a sail; and then best of all was a doll her mother had sewn for her from an old brown apron and stuffed with yarn. It had a skirt made from the sleeve of a red sweater, and a blue ribbon at the neck, and her big brother had drawn a face on it with coal and put on a patch of leather for a nose.

It was odd, but the old king listened patiently to all her chattering, and smiled. He was sure the little hand had claws, yet he let it pull and jerk at his mantle as much as it wished. But when Linda-Gold and the king came to the highway, and the mill was not far away, the king said goodbye. Now Linda-Gold could go home by herself.

But Linda-Gold was disappointed. She did not want to say goodbye so soon. She clung to his arm and tugged it, and begged him. How could he *not* want white bread, which was so good? It couldn't be true that he did not want to look at her fine toys! She would let him play with her doll all the evening, if only he would come home with her. She would give him a present — the boat with the burdock-leaf sails — because he had saved her from the wolf.

When none of this helped, she at last asked the king where he lived.

"In the castle," he said.

"And what is your name?"

"Old Man Greybeard."

"Good. Then I will come to visit you, Old Man Greybeard." And she took off her little blue checked scarf, and stood waving it as long as the king could see her — and he turned to look back quite often because he thought her the sweetest little girl he had met in a long time.

Even after he had returned to the castle, he still thought of Linda-Gold, wondering if she really would come to visit him. He was worried because she did not want to keep her little hands at a respectful distance, but he could not deny that he longed to see her.

The king was still thinking of Linda-Gold the next morning, and feeling sure that she would not dare venture out so far for fear of the wolf, when he heard a clear child's voice calling from the palace yard. He went to the balcony and saw Linda-Gold with a rag doll under her arm. She was arguing with the gatekeeper. She said she must speak to Old Man Greybeard about something very important.

But the gatekeeper just laughed at her and replied that no Old Man Greybeard lived there. Then Linda-Gold got angry. He mustn't say that, she insisted, for she herself knew very well Old Man Greybeard did live there. He had told her so himself.

Next she went up to a lady-in-waiting who had just come outside, and asked her advice. No, the lady-in-waiting had never heard of Old Man Greybeard, either, and she too laughed heartily.

But Linda-Gold did not give up. She asked the cook, she asked the steward of the household, and she asked all the courtiers, who had begun to gather in the courtyard to stare at her. She turned red in the face as they all laughed, and her lower lip began to tremble. Her eyes were full of tears, but she still maintained firmly in a clear voice, "He must be here, because he told me so himself."

The king called from his balcony, "Yes, here I am, Linda-Gold."

Linda-Gold looked up, gave a shout of joy, and jumped up and down in excitement. "Do you see, do you see!" she called in triumph. "I told you he was here."

The courtiers could do nothing but stare in surprise. The king had to command twice that Linda-Gold be brought to him before anyone obeyed. Then it was no less a person than the royal court's Master of Ceremonies who led her to the king's chamber. When the door opened, Linda-Gold ran straight to the king and set her rag doll on his knee.

"I will give you this instead of the boat," she said, "because I thought that since you saved me from the wolf you should have the best thing of all."

The rag doll was the ugliest, most clumsy little bundle imaginable, but the old king smiled as if he were quite delighted with it.

"Isn't she sweet?" asked Linda-Gold.

"Yes, very."

"Kiss her, then."

And so the king had to kiss the doll on its black, horrible mouth.

"Since you like her, you should thank me, don't you think?"

"Thank you," said the king, nodding in a friendly way.

"That wasn't right," said Linda-Gold.

"Not right? How should it be then?"

"When you say thank you, you must also pat my cheek," said Linda-Gold.

And so the king had to pat her on the cheek; but it was a warm, soft little cheek, and not at all unpleasant to pat.

"And now -" said Linda-Gold.

"Is there something more?" asked the king.

"Yes I would like to pat your cheek, too."

Here the king hesitated. This was really too much for him.

"Because, you see," Linda-Gold went on, "I cut my fingernails," and she held up both her small chubby hands for the king to see. He had to look at them whether he liked it or not.

And truly, he could not see anything unusual on the pink fingertips. The nails were cut as close as a pair of scissors could do it, and there wasn't the trace of a claw.

"You can't say I have claws now, Greybeard," said Linda-Gold.

"No ... hmm ... well, pat me, then."

Linda-Gold flew up on his lap and stroked the old sunken cheeks and kissed them, and soon a couple of tears came rolling down. It was so long since the old king had known love.

Now he took Linda-Gold in his arms and carried her to the balcony. "Here you see the one you have always longed for," he called to those in the courtyard.

A loud cry of joy broke out among them. "Hurray for our little princess. Hurrah! Hurrah!" they shouted.

Surprised and bewildered, Linda-Gold turned to the king and asked him what this meant.

"It means they like you because you have fine small hands which never scratch and have no claws," he said. Then he kissed the two little hands so that everyone could see, and from below the people shouted again, "Hurrah for our little princess!"

And that is how Linda-Gold became a princess and in the course of time inherited the realm of the old king.

The Queen's Pearl Necklace

Anna Wahlenberg

In the park of the king's palace, Estella, the little lady-in-waiting, sat and cried. Sounds of music and dancing came from the ballroom, but she had crept out side and run to a shady bank where no one could see her. She leaned her head against a tree trunk and big round tears ran down her cheeks and fell into her lap.

Suddenly she heard a strange croaking laughter, and there before her stood an old troll woman. "You're crying pretty tears, my lovely child!" she said.

Estella was so startled that she leapt up to run away. But the old troll woman held her back by the hem of her dress. "Believe me, I know why you're crying," she croaked. "I know why you're so sore of heart. It is because the young king will not dance with you."

"He doesn't notice me," gulped the little lady-in-waiting. "He dances with the other ladies-in-waiting, but not with me, because they stand in front of me, and I'm so small."

"That's just it," chuckled the troll woman and rubbed her chin. "But I might be able to help you dance with the handsome young king."

"Oh, yes! Could you?" Estella pleaded with gleaming eyes. The troll woman shook her head thoughtfully. Of course she could help — but did she want to? It would depend on whether or not she would be able to make pearls out of the girl's tears.

"Pearls from my tears?" Estella asked curiously.

"Yes, they're unusually large and clear," answered the troll woman. Then she stood up and with a piece of charcoal drew some strange lines under Estella's eyes. "Now just cry a bit and we'll see."

Estella blinked and squeezed her eyes shut, but in vain. Not a single tear came from her eyes. How could she cry on command? But the old woman knew what to do. She turned the charcoal around and Estella saw the other end was glowing red. She cried in alarm, for the old woman had touched her neck with the burning coal. Now her eyes filled with tears. The great teardrops paused for a moment in the corner of her eyes, solidified, and then rolled hard and shimmering white down her cheeks.

"See, see," said the troll woman and quickly gathered them up. "They are real pearls, just the thing to beautify myself for the troll's feast. If you will just give me all your tears, I'll help you get to dance with the king."

The little lady-in-waiting flinched. All her tears! That was terrible. "Will I never be able to cry again?" she asked.

"No, never again. But what of it? It's no pleasure to cry."

Estella hesitated. Without knowing why, it suddenly seemed to her dreadful never to be able to cry again. But the troll woman came close and said, "Perhaps I could do much more for you. I could perhaps arrange for the young king to fall in love with you and make you his queen."

"Oh!" sighed the little lady-in-waiting. She had never dreamed of such a thing. Now her heart burned with the desire to become the wife of the young king, and she would never find peace until her desire was satisfied.

"Well, take all my tears!" she said.

The old woman leapt into the air for joy, sat Estella down on the bank of moss, and spread her apron across the young girl's lap. Then she began to stroke her with the glowing coal until she wept with pain. Tears poured from her eyes, changing into the most pretty, white pearls which rolled into the troll woman's apron. She cried for a whole hour and then for another. Then the pearl-tears grew smaller until they dried up.

"There," the old one grunted as she took the apron and let the pearls run through her fingers. "Now I have them all! And you will receive what I promised."

She took needle and thread and strung some of the pearls together. She laid the pearl necklace around Estella's neck and tied the thread together.

"As you've cried so well, from now on you shall laugh well," she said. "And no need to worry about losing the necklace, for no human being can open the knot and the thread cannot break." Estella tugged a little at the necklace, but it remained firmly around her neck.

"Be happy with your necklace. It suits you! Farewell" said the old troll woman. Then she gathered her apron with the remaining pearls and limped away towards the mountain.

Estella stood in amazement. If she hadn't been afraid she would have gone after the old woman to remind her of her promise, for she had not grasped that the troll woman had already kept her word. So she slowly made her way back to the ballroom to join the other ladies-in-waiting.

At that moment the king was not dancing, but was joking with the young ladies who laughed at everything he said. Suddenly he listened and asked: "Who is laughing here so beautifully? It sounds like the rustle of pearls."

The ladies-in-waiting looked at each other. Each one would have liked to claim the compliment for herself. But none knew if she was really meant.

As the king got no answer he carried on with his witty remarks and the ladies-in-waiting giggled and laughed as before. He listened carefully, and when the pearly laugh sounded again he saw that it came from the little lady-in-waiting.

"Come here," he said, beckoning her forward. And then he asked her name.

"Estella," she answered. Suddenly she knew that the old woman had kept her word.

The king took her by the hand and danced with her. And when they rested he made her laugh again with his charm and wit. She was so pretty when she laughed, and each time the pearls leapt and glistened on her neck.

The whole evening the young king danced with no one else, and on the following evening it was the same. On the morning of the third day he went to his mother the widowed queen, and told he wanted to marry the little lady-in-waiting.

The queen was horrified, the ministers were horrified, and all the people were horrified. It was not dignified for the king to marry a mere lady-in-waiting. But the king was used to having his own way, and so it happened. Before the week was over, Estella had become queen. The greatest wonder was that everyone who had been so horrified soon loved the young queen. No one could resist her happy laugh which was infectious. Everyone joined in laughing and was merry. And the joy and the court spread over the whole land.

The greatest joy came a year later when Estella bore a son who was the most adorable creature under the sun.

Another happy year followed in the land, but then one tragedy came after another. Bad harvests followed diseases that spread throughout the kingdom. Many poor and sick came to the palace of the king to seek comfort. The king, his mother and the young queen did all they could to help. Their woes moved the king so deeply that he found comforting words for each one. His mother wept, but only the young queen did not weep.

Once, as a poor peasant told how his wife and children were near dying of hunger, there was a soft, suppressed giggle from the queen. Sympathy rose from her heart, and would have produced a sob, had the queen been able to cry, but the only sound she could utter was a giggle. The poor peasant was put out — he thought the queen was mocking him. All the courtiers looked at her, the king frowned. As soon as they were alone, he asked of what she was thinking to laugh at such a tale.

"I was thinking of something else," Estella answered, for she did not dare tell him that she had discarded her tears for laughs. He might, after all, take her for a witch.

Now she began to avoid unhappy people, and soon sad stories were not told in her presence, for she would get up and leave. This made people speak badly of her. They said she had no heart, and only wanted to laugh and be amused. Eventually the king began to believe in the murmurings, and doubted his wife.

Some time later tragedy befell the royal household. The king's mother took ill and died. The king mourned and did not leave her coffin. His young wife, though, was not at his side. How could the king understand that even now, she could not shed a tear? Or worse still, what would happen if a sob escaped as a giggle? At last the king sent for her, so that she could take her leave of the old queen. And as Estella stood before the coffin, he looked into her face devoid of tears.

"My sorrow and the sorrow of the whole kingdom are not yours," he said.

With those words Estella could not control herself and a loud laugh burst from her lips.

"Go!" cried the king, angry and bitter. "I cannot bear to see you!"

In her chambers the queen paced up and down, in vain tearing at her pretty necklace. She would rather be silent forever, if only she could be rid of the necklace. But the sorrow in her heart welled up and emerged as peals of laughter.

The courtiers before her doors heard her laughing to herself. They whispered to each other anxiously. The young queen was behaving rather strangely. Something was not right. So they ran through the palace telling all that the queen was possessed of an evil spirit. When the king heard this, he did not want to believe it, but he could not rid himself of the thought. Only after several days did he go to see his wife.

A short time later another tragedy came. The young boy took ill and the doctors feared he might die. One evening, as the king and queen were sitting by his bedside, the boy no longer answered and did not seem to recognize them.

"Lord, have mercy on us," said the king. "I think his soul is leaving him."

Then the queen could no longer suppress her sorrow and broke forth in peals of laughter. The king leapt up in horror. Now he was convinced she was possessed.

"Go out! Guards, send her out of the palace, and if she ever shows herself again, attack her." And the guards dragged her out of the palace into the forest and left her there. She wandered through the night, not knowing where to go, but not staying still until she fell exhausted to the ground. But the sorrow and pain inside her was worse, and it finally burst forth in wild uncontrolled laughter, and now there was no reason to suppress it.

There was rustling in undergrowth by the side of the mountain where she lay, and the old troll woman stuck her ugly head out. Estella had fallen in front of her cave. "Would you mind stopping this laughter?" cried the old woman, and struck the young queen with her stick.

When the young queen recognized the troll woman, hope rose within her, and she pleaded with her. "Give me back my tears, and I will never again trouble you! Give me my tears, so that I can cry for my dying child!"

"I cannot do that," said the old woman, "until you bring someone to cry at your laughter."

Now she is mocking me, thought the young queen, and beside herself with grief she laughed even louder than before. The troll woman covered her ears, shouting at Estella to stop and go on her way. But Estella could not stop and continued to laugh. At last she paused and said, "I will go, if you will only help me to see my child once more before he dies."

The troll woman's ears ached so badly that she agreed. "I will lend you one of my shadow-cloaks," she said, fetching a light dark grey cloak from her cave. She threw it over the queen, saying, "Now you can go to the palace. Knock on the doors and when they are opened, no one will see you for you are just a shadow. Slip in quickly while the door is open. Go where you will, but take care not to laugh, for in that moment the cloak will fall from you and you can be seen."

"I shall take care," said the queen, and rushed away. At the palace everything happened as the old one had told her. At her knocking the doors were opened, and the servants looked in vain for someone and did not notice the shadow slipping past them. At last she came to the room of the little prince.

The child lay still in his golden bed, the king sitting by his side. He had sent away doctors and nurses, and wanted to stay alone with his son. But he was so tired that he had fallen asleep on his chair.

The queen bent over the child and whispered his name. But he did not respond. She gently stroked his cheek, but he gave no sign of life. She laid her ear on his breast but could hear no heartbeat. She thought he was dead, and in her sorrow forgot herself and the world. A pearly laugh burst from her lips, the shadow-cloak fell from her disappearing like a grey wraith into the darkest corner of the room. But she noticed none of this, nor that the king had got up and was staring at her.

He saw how her lips quivered as if she were weeping, and how her whole body shook in anguish and how she wrung her hands. And all the while a clear, pearly laugh uttered from her lips.

"Estella," he said quietly. She gave a start and wanted to hurry away, when she saw a sudden change in his face. Large tears fell from his eyes and rolled down his cheeks.

"Forgive me," he said, taking her hand and kissing her. In the same instant her own tears flowed again and the pearly necklace broke, scattering the pearls on the face of the little prince where they changed into tears again as they had once been. They awoke the boy from his trance, and he opened his eyes. Seeing his mother, he held out his arms to her and sat up, restored to health and with rosy cheeks. The queen took him in her arms and cried with joy.

Her pearly laugh disappeared forever. She never missed that enchanted laughter. How much better it was to be able to cry!

The Crofters and the Gnomes

Anna Wahlenberg

A crofter and his wife sat at the dying embers of their hearth. The crofter was shaping a new handle for his axe, while the knitting needles flew back and forth in his wife's hands. Every now and then the knife and the needles would come to a standstill and the old couple would stare silently into the flames. It was a sad day for them. Andrew, their youngest son, had followed his brothers and moved to the city. He thought it would be easier to earn a living there than to stay and toil in the fields.

After a short time the old crofter fell asleep in his chair. His wife, however, remained wide awake with troubled thoughts chasing through her head. She worried about where her son could be. God forbid that something bad should happen to him, her dear young boy! She really couldn't grasp that Andrew was already seventeen years old and wanted to make his own way in the world. It didn't seem that long ago that he was sitting on her lap and she was teaching him to eat with a wooden spoon. When she thought back to those days, her tears began to fall and she reached for her apron to wipe them away.

Her apron though lay on the floor filled with brushwood that she had gathered in the forest, and so she had to lift the back of her hand to dry her tears. Just at that moment a gnome sprang out of the hearth, took off his red cap and offered it to her, saying: "Take my hat."

He stood on his tiptoes as if wanting to dry her eyes himself. The crofter's wife took the hat, but was so surprised that she kept it in her hand and forgot to dry her tears with it. She knew he was the house gnome and lived with his wife and children in the ridge of the roof. She had caught a glimpse of him now and then when he had helped in some way or another, but she had never seen him so close. Indeed it was said of old: these little people don't let themselves be seen unless sorrow and need come to the house.

"Don't grieve, crofter's wife," said the gnome. "You will see Andrew returning soon with a bag full of money, and he will rebuild the croft just as he promised."

"Ah, I fear he will have forgotten that," the woman sighed.

"Forgotten? This croft, which is the best in the world?" cried the gnome. "No, that would be impossible."

The woman's face lit up. How comforting that the gnome was so sure of the matter. But soon the fear that something might happen to Andrew rose again. And so she thought of asking the gnome to watch out for him a bit. She bent her head to the side, looked at him pleadingly. "Listen, dear gnome," she said, "could you not go and stay with Andrew as long as he is out there, and keep him safe, and see that he feels at home and comfortable?"

That made the gnome so angry that he snatched back his hat and was halfway to the hearth when he turned and snorted, "Has anyone heard of such a thing? Such demands!" To ask him to leave his home and family to babysit someone else's gangly youth. No thank you! And he disappeared.

The crofter's wife was dismayed and stared after him. Never fall out with the house gnome! And now her tears fell again. Now she had to get up and shake the brushwood from her apron to dry her tears. She buried her face in her apron and knelt crying in front of the hearth. Then she noticed that someone was breathing down the back of her neck, and there was the gnome again with sparkling eyes, his anger blown away.

"Look out there on the hillside," he said. As the wife looked out of the window, she saw a dwarf stepping away into the distance.

"That is my oldest son," explained the gnome, "going off to your youngest son."

The woman was so happy, she clapped her hands. Though she did ask whether the young gnome would really be able to find his way in the world. But that was no problem according to the old gnome. Gnomes could always find help — they asked stones and trees, fences and boats about those who had passed that way. And his boy would speak to the magpies to send home news of how Andrew was managing. As soon as the gnome had finished speaking, he was gone.

The old woman woke her husband to tell him of her news. He, too, was comforted.

But as day after day passed, their sorrow returned for they had no news of Andrew or of the gnome-boy. The magpies had brought no news, or they would have heard from the old gnome.

One evening as the old woman was stirring her porridge, she saw a red hat behind the hearth, and under the hat was a young gnome face. It was neither the old gnome's nor his wife's face, and this young elf was too shy to show more than his eyes and the tip of his nose.

"How in God's name are you here?" asked the old woman who had guessed it to be the gnome-boy. "Are you not supposed to be with my son, Andrew?"

"Yes, I tried, dear lady," replied the little one, hiding further under his hat, "but it wasn't possible."

Then he told of his journey to the city. It had been hard to find Andrew, and at last he had discovered the boy in a terrible place, for he had ended up working in a prison for trolls. To punish them for all their wicked deeds the people had

159

hauled the trolls out of the hills with chains and belts and thrown them into a dungeon. There they were given metal ore to chew, and as soon as they had done that it was taken away, and they were left hungry. One of the prison-warders was Andrew.

The gnome-boy had seen how wicked and cunning the imprisoned trolls were. If the warders did not watch out the trolls would catch their arm or leg and chew it up. It was terrible! No, a gnome simply couldn't live there, much as he tried.

Where Andrew lived it was not much better. He was boarding with another prison-warder and was sleeping in his kitchen. But it was really messy and dirty! There was no corner where a gnome could sit and feel at home. And there was such a lot of noise and arguing in the prison and at the house, so Andrew could not hear a word the gnome-boy whispered to him. He was just wasting his time there without being of the slightest use, so he had come home.

The old woman was so sad, she never noticed her porridge was boiling over. "Oh dear! What is to become of my boy?" she sighed, and it cut the gnome boy to the quick.

"Dear lady, Andrew will manage," he comforted her. "I could see how he counted his money in the evenings, and it was a considerable amount. I'm sure he'll come home soon and rebuild the croft." Then he disappeared behind the hearth.

Soon afterwards one of the neighbours rode to the city, and when he returned he had sad news for the crofters. Andrew had injured his right hand at work, and could no longer use it. When the wound healed, he left, and no one knew where he had gone.

When the crofters heard this news, they were so worried they abandoned their work and forgot to eat, and in the evening they sat by the hearth where only a few embers glowed, for they had neglected to put on fresh logs. So they did not notice the old gnome creeping into the room. They did not hear the words he whispered. All their thoughts were with Andrew. It was bad enough when he left home, but now their sorrow was unbearable. They wanted to go and look for him, but where should they begin?

The gnome hurried from one to the other, but in end the end had to be still in order to think, tugging at his beard in frustration that he could see no way to help. But at last his eyes began to sparkle like they did when he saw what to do.

Carefully he undid the knot in the apron of the crofter's wife, pulled the apron gently free, and hid it in his jacket. Behind the water barrel he fetched the axe which the crofter had put away, and tucked it into his jacket too. Then he crept out of the door into the night.

Now no-one had actually asked him to look for Andrew, but he did it nevertheless. He searched for him through the whole night and right through the following

160

day, and when it was evening again he found him in an old barn, where he was resting for the night on the straw. The bread that Andrew had bought with his last pennies was finished, and he was hungry and thirsty. But he would rather lie freezing and hungry in the barn than beg at people's doors. He seemed as unable to beg as he was unable to work. Next morning he wanted to go into the forest to find berries. And if he did not find any he would go hungry. No matter, the end would just come a bit quicker.

Andrew tossed and turned, shivering with cold, and the rough straws jutted into his face. The old gnome gathered a bit more straw and covered him with it, took the apron from his jacket and carefully tucked it under the boy's head, so that he had a soft pillow.

Andrew smiled in his sleep, for he was dreaming that he was a little boy who was being tucked up by his mother. And it was so pleasant, he wouldn't have changed his place for a king's!

After a while the old gnome pulled the apron from under Andrew's head, stuck it back into his jacket leaving just a corner of it in the boy's left hand. Now he dreamed he was holding on to his mother to stop her leaving. And the gnome stood up and took a few steps. Andrew followed in his sleep, dreaming that he was following his mother. He followed after when the gnome opened the barn door, and then along paths and roads, through forests and over the hills. All the while Andrew slept, dreaming that he was following his mother's apron strings.

Only when dawn came and they were at the croft, did the gnome stop. Andrew woke up, looking around in wonder. How had he come home? And why was his mother's apron in his hand? He saw the gnome — in the past he had merely glimpsed a creature hurrying by — and understood who had shown him the way home. Then after casting his eye around the croft and the land, the logpile, and everything else that was so familiar and dear to him, he nodded to the gnome.

"Thank you for bringing me home," he said. "It was good to see all this once more, but now I have to go again." And he turned his back on the croft. If he wasn't able to work, he would rather stay away.

But how strange! He couldn't move his feet from the ground. Huge clods clung to his boots. When he scraped away the clay and took a few steps, he got stuck again.

Then he heard the gnome laughing behind him. "Andrew, my boy. Why don't you try and walk towards the croft?" he suggested. Andrew tried, just to see what the strange fellow was on about. But what was happening? As soon as he turned back to the croft, his feet danced over the ground, but when he turned away again, heavy clay stuck to his boots and glued him to the ground.

"There, you see!" said the gnome. "You don't have the wit to understand that you're to stay here. Year after year the ground's been lying fallow waiting for you to dig it, and the trees are waiting for you to fell them and rebuild the croft."

Without a word Andrew stretched out his right hand which had no fingers, and could not hold anything. But the gnome just laughed kindly, as if to a small child who had just grazed himself.

"I see the wicked trolls have nibbled at you," he said. "Come, let me blow it better to stop it hurting." And he blew on the old wound while he pulled the handle of the axe from his jacket.

"Here, let's see if you can hold this," he said and pressed Andrew's hand around the shaft. "Just think that you can do it! For what you really want, you can do."

When Andrew saw his father's axe, his heart warmed. How he would love to hold it. He tensed all his muscles to try. And to his surprise he felt how his fingers grew again and went round the shaft. He could not see them, but they seemed to be there. Then he held the shaft tight, lifted the axe and swung it.

"See, it works," said the gnome. "Now you've got gnome fingers, which are not that bad."

Andrew took the axe to a tree and felled it in no time. The next fell just as quickly. He chopped trunks and roots. Never before had the work been so much fun!

Meanwhile the crofters sat inside and listened. Someone was on their land and seemed to be helping himself to their trees! They hurried out, but when they beheld the sight, they were rooted to the spot. It was their Andrew who was felling the trees at speed, though they could not understand how the axe stayed in his hand, for one cannot see gnome fingers. Behind him were the old gnome, his wife, and a host of little gnome children who were clearing the trunks and branches, which Andrew had felled.

"Andrew, Andrew!" his mother called. Then Andrew turned and hugged his parents, and went with them into the hut. As he stepped over the threshold the fire in the hearth flamed up, the pot began to boil, the spinning wheel turned, and the clock in the corner struck the hour to welcome him. And from every corner little gnome-heads peeped out to welcome him home.

From that day on, the gnomes were no longer shy of the crofters who would often see them as they worked. They guided the plough, they stacked the hay in the fields, they swept the hut. All the work went quickly and easily, and soon the little croft became a good farm. Andrew no longer understood why he had ever wanted to work in a troll prison, since now he could live and work happily with the gnomes on the farm.

The Prince Without a Shadow

Jeanna Oterdahl

Once upon a time, there was a handsome young prince who was the joy and pride of the whole kingdom. No one was as joyful and enlightened as the young prince. But his best side was his good, warm heart. If others were not well, he knew no peace, and if he saw want and suffering, he tried to help. So it was that peace and prosperity ruled in the whole kingdom. When the prince crossed the marketplace, crowds followed to greet him. Little girls threw flowers, boys cheered, and the prince greeted everyone with his soft smile which would melt the heart of the coldest misery-guts.

However, the king and the queen had another child, a little princess of five years, who was sickly and pale. Usually she sat in her high armchair by the window playing with flowers that her brother had picked for her in the palace gardens. Every now and then she would smile wanly at the children outside. Sometimes the prince would take her out in a richly decorated carriage pulled by two fine horses. But the princess took no joy in this. She was too sick and tired, and everyone was heartbroken to see her so.

It was most difficult for the king and queen who dearly loved their healthy, happy son, but could not help loving their sickly, sad daughter all the more. All the doctors of the kingdom had been summoned to give their advice and had prescribed drops and ointments from all over the world, but in vain. The princess became paler and weaker, and soon it looked as if she would die. The queen stayed with her day and night, the king in his sorrow forgot to rule over his realm, and the young prince racked his brains to think of some way of helping his little sister.

One night the prince and the queen were at her bedside. At the door sat a page but, though he kept his hand on his dagger, he had fallen asleep. Even the two chamberlains had fallen asleep in front of the fire. It was quite still in the room, only the breathing of the sleepers could be heard. The queen who had not slept a wink all through the previous night finally slumped back in her chair and nodded off. Only the prince was awake — wide awake — and watched the moonlight shining into the room and on to his sister's face, filling it with light.

After the prince had sat for a long time without moving, he went to the window to stretch his legs. The stars in the sky showed him that it was midnight, and just then the watch in the tower blew the midnight horn. When the prince turned to go back to his seat, he saw a strange figure sitting in a grey coat with the cape pulled low over its face.

That must be Death, the prince thought fearfully, afraid that he had come to take his little sister. Then the figure looked up with a strange expression on its face, and said: "I am not Death. See, I have neither scythe nor hourglass. I am the man who gathers shadows. If you will give me your shadow, your sister's illness will vanish and she will become the most beautiful princess."

"My shadow?" asked the prince, and he saw how the moonlight made it long and black on the floor. "Why do you want my shadow?"

"That is my business," the stranger answered, giving him another strange look. "Either you give me your shadow and your sister regains her health, or you keep it, and she remains ill. Incidentally, Death is close by — I just saw him at the city gates."

The prince looked at his pale sister, and then at his own shadow. As far as he could remember he had never had any use for his shadow. Why should he not be able to survive without it? And what a joy it would be to have a strong and healthy sister, and to see his parents happy again. All the people would say, there goes our noble prince who saved his sister by giving away his shadow.

"No, no!" said the stranger. "If you agree to the exchange, you must swear never to tell a soul what we have agreed tonight. And if you break your promise, your sister will in an instant fall dead."

"You seem to be able to read my thoughts," said the prince. "I feel uneasy about that. However, I agree to the exchange. Take my shadow and make my sister better. I promise you not to say a word to anyone."

"Then we are agreed," said the stranger and rose from the chair. He was as thin as a shadow himself. Then he bent over, picked up the prince's shadow and put it in his bag. He then disappeared so quickly that the prince did not see where.

The prince looked around the room in surprise. Nothing had changed. Everyone was asleep, and the sand ran through the hourglass as before. Only one thing was different — no matter which way the prince turned he could not see the smallest trace of a shadow.

"Ah well!" said the prince to himself. "What use is the shadow to me? If my strange visitor keeps his word, I shall manage without it." And he leaned over the bed to look at his sister, and leapt with surprise to see the change. The pale cheeks had some red colour, her fine lips were now rosy and smiling. The girl was breathing steadily and seemed healthy as if resting after a long day of play. The prince was so happy he forgot all worries about his shadow. He sank into his chair and cried for joy.

Next morning when news of the wondrous cure of the princess was spread about there was great joy in the palace, in the city, and in the whole kingdom. The king and queen could hardly believe their eyes when they saw her running around in the

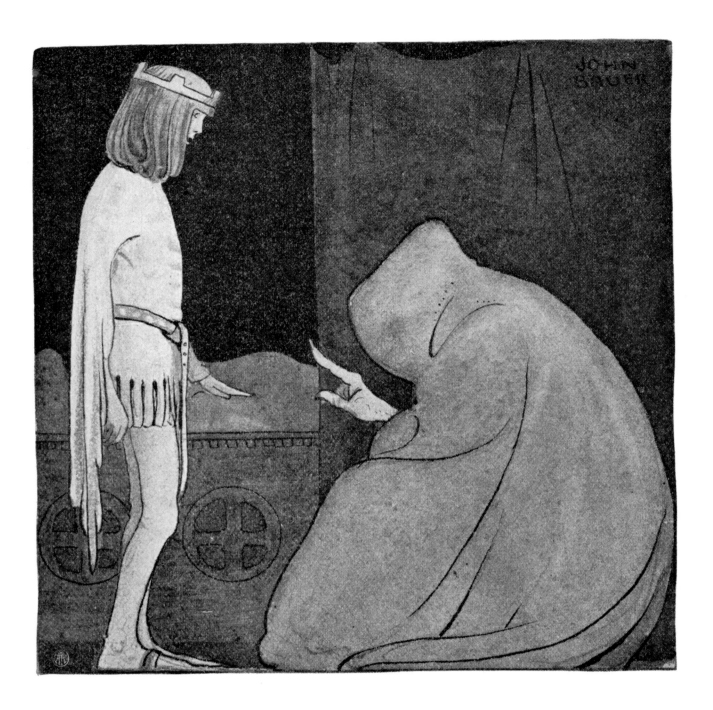

palace gardens. When the prince took her for a ride in the carriage, she asked to take the reins herself, and called "Gee up!" to the horses, so loudly it could be heard afar. Children waved at her while she stood on the coach-box throwing them raisins and pepper-cakes.

Everyone was so astounded about the princes they had no time to notice anything about the prince's shadow. He even had no time to think of it himself. However, after a time when the healthy princess was seen more regularly, he did observe a kind of absence or emptiness, particularly in the evenings when other people's shadows grew into long giants. It was unpleasant to have the sun in his back, and he tried as often as possible to face the sun, so as not to be reminded that he was now different from other humans.

But people began to notice. The ladies of the court began to whisper in corners, and the courtiers looked at him strangely when he passed.

One evening as he was riding his white horse, children surrounded him joyfully as usual. He was feeling lighthearted, for he had briefly forgotten what was troubling him. But as he bent down to lift one of the young ones into his saddle, a shrill little voice exclaimed: "Look, look, the horse has got a shadow, but the prince doesn't have one."

And in no time a hundred little voices were calling: "The horse has a shadow, but the prince doesn't!"

Now it's over, thought the prince, and he spurred his horse on to ride back to the palace like the wind.

The next day the whole city talked of nothing else but that the prince had lost his shadow through some kind of wizardry. It was as if they had completely forgotten that he was their beloved prince whom they had worshipped. Now they stuck their heads together to discuss what unimaginable treasures and advantages the prince must have gained in selling his shadow. For it was clear that he must have profited from it somehow. At every street corner they spoke of it, and it did not take long before children were pointing at the prince when he went out on one of his ever more seldom walks. Some even threw stones after him and cursed him. All this made the prince so heavy-hearted that he was barely to be recognized, and the little princess cried at the change in her merry brother.

When the prince saw that even his father and mother were affected by the suspicions and talk of the town, he decided to leave his home and kingdom for ever. So he went to his parents to take leave.

"Dear mother and dear father," he said. "I see that you too are dissatisfied with me. So I want to go out into the world and no longer trouble you with my presence. Give the kingdom to my sister instead. Accept my thanks and farewell!"

When the king and queen heard that their hearts softened, and the queen began to weep. "Just tell me, my dear son, how you are different from other people. What have you done with your shadow?" she asked.

"My shadow has gone," answered the prince, and sunk his head. Then the king became angry. "Away!" he said. "We can all see that! What we want to know is where it is."

"I don't know," said the prince. "I only know it's gone."

"You are the most obstinate and ungrateful boy who ever lived!" the king exclaimed, and rose from his throne. "Leave my kingdom, and never return!"

The poor prince bowed again before his parents, kissed his little sister in parting and cut one of her locks as a keepsake. Then he left.

He wandered far and wide, until he no longer heard his own language spoken, and then he wandered through a further three kingdoms. In the fourth kingdom he came to a wild oak forest.

"Here I will stay," he said to himself. "Here in this forest among the wild animals. Perhaps they will be more charitable than people."

The prince had not long left his home, before his parents regretted their hardness. "He may have lost his shadow," the king mused, "but what of it? It is even quite proper that the prince is different from the crowd. Was it perhaps a special blessing of a powerful fairy? I shall send out messengers through my whole kingdom and in the neighbouring ones to find him. His start is not so great that we would find not him."

"Yes, do that," sighed the queen. "Fetch our son back, or I will not have another happy day."

Five hundred riders were sent forth through the whole kingdom and the neighbouring realms to find the prince and fetch him back. But day after day passed, month after month. After a year, most of the riders had returned, without any of them having found a trace of him or even heard word of him. After three years the last rider returned. He said that more than a hundred miles/leagues from the kingdom he had found a child who said it had seen a youth without a shadow. But the child had no idea what became of him, and all inquiries were fruitless. That was the best the riders could do for the king and queen.

Over the years the little princess now grew into a beautiful girl — but she was not really happy. She could not forget her brother who had always been happy and kind to her, and she kept wondering how she could find him again. One day she sat at the feet of her parents, as she liked to do.

"Last night I had such a strange dream," she said. "I was a little girl again, and ill, and my dear brother was watching by me. My mother and all the servants had gone to sleep, only he was awake. Suddenly a man in a grey coat appeared and made a bargain with my brother. He would make me better if my brother would give his shadow. Mother, father, what do you think of my dream?"

The king and queen paled with fright. "Now I remember," said the queen, "it was during the night you recovered. The servants had nodded off one after another, and finally I fell asleep too. Around this time we noticed that your brother's shadow had disappeared. It must be the truth which is showing itself in your dream."

Thereupon the king made the dream known in every church of the land, and it did not take long to restore the love and worship that everyone always had for their prince. At every street corner, people stood and discussed what they could do to find the prince again. The princess, however, went to the king and asked: "Father, let me go and look for my brother who left because of me."

When the king saw her determination, he had to agree to let her go. He wanted to give here a great company of followers, but she asked to go alone. She dressed as a simple shepherdess and only kept her pearl necklace which she had worn as a child. She thought her brother might recognize her by the necklace. Then she bade farewell and went on her way.

Mile after mile she walked and soon she was out of the kingdom. She asked everyone she met after the prince without a shadow. No one had heard of him. Most thought she was mad and gave her some milk or a piece of bread and let her sleep in the hay. But the princess did not give up hope.

It was late one evening when she came to a hut in the forest. She knocked at the door and on entering saw a red-eyed old woman who was so wrinkled she must be a hundred years old. "Good evening, dear mother," the princess greeted her. "As you are so old, you will be wise. Tell me, have you ever heard of the prince without a shadow?"

The old one looked at the princess and nodded. "So you are the sister," she said. "I knew you would come, but it took a long time."

When the princess heard that the old one knew who she was, she felt so happy that she threw her arms around her, saying: "Show me the way to my brother and you will get anything you wish for!"

But the old woman told her things could not be rushed like that. Only his own shadow would know the way to the prince. But the shadow was with the man in a grey coat who lived at the end of the world.

So the princess asked the woman to show her the way to the end of the world.

"What will you give me if I show you the way?" asked the old one.

"Anything you want," replied the girl, who thought nothing would be too valuable to give for this.

"Give me your beauty," said the old one. And as the princess agreed, she passed her hand three times over the face of the girl, and in an instant the beauty had passed from one to the other. The princess' eyes were small and ugly, her cheeks were grey, her mouth as wide as a toad's, and her golden locks turned into matted straggles. The princess sighed when the old woman handed her a looking-glass, but then she laughed again.

"It's lucky I have the pearl necklace," she said, "for otherwise my brother would not believe me to be his sister."

The old woman went to get a ball of wool from a chest. "Throw the ball in front of you when you leave tomorrow morning. It will bring you to the end of the world."

The princess thanked her, and next morning, after she had rested, she did as the old woman had told her. The ball rolled in front of her, no faster than she could walk. And when she wanted to rest, she caught the ball easily and put it in her pocket. So she continued her journey day after day. How long she went on like this she no longer knew.

One day as she was going through a dark forest, a troll suddenly jumped in her path, picked up the ball of wool and swung it over his head, laughing loudly. The princess was so startled she did not know whether she was coming or going.

"Good day, Mr Troll," she said with a quivering voice. "Please give me my ball of wool back. Without it I cannot find my brother." She knelt before the troll, weeping bitterly.

"What will you give me for it?" asked the troll.

"Whatever you want," she answered, for nothing would be too valuable.

"Give me your youth!" said the troll. Then he passed his hand three times over her head and the princess felt a coldness pass through her. Her limbs became stiff, and her skin wrinkled.

The troll gave her the ball of wool, but when she rolled it, she found she could only follow it half as fast as before.

"Dear little ball of wool," she called, "please roll a bit slower, I'm an old woman now."

The ball listened and immediately rolled so slowly that the princess could follow it. She had to rest more often, and often she would ask herself whether this road would ever come to an end.

Finally she came to a great blue shimmering sea. Far out on a peninsula stood a castle, and the ball of wool came to a rest in front of the gates. The princess knew this was the castle at the end of the world and the home of the man with the grey coat. She lifted her old stiff hand and knocked on the gate. The man in the grey coat opened the door himself.

"At last you are here," he said, "just as I expected. But you don't think I'll give you the shadow of your brother without getting something in return?"

"No," answered the princess. "I have learned on my way here that one does not receive things without giving something in return. I know that you want from me what you gave my brother that night in return for his shadow. So take my health and let the shadow of my brother show me the way to him."

The grey man laid his hands on her head and the princess felt the illness taking hold of her.

"I hope I can survive until I find my brother," she thought. The shadow of her brother had immediately appeared on the ground beside her. It was the shadow of a slim youth, just as she remembered him. Silently and slowly the shadow moved over the ground and the sick, old woman followed it with unsteady steps.

After they had travelled a long time, they came to a clear spring. The princess was thirsty and she bent achingly over to drink. When she saw her old, feeble face, she was startled and said to the shadow: "I will not be able to tell my brother who I am. It would make him too sad to see me like this. Good shadow, promise me you won't betray me!"

The shadow appeared to nod, and she was satisfied.

After countless miles when the princess could hardly take another step for tiredness, they came to a deep forest. The shadow glided silently over the grass, and the princess followed, though every step brought her pain. Finally the shadow stopped at a low hut made of woven branches. A young man with a sad face sat in the doorway and fed the wild animals gathered around him. The shadow glided behind him, and the princess recognized her brother. She stood before him and spoke his name.

"Who are you, that you know my name?" he asked.

"Call me your unknown friend," she replied. "I bring greetings from your home and from the whole kingdom. You are welcome to all, and they long to see you again, and to hear that you forgive them."

174

"I have been persecuted from my country, for I had no shadow. And because I shall never get it back, I will never go back," the prince said solemnly.

"Your shadow guided me here," said the princess. "Turn around and look!"

Then she told him how the king and queen missed their son and regretted their harshness, and how they had tried to find him for many years. Only about the princess did she say nothing, and evaded all questions which the prince asked about her. At last she persuaded the prince to return next morning to his kingdom with his shadow, in the company of the old woman.

Overnight he let her rest in the hut on a bed of soft moss and leaves, and next morning he called to a stag to help her so that she would not have to walk any more. As he lifted her on to the stag's back, he recognized the pearl necklace and said: "That is my sister's necklace. How do you come to have it? Tell me of her as we walk."

The princess thought he would never leave her in peace with questions about his sister if she did not put an end to them. So she said: "Your sister has been dead for a long time."

When the prince heard this, he put his hands to his face and wept. "Now I understand why my shadow has returned to me," he said. "But I would rather have lived the rest of my life without it, if I knew that my sister was alive and happy."

Hardly had the prince spoken these words, when she felt her health returning. Now she understood that the power of the grey man had been broken.

After a time they came to a dark forest, and the princess recognized it as the place where she had met the troll. And she saw the troll in a thicket, beckoning to her, as if he wanted something from her.

"Let me get off here for a while," she asked the prince. "I have an old acquaintance here in the forest, whom I must visit."

The prince helped her down, and sat down to wait. But when she came back, he hardly recognized her. She walked quickly and easily and swung herself onto the stag without help. Then she smiled at him from her ugly, though strangely younger face. He opened his mouth to ask her questions, but she stopped him, saying: "My acquaintance had to pay me my due."

They continued their journey, and after a time came to a tumbledown hut where the hundred-year-old woman lived. The princess jumped from the back of the stag and went into the hut, to return the grey woollen ball, which had helped her so much.

When she came out of the hut, the prince could not believe his eyes. Instead of an ugly girl with straggly hair and a wide toad's mouth, there was a beautiful maiden before him. Only her old clothes, the shoes and the pearl necklace reminded him of his companion.

The princess went to him, took his hands and said: "My dear brother, now the last of my debts has been repaid. Do you recognize your sister?"

The prince who had slowly begun to understand all that had passed, took his sister into his arms and cried for joy.

"How could I ever have been happy at home, without my little sister at my side?" he asked, and he played with the pearls in her necklace as he used to do. "Now we shall always be together!"

176

And he showed her the lock of hair which he had kept when he wandered out into the world.

At last they came to their kingdom and home. There was great rejoicing about their return, and no one was in the slightest bit worried any more about whether the prince had a shadow or not.

The Boy and the Trolls, or the Adventure

Walter Stenström

Once there was a clever and lively boy who wanted an adventure, so he took the shortest possible cut to adventure: right through the deep forest.

"Hello!" he called. "Hello! Where can I find an adventure? It is so boring at home, and nothing ever happens. Well — except that the good queen died and all the country mourned. The king and the princess mourned and the people mourned. But then the princess got a stepmother, and now it is she who rules. Everybody believes she is a witch, but nobody knows for sure."

And the boy wandered deeper and deeper into the forest.

"Hello!" he called. "Hello! Where can I find an adventure? Mother gave me seven sandwiches when I started out, but now there are only two left. Won't an adventure come soon?"

It grew late in the day, and the boy trudged even deeper into the dark forest.

"Adventure!" he called. "Come on, adventure! There is nothing but sadness and sorrow at home. A few days ago the princess disappeared. She was picking flowers in the meadow, and suddenly she was gone. Some believe that the queen bewitched her and spirited her away, so that her own daughter might be the princess of the realm. But nobody knows for sure."

Dusk was falling by then, and the boy had eaten his last sandwich. He was tired from his walk, and sat down on a stone to think.

There was a rustle among the twigs and leaves. But he was not afraid. He sat waiting for the adventure he had gone out to seek.

Then a troll came lumbering by with a sack on his back. It was the Big Brother troll, the oldest of three brothers. He was as ugly as sin, and the ugliest part was his long, hairy ears that almost dragged on the ground. "Klafs, klufs, klafs, klufs," the troll panted as he walked along.

"Good evening, Uncle," the boy greeted him. The troll stopped, flapped his ears, and squinted at the boy.

"My, a dwarf!" he said

"I'm not a dwarf, I'm a boy."

"My, what a boy! Such ugly little ears you have. Look at mine. Those are what I call ears! How could the princess turn me down when I have such beautiful ears. What ugly little ears you have!"

"I like what I have," said the boy. "What do you have in your sack?"

"This sack is full of silver I have been collecting, and in addition I have a delicious snake for the princess to nibble on."

"Which princess is that?"

"Do you think I'd tell you?" The troll flapped his ears and looked slyly at the boy. "I could change you into a black raven if I wanted to," he said. "But I suppose you'll just have to stay as ugly as you are. If you see my brothers, tell them I've gone home to the mountain. Goodbye."

"Goodbye, Uncle," said the boy.

The troll left the boy sitting by himself on the stone. How the twigs and leaves rustled and crackled! But he was not afraid.

Another troll came plodding past with a sack on his back. It was the middle-sized troll. He was as ugly as sin, and the ugliest part of him was his warty chin, so long it almost touched the ground.

"Klafs, klufs, klafs, klufs," he panted as he walked along.

"Good evening, Uncle," said the boy.

"What! A little tomte," said the troll. He put his chin to the ground and squinted his eyes.

"I am not a tomte. I am a boy."

"A boy!" said the troll. "What an ugly little chin you have! Look at mine. It is fine and well shaped. How could the princess turn me down when I have such a beautiful chin! Now *yours* is what I call an ugly chin."

"I'm content with what I have. But what do you have in your sack?"

"This sack is full of gold that I have been collecting, and in addition I have a fine green frog for the princess to nibble on."

"Which princess is that?"

"Do you think I'd tell you?" said the troll, squinting his eyes cunningly. "Have you seen my big brother?"

"Yes, indeed. He asked me to tell you he had gone home to the mountain."

"Then I must hurry," said the middle-sized troll. "If I had time, I would change you into a crow, but I'm afraid you will have to stay as ugly as you are."

The troll lumbered on, leaving the boy sitting by himself on the stone. The leaves and twigs rustled and crackled again.

A third troll appeared with a sack on his back. It was the littlest brother troll. He, too, was ugly as sin, and the ugliest part of him was his long blotchy nose. "Klafs, klufs, klafs, klufs," he panted as he walked along.

"Good evening, Uncle," said the boy.

"What a little hobgoblin," said the troll, sniffing with his long nose.

"I'm not a hobgoblin, I'm a boy."

"A boy indeed!" said the troll. "What an ugly little nose you have! Look at mine. That's how a nose *should* look. The princess couldn't turn me down with such a beautiful nose. That is an awful little nose you have."

"I'm content with what I have," said the boy. "What do you have in the sack?"

"This sack is full of precious stones that I have been collecting. And in addition, I have a juicy, fat toad for the princess to nibble."

"Which princess is that?"

"Do you think I'd tell you?" replied the troll, squinting slyly. "Have you seen my brothers?"

"Yes, indeed," answered the boy. "They asked me to tell you that they have gone home to the mountain."

"Well then, I must hurry," said Little Brother troll. "A pity it's so late, or I would change you into a magpie. But you will have to stay as ugly as you are." And so this troll, too, clumped off.

Adventure, thought the boy. It's beginning. And if I follow the trolls, I will probably find more of it. So he crept off after them as carefully as he could. My, how the twigs and leaves rustled! But the boy was not afraid.

The trolls' castle was on a grey mountain in the very midst of the forest, and a princess was being held prisoner in one of its chambers. It was the same beautiful little princess who had disappeared while picking flowers in the meadow.

The chamber opened on to a balcony that had stairs leading up to it. High up on the wall was a single small window through which a star twinkled. The princess sat on a couch of soft moss, which seemed hard enough to one accustomed to sitting on silk and eiderdown. In front of her was a table laden with food — dragon blood pudding, mud soup with frogs' legs, roasted bats' ears, and porridge made of poisonous black henbane. The princess could eat none of this, of course, and would not even touch it.

She did not dare to speak out loud, but whispered to the star over and over, "When are the elves coming? Are the elves coming soon?"

Yes, they were. Now a whole flock of elves flew through the narrow window and kissed the princess on her eyes and cheeks. They had brought her fruit and berries to eat, as much as she wanted. Then they floated away, taking the terrible troll food with them.

Now the hinges of the chamber door squeaked, and old Mother Troll scurried into the room. She was uglier than you can imagine for she had ears as long as the big troll's, a chin like the middle-sized troll's, and a nose like the little troll's.

"Ugh!" she said. "Fresh air! I must hold my nose. Why don't you close the shutters, or else come to my room. The air there is wonderful. The shutters have not been opened for a thousand years."

"I like to look at the stars," said the princess. She did not dare say that thousand-year-old air made her choke, for that was something Mother Troll did not like to hear.

"Looking at the stars!" exclaimed the troll mother. "What foolishness. What is there to see? My room is full of silver and gold and precious stones. They shine more brightly than any star."

"Did you like your meal?" she continued, looking at all the empty dishes. She fluttered about the room, laughing raucously. She did not know that the elves had brought the princess berries and carried off the troll food.

Suddenly there was a bang on the door.

"That sounds like my big son," said the troll mother, and went to open the door.

The big troll entered, said good evening, and put down his sack. "Here, Princess, I have brought you something to nibble," he said, holding up a snake.

There was another knock on the door. "That sounds like my middle son," said the troll mother, and went to open the door.

The middle-sized troll entered, said good evening, and put down his sack. "Here, Princess, I have brought you something to nibble," he said, and held up the frog.

There was a third knock on the door. "That sounds like my little son," said the troll mother, and went to open the door.

And the littlest brother troll entered, said good evening, and put down his sack. "Here, Princess, I have brought you something good to nibble," he said, and held out the toad.

The princess had to say thank you and accept what they offered her.

The elves will be back soon, she thought. They will come and take away these horrid snakes and frogs. I'd rather die than eat them.

The troll mother was flying around the room, still laughing uproariously. "I am so happy, I am in real troll spirits," she said. "Let's announce the engagement tonight. The princess is going to marry one of my sons. She can pick the one she wants. Or perhaps she wants all of them, but she can only have one." And she laughed so hard that she had to hold her sides. The troll brothers smiled broadly, pleased because each of them believed the princess would choose him.

The princess herself felt afraid and sad. She had no friends near her. The elves were gone, and only the star twinkled in the sky.

"Look at them," the troll mother urged. "Look at my sons. Handsomer trolls can't be found this side of the moon. But then, of course, they take after their mother. Look at them, little princess."

But with tears in her eyes the princess gazed at the star. No one could have been more unhappy, and she did not know how to escape. There she was, imprisoned among trolls in a castle on a mountain.

Outside the small window another troll was nodding at her. He looked a little like a boy, but the princess was sure he was a troll.

"Well, which one do you want?" continued the mother. "I don't care which one you pick, but choose well. They all know troll magic, and they are all marriageable age. Little brother, who is the youngest, will be 947 years old next week. And with luck, they will all live thousands of years more. Trolls have only one thing to fear."

"What is that?" asked the big brother troll.

"Haven't I told you?" said his mother. "Well, it is high time you learned. There is a rhyme that can destroy us, and I always feel ill when I say it:

Come, fresh winds, and blow away
Long ear, huge chin, big nose.
Come, west wind, and sweep away
All these trolls from mountain grey.

"Ugh!" said the troll mother. "It makes me feel sick. But I'll feel better soon. Don't be afraid, my sons. It doesn't work when just anybody says it."

"Who has to say it to make it dangerous?" asked the middle-sized troll.

"Don't you know that either?" said the mother. "When a boy who is not afraid of either darkness or trolls says it, then it is dangerous. But I have never met such a boy, and don't expect to either. And if you meet one, all you have to do is cast a spell on him and change him into something else before he has a chance to open his mouth."

"I met a boy in the forest this evening," said the big troll.

"I did, too," said his little brother. "And he was not afraid of trolls."

"Or darkness," added the middle-sized troll.

"You're frightening me!" cried their mother, jumping about the room. "Why didn't you cast a spell on him?"

"We were in a hurry," said the sons. "We wanted to come and see the princess."

"I feel ill," complained the troll mother, "but I hope it will pass. Of course, we have nothing to fear because that boy does not know the formula. Now I feel better." She laughed loudly again, and moved around the room.

"But we are forgetting the engagement," she continued. "Has the princess made up her mind yet?"

But the princess was still looking at the star. Big tears rolled down her cheeks. She was the saddest princess in the world, with not a friend to turn to. Outside the window, the troll looked at her kindly and nodded in a friendly way. Indeed, it was strange how much he resembled the gatekeeper's son at the castle, with whom the princess had often played. Of course, she told herself, she was only dreaming. No one could save her now.

"Well, why don't you answer?" said the mother. "Are you asleep? I'll give you a little pinch to wake you up." And she pinched the princess so hard on the arm that she had to scream aloud.

"Is the princess too shy to choose?" asked the mother. "Well, then, I shall make up her mind for her. She will marry my big son because he is oldest. Will that do?"

"No," said the princess. "No, no. I won't marry any of you ugly trolls. I want to go home. I don't want to eat snakes and frogs, and I don't want to breathe thousand-year-old air."

"So! So!" screamed the troll mother. Her face turned green with anger, and she spat out her words. "Is that so! Well, you will never return home. My sister is queen of the castle now, and she is as powerful a troll as I. She sent you here, and she does not want you back. A troll child is going to be princess and inherit the realm. Ha, ha, ha! You will never go back.

"And now," she added, "you stay with me in my room. The air is lovely there — just right for a princess. Then you will marry my big son. But first you must learn some manners. You need a pinch or two and a taste of the switch I have in there." With that, she gripped the princess's arm hard, and pulled her behind her. "Get to my chamber," she shouted. "You won't sit on soft moss there."

At that moment, however, something unusual happened. A voice was heard from outside the window. It was an ordinary boy's voice, but the troll mother let go of the princess's arm at once, and she and the other trolls stood as still as if they had been turned to stone.

Come, fresh winds, and blow away
Long ear, huge chin, big nose.
Come, west wind, and sweep away
All these trolls from mountain grey.

And a fresh wind came and blew the door wide open. The troll mother and her big son, middle-sized son, and little son were whisked out so fast you could not tell where they went. Yet the wind never touched the little princess.

A moment later, a boy stood at the door. It was the gatekeeper's son from the castle, the boy who had set out in search of adventure. He greeted the princess politely.

"Don't be afraid, Princess," he said. "The trolls are gone now, and will never return. We can go back to the castle and take all the gold and silver and precious stones with us."

"Thank you, dear boy," said the princess. "I have been sad and frightened. And I thought you were a troll."

The boy laughed loud and long, and when he stopped he sighed and said, "At last, a real adventure." He sounded so pleased.

Back in the kingdom, in the palace and the city, everyone was astir, for the queen announced an end to the mourning for the old queen and the lost princess. That same day all the realm would learn that there was to be a new princess: she was the new queen's daughter and the king's stepdaughter.

The old king was sitting in a corner playing with his sceptre and orb. Sorrow had weighed so heavily on him that he had become like a child again. All the king did now was say "Yes, yes" to everything the new queen suggested. It was she who really governed the kingdom.

"The queen is a troll! She is a witch!" the people thought. Yet no one knew for sure, and no one dared say so aloud.

In a room in one of the royal chambers, the queen was helping her daughter to dress. All the ladies-in-waiting had left. "Shut the windows and doors tightly, and go," she had told them, so they had seen to it that all the doors and windows were well fastened, and then had gone away.

"Ugh, how awful! Fresh air!" observed the queen when she and her daughter were alone. "I feel quite ill. But soon everything will be different. Tomorrow I shall command everyone to nail all their shutters down. Then I will build a wall around the whole country, so high that fresh winds can't get in. Now, my little troll girl," she concluded, "just once over with the sponge!"

"No!" screamed her daughter. "No, no! I don't want to wash."

"You won't have to soon, my sweet," said the queen. "Only this once. When I am proclaimed queen, you will never have to wash again. We will have all the sponges burned. We will put locks on all the wells. It's only people who have these silly notions about clean noses. Now behave. Don't scream so."

But her daughter screamed all the more. You would have to be a troll child to understand.

"Now, it's done," said the queen. "You look the way people expect you to, although I must say, I thought you looked much sweeter before."

The troll girl was dressed in the princess's most beautiful gown. She was no prettier, however, for even silk and velvet will not do much for a troll.

"Put some garlic and stinkhorn drops on your handkerchief," suggested the queen. "It will be good to have when we are out in the fresh air."

Then the queen and her daughter walked on to the castle terrace where the ceremony was to take place. The king came, too, and sat on a throne next to the queen, while the troll girl sat at their feet. Behind them were courtiers in lavish costumes and soldiers with shining swords and halberds. And behind the soldiers stood the common people of the realm, crowded together in their gayest clothes, since they were no longer allowed to wear mourning. Trumpets blared, and flags and pennants were waving in the wind.

Yet none of the gaiety was real. The king looked gloomy, and sat playing with his sceptre and orb. The courtiers seemed afraid, and the soldiers had to try hard to stand straight. On all sides, the people seem disheartened and sorrowful.

And so they were. They were still mourning for their good queen, who had died, and her beautiful daughter the princess, who had disappeared. And they were mourning for their kind king who had become so childish. They were frightened of the new queen and her daughter, who would now be princess of the realm.

188

"How ugly she is," they whispered. "She looks just like a troll child. And to think she will be our princess!"

"And she and the queen are acting oddly. Look, they sit with their handkerchiefs pressed to their noses as if they are ill."

The queen and her daughter were not ill, but they were suffering dreadfully from the fresh air, and if they had not put the garlic and stinkhorn drops on their handkerchiefs, they would not have been able to bear it.

"I think we can begin now," the queen whispered to the king.

"Yes, yes," said the king.

And so the trumpeters blew once again, after which the queen rose and gave a speech. She spoke eloquently of the queen who had died. Large tears rolled down her cheeks, although no one believed they were genuine. She spoke of the lovely princess who had disappeared, and again her eyes were wet, but no one believed she meant it.

Now, she said, the king was proclaiming her daughter princess, and she would inherit the realm. The queen would rule until the princess was old enough to govern. All this was as their king wishes, she said, for he felt old and tired, and longed for peace and quiet.

She would be a good queen, she assured them. Indeed, she knew better than most what the king's subjects wanted. If only they would be willing and obedient, everything would go well. Any disobedience would be punished.

When the queen had finished, the prime minister stepped forward and placed a crown on the daughter's head. Then he called for a cheer from the people, and he himself cheered as loudly as he could. The courtiers shouted hurrah, because they didn't dare keep silent. Yet the king's subjects said nothing; their hearts were too full with sorrow.

There was another reason why they did not cheer. Something else had caught their attention.

A long procession of wagons, each pulled by two horses, was rolling along the main highway towards the castle terrace. In the first wagon sat a little girl who looked very like the lost princess, and next to her sat a merry young boy. Had it not been so hard to believe, you would have said he was the son of the castle gatekeeper.

Wagon after wagon followed, and out of every three wagons, one was loaded with silver, one with gold, and one with precious stones. The crowd, scarcely believing their eyes, made way for the procession.

"Isn't that the real princess?" they whispered to each other. "Isn't that the gatekeeper's son? Do you see the silver, gold, and precious stones?"

The gatekeeper and his wife were also watching the wagons pass. "Of course it is our son. Of course it is the real princess," they said.

The crowd began to cheer lustily and wave their hats in the air. They cheered and cheered, they were so happy.

Are they really cheering for me? wondered the queen. For me and the new princess?

Then she caught sight of the long procession, which had stopped at the main gate. Of all things! she thought. There sat the real princess whom her troll sister had imprisoned on the grey mountain. How had she ever come back? The queen's face turned green with rage.

Then the gatekeeper's boy began to speak. "My King and all your people, good morning. I've brought back the princess, and I have had a real adventure."

"Hurrah! Hurrah!" shouted the people.

"The queen on the terrace," the boy went on, "is really a witch. She is sister to a troll in grey mountain. And her daughter is really a troll child."

"Just as we had always thought," exclaimed the crowd.

At that instant something very strange happened. The old troll and her daughter suddenly looked different, or else people at last saw what they had not seen before. Both of them now had hairy ears so long they almost touched the ground, and their chins and noses were so large and ugly, it was enough to frighten you. They were fluttering about, flapping their ears like wings, and hissing through their teeth with rage. It was horrible!

In his confusion, the king dropped his orb and sceptre, and the courtiers yelled and hid under the chairs. The soldiers forgot their courage and prepared to run away, and the king's subjects huddled together in fear, hiding behind each other.

The only one who was not afraid was the boy who had gone out looking for adventure. He knew what to say, and he said it:

Come, fresh winds, and blow away
Long ear, huge chin, big nose.
Come, west wind, and sweep away
All these trolls from mountain grey.

Then a wind came rushing past, and caught the trolls by their large ears, and in a twinkling they were gone! It happened so fast that no one knew where they went. But the wind did not touch anyone else — not the king or the princess or the boy or the courtiers or the soldiers. All around, people cheered and laughed. The soldiers, straight-backed once again, presented arms, and the courtiers crept out from under the chairs and began to discuss the weather as if nothing had happened.

The old king took his daughter in his arms and wept with joy. He seemed now to have regained his reason, the spell was broken. Now he would no longer sit playing idly with his sceptre and orb.

He kissed the princess on the forehead and embraced her again. Then he gave the boy a good hug, as indeed he deserved.

"Long live the King!" shouted the crowd. "Long live the Princess! Long live the boy who went out looking for adventure!"

"Yes, it was a fine adventure," said the king so loudly and clearly that everyone could hear him. "It was a fine adventure, and a fine adventure deserves a fine ending. I can see that the Princess feels the way I do. This boy shall have the Princess's hand as his reward, and inherit the realm after me. He is not afraid of trolls or darkness, and he likes fresh air and baths. I am sure he will make a fine king."

The boy thanked him politely and did what he thought was most fitting: he kissed the king on the hand and the princess on the lips. "I shall be kind to you, little Princess," he said. "I will take care of you and protect you from trolls, and while I rule, you will always sit on eiderdown and silk."

And so one adventure ended and another began, just as it happens in life.

The Maiden in the Castle of Rosy Clouds

Harald Östenson

They had been working ever since morning, and by evening the whole meadow had been cut. Now everyone had gone back to the farm; that is, all but the youngest. He did not live in the neighbourhood, but travelled from place to place, working by the day. Now he lay on the ground, sound asleep, with some new-mown hay under his head.

He slept, and then he began to dream, and soon he saw a young girl in a white gown walking slowly towards him. Her eyes shone like stars, and there was something so pure and fine about her that he thought she might be an angel.

"Who are you?" he asked.

"I am the maiden of the Castle of Rosy Clouds," she answered.

"Whoever wins you will never know sorrow," said the young man.

"If you want to win me, you must look for me," said the girl. And with that she disappeared.

The young man sprang to his feet and looked around eagerly, but there was nothing to see.

Everything went on as it had before. The young man worked day after day, yet he could never forget his lovely dream of the maiden from the Castle of Rosy Clouds. Wherever he went, he asked people where the castle was, but most of them just laughed at him.

"He is mad, poor boy."

One or two people, however, patted him on the shoulder and gave him a friendly smile. "You set your goals high, don't you?" they said.

A long time afterwards, the young man came to a small cabin rotting with age and almost hidden by rocks and underbrush. It was a bleak evening, so he knocked on the door and asked if he could have shelter for the night.

Yes, he could, said the old woman who lived there, but it would be very plain fare.

Never had the young man seen anyone so old, wrinkled, and stooped as that woman. But then, she was over a hundred years old.

He could see that she had hardly any food, so he offered to share his own with her. Then they began to talk, and he asked her about the maiden in the Castle of Rosy Clouds.

"I declare," said the old woman. "Are you really asking about her? It was many a yesterday since anyone asked me *that* question."

"Well, I don't know the way to the castle," she continued. "And it won't be easy to get there, either, if all you have are your two empty hands. If I remember correctly, there was an old rhyme I heard when I was young, and many strange things are necessary to go there. How did that rhyme go?

Do you want to find the maiden in the castle of clouds?
If you want to win the maiden in the castle of clouds
First you need a stallion grey
Who midst the clouds can find his way.
You need a red mantle, like that of a squire
To keep you safe from embers and fire.
And you need the sword that is known as Gull
To split the iron serpent's skull.

"Yes, that's the way it ran," said the old woman. "So I think you had better forget all about going there."

Yes, thought the young man. I don't know how I could get all those wonderful things. And I have no money, so there is no chance for me to buy them, either.

But all night he dreamed about the grey horse, the red mantle, and the sword known as Gull.

He stayed with the old woman for a few days, and helped her repair her cottage and dig her little garden. Then he went on his way.

One evening three years later, he found himself in a wild and desolate mountain region, where dangerous gorges and dark ravines opened on every side. Suddenly he heard a desperate cry and saw an old woman rushing towards him. Just behind her was a large snake. Its back and great head were covered with thick, horny scales, and a high comb of jagged barbs ran along its back.

Now I could use the sword Gull, he thought. But since all I have is my sheath-knife, I'll have to make do with that. I can't let the snake eat the old woman. And he rushed forward, waving his knife.

When the snake saw the boy coming it forgot the old woman, who quickly hid among the boulders, and turned its horrid head towards him. The snake seemed ready to devour both the boy and his sheath-knife.

But when it was quite close, the boy felt something strange happen to his hand. Suddenly his sheath-knife had disappeared, and he was holding a sword with a long, shining blade instead.

He gave a mighty blow, and the snake lay dead.

This must be the iron serpent, thought the young man. So the sword in my hand

194

is probably the sword Gull. But where did it come from? He looked around, but all he could see was his sheath-knife lying on the ground.

I suppose the sword is mine, since I am holding it, he thought, and so I will take it with me. And he continued on his travels, and more than once the sword served him in good stead.

He had had it for six years when one day he came to a village where a large house was on fire. Flames blazed on every side. All the villagers seemed to be safe, however. Then suddenly the face of an old man with a snow-white beard appeared in a window on the top floor of the house.

A cry of anguish rose from the villagers.

"It's old lame Father Lars. We forgot him!"

Had the old man jumped from that height, he would have been killed; yet no one dared brave the flames to help him.

But rescue was coming. Here was a young stranger pushing his way through the frightened crowd.

"The ladder, up with the ladder!" he commanded.

But the tallest ladder had already been burned, and the other one only reached to the second floor.

Then he dashed in among the smoke and flames, and up the stairs.

The villagers saw him at the window. He lifted the old man up as he would a child, but at that moment flames engulfed them and they could not be seen.

"They are lost, they are lost!" cried one of the villagers, while all the rest stood staring.

But after a while the stranger came rushing down the stairs with the old man in his arms. Neither had been hurt badly and around them fluttered a wide red mantle.

A cheer rose from the crowd, and with loud hurrahs they hurried the courageous stranger to the best house in the village.

Even I don't know how I escaped unharmed, thought the young man. Then he saw the mantle in which he was still wrapped. Oh, this must be the mantle like a squire's, he thought, which will protect me from embers and fire, as the rhyme said. Now I have both the sword and the mantle. Who could have given them to me — and just when I needed them most?

That was a question he could not answer, and he had no time to wonder about it, either, for all the leading townspeople were coming towards him, one after another, to congratulate him and wish him well.

And so years passed, and the young man wandered far and wide, worked well and usefully, and did many brave deeds, but no one had anything more to tell him about the Castle of Rosy Clouds.

Nine years had passed since he had received the mantle, when once again he

196

found himself in a mountainous region. This time he was not alone; a friend had been travelling with him for some time. His friend often asked him about the secret of the sword and the mantle, and at last the young man told him everything.

The next morning when he awoke, his friend was gone, and so, too, were the sword and mantle.

My best friend robbed me, he thought sadly as he proceeded on his journey. And he was just climbing a hill when he caught sight of his friend carrying the sword and mantle. Something very strange happened. The mantle spread out like two enormous wings, and lifted his false friend into the air. His friend struggled and cried out and kicked wildly with his legs, but despite all his efforts he could not get free. He was as helpless as a rabbit caught by an eagle.

The mantle soared high over a wide, deep chasm, and when it reached the other side, it dropped the friend down. He fell headlong to the ground and was clearly badly hurt.

How can I help him? thought the young man. If I leave him there, he will bleed to death. I must try to jump over to the other side of the chasm. It is the only way. So, straining every muscle, he made a running start and jumped. At once it was clear that he had not jumped far enough.

Expecting to plunge down and to the bottom of the abyss, the young man closed his eyes. Then suddenly he was sitting on the back of a grey horse, which, swift as an arrow, carried him safely to the far bank.

Hurriedly, he tore off pieces of his clothing to bandage his friend's wounds. He was so anxious, and so preoccupied with what he was doing, that at first he did not stop to think how miraculous his adventure had been.

Only when he had stopped the bleeding did he look round at the horse standing by his side. His sword and mantle lay on the ground not far away.

This must be the grey stallion who can find his way midst the clouds, he thought. He put on the mantle, sheathed the sword at his side, lifted his friend in front of him on the horse, and rode away. At the next town, he stopped, and did not leave his false friend until he was well.

Many long years passed after this. The young man's cheeks were furrowed now and his hair had turned grey but he had never stopped looking for the Castle of Rosy Clouds.

At last, one evening, he saw in the distance a golden castle rising against the rosy evening sky.

He began to ride towards it on a silvery, shimmering road that led up among the hills and vales of the clouds. Suddenly a terrifying coal-black giant blocked his way. The giant's eyes flamed, and he shook his enormous fists as if he were going to smash both horse and rider. But not for a moment was the rider afraid. He spurred his grey horse straight towards the giant. The horse reared on its hind legs and laid back its ears, eager for battle. And just as the rider grasped the hilt of his sword, the giant disappeared.

Now he was riding, jubilantly happy, on the airy, billowing highway towards the shining golden Castle of Rosy Clouds. The drawbridge was down, and the lovely young maiden with brilliant starry eyes came out to meet him.

She put out her hand and said, "You have found me, and you have won me."

The rider sighed and answered, "But it took so long. Now I am old and grey."

The maiden only smiled, and held a silver mirror to his face. And once again he was a handsome young man, tall and slim, with rosy, unlined cheeks.

And hand in hand he and the maiden entered the castle.

Agneta and the Sea King

Helena Nyblom

It was a summer's day hundreds of years ago, and the world was as beautiful as it is today. The forest was just as green, the meadows were covered in flowers, and the roses and lilac bushes in the gardens gave out the same wonderful scent. Over all this splendour arched the same blue sky and the summer clouds scudded across it.

At that time there was a castle on an island in the middle of a lake. Firm and stately the red stone walls rose with a radiant golden roof crowning them.

Now the sun was just about to set and the whole sky glowed like a golden sea. Not a soul was to be seen, the castle stood closed and forbidding, only a nightingale sang her song from a high lime-tree in the garden behind the castle. All was still, not a murmur was heard. The forest was reflected in the still, clear water of the lake. The scent of summer hung heavily, but no one was there to notice it.

Suddenly a little side door of the castle opened, and a young girl stepped out. Carefully she went down the steep steps, walked across the courtyard, went through a gate in the wall to the pier which jutted out into the lake. At the end of the pier she stopped and looked across the water.

She was Agneta, the daughter of the lord of the castle, his only child and comfort for the loss of her mother who had died many years earlier. She stood quite still watching the flaming red sun sink into the lake, and asked herself what it must be like in the magical realm of the clouds which changed their form and colour every moment.

But then something happened that brought her attention closer. At her feet the waters stirred as a strange form swam towards the pier — was it a large fish, or was it a man? Agneta was about to run back to the castle when the strange figure raised its hands, and revealed a face of such deep sorrow that she stood there and asked in a quivering voice: "Who are you? And how did you get here?"

Large dark eyes looked back at her like the sad eyes of a doe, and around his mouth was a strange smile, but he gave no answer.

"Just tell me who you are!" Agneta repeated. "If I can help you, I will gladly do so, and if I cannot help you myself, perhaps my father can for he is a powerful man."

Then the stranger began to speak: "No, you. You alone can give me peace and happiness."

His voice was mild and gentle like a breeze rustling in the sails of a ship. And again he raised his arm in supplication. Agneta had never seen a more beautiful face. Heavy, wet locks framed his cheeks, his purple lips opened to a gentle smile. Most wondrous of all, though, were his eyes. Agneta had never thought eyes could express such sorrow and tenderness. They were like the depths of the sea which had so often captivated her gaze — one moment dark and mysterious, the next filled with glistening sunlight.

Agneta stepped on to the furthest stones at the edge of the water. "Tell me who you are," she demanded a third time.

Then he replied with a soft voice: "I am the sea king and have lived for hundreds of years in this lake. Long before the castle of your father was built, this was my kingdom. I saw how the scrub on the shore grew into a forest, which now reaches to the sky. Long ago the lake was much bigger and reached far into the land, but it shrank, as does everything that comes into contact with human beings. And nonetheless there is not a lake in the whole wide world as beautiful, as still and as deep as this one."

"Is it not strange down there among the reeds and the water-plants and all the creatures of the lake?" asked Agneta.

200

"You humans always think like that about places you don't know," the sea king answered. "Actually it's beautiful down there! Much more beautiful than up here on earth. The sun shines twice as clear through the water without burning. And when storms and rain rattle at your houses up here, the bottom of the lake is quiet and still. But much as I'd like to describe my realm, I can only give you a faint impression of what it is really like. You have to see it yourself to believe it."

"But we humans cannot live at the bottom of the lake," said Agneta, and took another step closer to the water.

"That's just what you think, because you have never tried it," said the sea king with a laugh. "I could take you down into the depths without harming you. And I could show you things more wonderful than you can possibly imagine."

He had laid his hands on her little pearly shoes, and looked at her pleadingly.

"No, I don't dare!" sighed Agneta. "My father would get worried and start searching for me. And I want to go home now before the sun sets. Good night!"

"Will you just leave me like that?" called the sea king in a voice full of pain. "Shall I just return to my realm as lonely as ever? At least give me a keepsake to comfort me on my way. Give me the lime blossom you carry in your hand. As long as the scent lasts I shall believe you are close to me."

Agneta stretched out her hand with the lime blossom and said: "Gladly will I give you that. Here, take it."

The sea king reached out for the blossom and took hold of Agneta's hand. Then he reached for her waist and lifted her up in his arms. She struggled and cried, but he dived down into the depths with her. At the same moment the sun set and soon the clouds paled and night fell.

When Agneta did not come home, her father became terribly anxious. He sent a whole party of servants into the park and forest to search for her, but in vain. Finally a little boy found Agneta's pearly shoe by the stones of the pier, and this brought sorrow and tears to the old knight. He feared she had drowned and for days the lake shore was searched in the hope of at least finding her lifeless body. But even this wish was not granted.

Within a few years he aged, and was indifferent to all that happened around him. Usually he walked up and down the pier. On sunny days he looked into the depths of the lake, and some nights he stayed there in the moonlight, moving like a shadow, or standing like a stone, staring hopelessly into the dark waters.

Agneta though had not drowned. She lived in the depths with the sea king and was happy. At first she had been afraid when the sea king pulled her to the depths, but as soon as she reached the bottom, her fear disappeared and the king seemed even more handsome than before. As a water-lily only shows its beauty when swimming on the waves, so the sea king only revealed his true nature in the depths.

And he had not promised too much. Around her little waves sounded like harps.

At night when the moon rose the water shimmered like silver, and when the sun rose, everything was illumined in enchanting colours. In a moment thousands of blue sparks lit up, then the light flamed like gold, or glowed turquoise. Then again everything became pale and flowed in lilac streams like summer clouds in the sky.

Wandering among all the strange flowers that grew on the floor of the lake, she would pick a whole bunch and made herself a crown. But when she smelled them, she noticed they had no scent. Like birds of the air, fish glided over her head. There were whole schools of golden fish bright with sunlight, there were carp with red fins, silvery trout and strange silly burbot, motionless in the water with only their gills moving as if talking to themselves.

202

Now the sea king led her deeper still.

"This is my banqueting hall," he said, "and this is where we shall celebrate our wedding."

She looked around and found herself in a deep green vale. High above her a crystalline green dome seemed to arch with a great golden lamp in the centre. This was the sun shining through the waters.

Then the sea king reached for his harp and said: "Now I shall play for you."

At the first note Agneta thought her heart would break. The sound was wonderful and painful at the same time, and her eyes filled with tears. But when the sea king began to sing, all sorrow and pain vanished, and all joy as well, for everything was forgotten. She forgot her father's castle and her happy childhood. She forgot her father's love and the memory of her mother. She forgot that she had grown up on earth and had once looked up at the sky. She forgot the summer roses in the castle gardens and she forgot the snowflakes of winter, the incense in the church, and the candles on the altar. The only thing she remembered was the sea king, and she longed for nothing else but to be at his side for the rest of her life and to hear him playing.

When he had finished playing, he said to her: "Now you shall be my queen and stay with me for ever. Do you wish for that, my dear Agneta?"

"Yes, yes!" she cried.

The sea king made her a crown of white water-lilies and set it on her head, and from that moment on she was his queen.

In time she got to know the whole kingdom of the sea king. It was much bigger than she imagined. Following a river, it was even possible to reach the sea. What joy it gave them both when the sea king embraced her waist and they glided along the river like birds flying through the air. The reeds at the water's edge bowed low as they passed. The river became broader and broader until it opened into the wide, infinite sea.

But Agneta was not allowed to come to the surface of the water, for the sea king feared that she would remember everything she had left behind on the earth, and that she would long for it again.

For seven years Agneta was the wife of the sea king and in that time gave birth to seven sons. All seven were like their father, and had the same big, dark sad eyes. The youngest was still in the cradle.

One Sunday morning, Agneta stood at the reed cradle and sang for the little one while the other children were outside playing among the waves. She did not know it was Sunday, for all the days, all the years had become the same. But now she distinctly heard the sound of bells —"Ding, dong, ding, dong" — reaching to the very bottom of the lake. She lifted her head and listened.

"Those are bells!" Agneta thought. "I have heard those before ... but where?"

And suddenly the image of a church rose before her inward eye, the arches, the candles at the altar, the loud organ. With a sigh she left the cradle, went to the sea king and asked him: "Let me go up to the church! Please let me go! It has been such a long time since I've been there."

The sea king looked at her in alarm. How had she suddenly remembered her earlier life?

"You want to go to church? Why specially today?" he asked.

"I suddenly feel such a longing for it," she answered. "I feel as if I would die if you don't let me go."

"Fine. You shall go," replied the sea king. "But you first have to promise me to come back before evening. All your children will long for the hour of your return."

"Of course I'll return!" said Agneta and smiled. "Do you think I could be happy without you, without the children, without the youngest in his cradle?" And she bent down and kissed the sleeping boy.

"Good. Then follow me," said the sea king. Like an arrow he shot up to the surface with her, and sat her on the end of the castle pier. Then he disappeared back into the depths.

Agneta's head was suddenly all mixed up. She shaded her eyes with her hand, for the sun was so much stronger than she was used to, and everything around had such clear and bright colours. When she looked again, she recognized her father's castle, rising strong and mighty as at the time she had left, and from the gardens around the park came the scent of lime-blossoms and roses. The swallows flew swiftly over her head with loud cries, and the sound of bells filled the air. Now she saw the church — the door was open — and as quick as she could she ran there.

The service had begun. Among the people kneeling was an old man, dressed in the fine garb of a knight. His beard was long and white, and his face was buried in his hands. But Agneta recognized him immediately. It was her father. She saw how the tears ran down his hands and his chest laboured as he breathed, and she knew why he was so sad. At the back of the church where she stood, she sank to her knees and wept as if her heart would break.

The service lasted a long time. The clouds of incense rose and the candles on the altar burnt low, the organ played louder and louder, and song filled the building. But then it was as if a cloud passed outside. The church became dark, and Agneta saw how the pictures of the saints turned away. Then she noticed that the church door had opened, and the sea king stood there.

"Agneta," he whispered, "come with me. You have been away for so long."

She did not answer, but buried her face in her hands. Then he touched her shoulder and she felt a shudder of fear go through her body.

"Agneta," he pleaded with a soft voice. "Your children are longing for you! Don't let them wait for you in vain."

She shook her head and folded her hands.

"Agneta," he said again, and this time his voice sounded so sad, that she could hardly bear to listen. "The little one in the cradle is longing for you. He is crying, because he cannot see you."

Now Agneta turned to face the sea king. Her face was white with pain, but she said with a strong voice: "They shall wait in vain! You, too, can wait in vain for as long as you want. None of you will make me return to your realm. Leave me!"

The sea king sighed so deeply, that all the candle flames in the church quivered.

"Agneta, look at me," he pleaded.

But she did not raise her face. She kneeled on the spot as still as a statue. Then the sea king slowly departed. Agneta felt a cold draft as he opened the door. As soon as he had left, the pictures of the saints turned to her again. The sun shone out from behind the clouds and filled the church with its warm rays, and everyone stood to leave. When Agneta's father came to the church door, he stood rooted as if seeing a ghost. Was it possible? Could it be his long-lost daughter?

Agneta went to him and threw her arms around him, saying, "Yes, it's me, your Agneta. I was away for a long time in the castle of the sea king, but now at last I have returned to earth, and will stay here."

And hand in hand, rejoicing, father and daughter went outside into the warm sunshine.

The Golden Key

W.E. Björk

Lena, the shepherdess, sat in the meadow and sang while she watched the Queen's sheep. It was mild and still and the light of the evening sun glinted golden on the windows of the castle. No cart or riders were to be seen on the wide road across the valley, just three old ladies who seemed to be walking from afar.

One of the castle windows opened and the cook called to Lena: "Listen, girl. You have much too beautiful a voice. If our dear king were still alive, he would have had a shining gold ducat for you. How times have changed since the queen has been in power! But if you come inside, you can have a good meal. The queen won't know for she is out hunting."

"I thank you," answered Lena, "but I'm not hungry just now, and anyway I like singing and don't expect any reward for it. But if you want to make me happy, give something to those three old beggar-women walking along the road."

And she continued to sing, so beautifully that the cook and all the kitchen-helpers felt tears coming to their eyes. And they whispered to each other, "See, is it not enchanting how she sits and sings? As beautiful as the queen, yes, like a queen herself."

The three old women in the meantime had left the road and were making their way to the castle. Their wide coats were rough and worn and they had pulled their hoods down over their faces. They were bent, clutching their sticks, and talked loudly together in a language which Lena did not understand.

"Take this loaf of bread," said the cook to them as they came near. "And thank Lena for it."

At that moment the sound of horns, horses' hooves and baying dogs came closer through the woods. The hunting party was returning at a gallop with the queen at its head. Yes, she was beautiful, the most beautiful in the land, as the courtiers used to say. And that was no lie. But she was wicked as well. As wicked as no other woman in seven kingdoms, whispered the courtiers to each other. And that too was no lie.

On seeing the queen ride up, the cook paled and slammed the window shut. But too late. The queen had seen him handing out the bread.

"What's the meaning of this?" she asked him. "Are you wasting my bread on beggars?"

She rode to the three old women and looked at them angrily, crying: "What sort are you, that you are not ashamed to be creeping around my castle begging from my servants?"

"We are not here to beg," answered one of the women without lifting her head, "but to distribute gifts."

The queen laughed mockingly. "Listen to these scarecrows! And for whom do you have gifts?"

"For the one who is worthy," said the second woman.

"Just listen to them!" cried the queen. "And who should that be?"

"Not you, your majesty," the third woman answered.

The queen raised her riding whip to beat them, but it broke in her hands.

"Set the dogs on them!" she commanded. But the dogs crept behind the backs of the courtiers and would not stir from the spot.

"Leave my kingdom!" shouted the queen furiously. "And never let me see you again."

"When the measure is full, you will see us again," said the first woman. "And then your fall is not far off."

"I shall chain you in the deepest dungeon and leave you to rot," the queen roared in a rage.

"When the time is ripe," said the second woman, "we shall heal the wounds which you have inflicted."

"May you know every evil in the world, may nightmares haunt you and pestilence strike you!" cried the queen in a fury.

"When the hour comes," replied the third woman, "you yourself will be nothing more than a bad dream."

And with that the three women slowly made their way through the hunting party, without anyone making the slightest attempt to hold them. They walked away down the road, their coats flapping like big, dark wings. And they talked again in a strange tongue.

But Lena the shepherdess quietly followed them, and when they were far enough from the castle, she ran up to them, tugged at the coat of the first, calling: "Old mother, look what you dropped on the meadow."

And she held up a key, a fine key made of pure gold.

"You have good eyes, my child," answered the old woman.

"I saw it glisten when it fell." And then added abashed, "But I did not dare say anything in front of the queen."

"Come with us to the fork in the road," said the second woman.

"If you will risk it," added the third.

And Lena went with them. But when they came to the fork, the women went neither to left nor right, but straight on over the meadows to the sea. There they rested. But what was that? Could it be, or was the setting sun playing tricks? The rough worn shoes of the women glistened as if they were made of diamonds. And the coarse coats — she must have been mistaken -now were of finest silk. They threw back their capes, and Lena saw the fine faces of good fairies. The first took the golden key and turned it three times in the air. There was a rumbling as if a heavy gate was opened. She saw a bridge in seven shining colours — like a rainbow, as she had often seen from afar. This one, though, came to an end here on the beach at her feet. The fairies walked on with Lena over the bridge. It was broad and long and many riders and walkers were crossing it.

"Who are those lovely, happy children?" asked Lena. It seemed as if she had seen many of them before.

"These are the beautiful dreams," answered the fairies. "Every night they come from their pleasure garden above the clouds and visit the earth."

"And nightmares?" asked Lena. "Where do they come from?"

"They come from the realm of shades, deep under the earth. There they sit imprisoned during the day, but when night falls they are freed. Then they go out and frighten those whose minds are not set upon the good."

At last they came to the end of the bridge, and entered the pleasure gardens above the clouds. But as soon as they set foot here, the fairies disappeared, and Lena remained all alone.

She stood in a deep forest, where she glimpsed deer grazing among the trees. Brightly coloured birds flew from branch to branch. Flowers adorned the path and rang like fine silver bells in the wind.

"This has to be a dream," thought Lena, "but what a beautiful dream!"

Music and joyful voices drifted from afar, and she made for the direction whence they came. Soon the forest thinned, and between the trunks of the trees she could see a clearing where couples were dancing to strange music. The music came from the branches of the trees. And looking up, she saw hundreds of birds singing merrily. And thousands of bees hummed in deep harmony.

The dancers were pretty maidens and handsome knights. When Lena saw the beautiful ladies, she was sad. "Oh, if only I were not poor and ugly!" she thought. "I shall never be able to dance in fine company like that."

Then she discovered one of the knights who stood apart and was not joining in the dancing. The longer she looked at him, the more handsome she found him. "He is probably more elegant than the others," she thought. Again she became sad when she remembered how insignificant she was.

"At least I shall wash my face and comb my hair," she thought. She went to a spring, which she heard splashing near her. She leaned over the surface of the water — and leapt back. Who was that in the reflection? She leaned over a second time, and again it seemed as if the face of the queen was looking at her. She blushed. And the face in the pool reddened. She nodded, and in the same instant the other head nodded.

"It's only a dream," whispered Lena, "but it's a nice dream."

But when her hands brushed over her dress, she heard the rustle of silk. She rose again and went back to the clearing. Hesitantly and modestly she stepped out of the forest.

In the same instant everything became still, the dance stopped and everyone turned to look at her. She turned and wanted to flee, but the dancers hurried after her and pulled her towards the sunny, fragrant meadow.

"Little sister," the beautiful ladies called, "come and play with us! You are the most beautiful of us all." The lonesome knight came to her, gave her a hand, asking, "Come dance with me, with no one else but me."

She wanted to shout back, "But don't you know I'm just Lena the little shepherdess?" but her lips were as if sealed.

The party lasted all night. They danced on the meadow and Lena sang. The birds fell silent at Lena's song.

"Little sister, your voice is higher and clearer than ours," they said.

"Little sister," the dancers said, "It is wonderful to watch you dance."

Lena and the lonesome knight danced until they were tired of dancing. Then they went walking arm in arm, and the knight did not move from Lena's side. They spoke of everything with one another, except about things beyond the fairy land.

Suddenly a cool wind blew through the pleasure garden and Lena found herself standing with the three fairies at the rainbow bridge.

"You are our dearest child," said the first. "Here is the golden key."

"You are our dearest child," said the second. "Every night the key will open the door to the pleasure gardens, while others will simply see you sleeping."

"You are our dearest child," said the third. "But if you tell anyone what we have given you, you will have to return the key."

Lena wanted to thank them, but they had disappeared. She looked around for the lonesome knight, but he too had vanished. The rainbow bridge shook and swayed and a mist swirled around.

Lean woke up on the shore where she had been the evening before. It was morning and the sun shone brightly. She sat up, rubbed her eyes, and looked at her simple poor clothes. What strange things had she dreamt last night?

Then she saw something glistening. The golden key! Now she remembered everything. She hung the key from a string round her neck and tucked it under her clothes.

From that time on Lena herded the sheep during the day as she had always done. In the evenings, as soon as she was alone and no one could see her, she took the key, turned it three times in the air, and walked over the rainbow bridge to the pleasure garden.

Soon it was rumoured in the kingdom that the queen wanted to marry again. Many kings and princes had asked for her hand, but until now she had declined all their offers. At last, it was said, a young king had appeared who took her fancy. Many curious people had gathered around the castle to try and catch a glimpse of the young man who had gone riding at the side of the queen. The queen smiled at him sweetly, and he could hardly take his eyes off her.

Lena the shepherdess stood among the curious crowds. But when she saw the young king her heart grew heavy. It was none other than the lonesome knight.

"You're mistaken!" she wanted to call out. "You're mistaken. She is not the one you saw in the pleasure garden!"

But she had to remain silent, so as not to lose the gift of the fairies.

The next day, when the young king and the queen rode past, Lena jumped in front of the horses and fell to her knees. She just wanted the king to see her face and remember her.

"What does she want?" asked the queen, bringing her riding whip down on Lena's back. "Lock her up in the castle till I deal with her." The queen's servants dragged her off. The young king, however, rode on in thoughtful silence and the queen tried without success to make him smile.

When they reached the castle, the queen waved to her steward and told him to punish the girl. The steward had Lena's long hair cut, and had her face rubbed in a cream which made her look dirty and ugly.

"Now your face won't turn anyone's head," he said with a sneer.

The next day the young king from afar rode away and the queen went around moodily awaiting his return. Lena sadly watched over her sheep, and hid her face whenever anyone passed. But every night the golden key opened the gate of the pleasure garden, and there her face was beautiful and clean, and the lonesome knight came to her. They walked in the shade of the trees and spoke of a thousand things, only not about what was closest to Lena's heart. Her lips were sealed when she thought of that.

After a time the young king from afar came again to visit the queen. When he went out riding with the queen, Lena hid her ugly face and wept.

In the evening the queen held a banquet. Through the open windows the guests could be heard merrily chatting, while at the head of the table the queen sat smiling at the young king. He smiled back and looked at her as if she was from his happiest dreams.

Suddenly from below the castle windows, the sound of singing came to the banqueting hall.

"Where does the sun set?" sang Lena, "Where is the sky always blue? Where does the wind blow through a forest of songs? Where does my dearest dance with the sun in his hair? Where, where?"

The guests in the hall admired the beautiful voice. The young king, however, merely drooped his head in silence and stared down without hearing the pretty words the queen was whispering to him. Then the queen paled with anger and called the steward. He went to Lena and had her tongue cut off.

"Now you won't turn anyone's head with your singing," he said with a sneer.

The next day the young king from afar rode away and the queen went around moodily awaiting his return. Lena sat silently and sadly with her sheep, wondering how she could make the knight whom she loved so greatly see his error. Every night when they met in the pleasure garden, she spoke with him, but could tell him nothing of the world beyond the garden.

After a while the young king came again to visit the queen, and this time the betrothal of the couple was announced with great ceremony. In the evening the couple stepped on to the castle balcony to wave at the jubilant crowds. And there on a meadow in the moonshine a girl began to dance. Lena danced as if she was in the pleasure garden on the other side of the clouds, she danced to a magical music as only the fairy's beloved can do.

A murmur of amazement spread through the crowd. The king, however, put his hands to his face and wept. Then the queen was beside herself with anger. She called the steward who went to Lena, dragged her away and had her feet cut off.

"Now you won't turn anyone's head with your dancing," he said with a sneer.

The next day the young king from afar rode away and the queen went around sulkily awaiting his return when the wedding would take place. Lame, mute and ugly, Lena sat with her sheep, utterly miserable. Every night was blissful and splendid, though she felt like weeping.

After a time the young king came again to celebrate his marriage to the queen. On the wedding day the king and the queen stepped into a golden carriage to ride to the church. The queen smiled at the crowds who lined the streets in jubilation, and the young king only had eyes for his bride. As they walked up the steps to the church, something was in their way. Lame, mute and ugly, Lena had dragged herself to the steps and stretched out her hand with the golden key to the king.

"And even if I never again see the pleasure garden, and will always stay lame, mute and ugly, I must warn him!" she thought.

When the young king saw the key, he let out a cry of astonishment.

"Out of the way, ragamuffin!" screeched the queen. "Steward! See that she never again bothers me!"

Then there was a loud roar. The three fairies came through the air in a carriage pulled by white swans.

"The measure is full," said the first. "Your majesty, the hour of your downfall has arrived!"

"The time is ripe," said the second. "Now we shall heal all the wounds which you have inflicted."

"The hour has come," replied the third woman, "May you be nothing more than a bad dream."

At these words, the queen was transformed into a dark cloud which blew away into the realm of shadows deep under the earth.

"You are very beautiful, my child!" said the first fairy, and the dirt from Lena's face melted away and her hair fell like soft silk over her shoulders.

"Your voice is high and clear!" said the second, and Lena uttered a joyful cry.

"Your dancing is delicate and graceful, my daughter!" said the third, and Lena's feet were healed.

"But you betrayed the secret of the fairies," said the first.

"The key no longer is yours," said the second.

"Never again will you go over the rainbow bridge to the land beyond the clouds," said the third.

"Here!" called the king, and pulled a golden key which was exactly the same as the other. "Take this one too. What should I do in the pleasure garden, when the one whom I love is no longer there?"

Then the fairies took his key too, stepped into their carriage and flew off.

"Don't be sad about the pleasure garden!" said the young king and kissed his shepherdess. "We shall make our own garden of pleasures here."

Then they celebrated a splendid joyful wedding. Though whether their pleasure garden was just as good as the one on the other side of the clouds, is hard to say. Have you ever been there?

Bella's Glorious Adventure

Helena Nyblom

Once upon a time there was a little princess. She was four years old and was called Anna Jolenta Isabella Elisabeth Maria Catherine Ines Beatrice, for she had such a lot of godmothers after whom she was named. However, she simply called herself Bella, and all her childhood she kept this name.

She lived with her parents in the royal palace at the edge of a huge forest. Every evening on the stroke of seven o'clock her Nanny brought her into the palace from the garden where she used to play all afternoon among the fragrant flowers. Then she bathed in a marble bath set in a sumptuous bathroom.

Now of course much more goes on inside children's heads than grown-ups can ever guess, and the little princess had her own thoughts.

"It is boring going to bed every evening when it is still light outside and all the grown-ups are walking around talking and laughing," she said to herself one evening. "I don't want to be put to bed by my Nanny yet."

She looked around and saw a little footbridge over a stream. On the other side the path led into the huge dark forest and soon disappeared among the trees. The little princess sat quite still on the lawn playing with a few pebbles that she had found. Her Nanny, sure that she was happily occupied, went off for a moment into the palace. As soon as the Nanny had disappeared from view, Bella jumped up, ran over the little bridge and into the wood as fast as her feet would carry her. She only stopped when she was well inside the forest. There thick pine trees surrounded a mossy clearing. Bella's face was red and she was quite out of breath from running.

"It's lovely here," she called out loud and clapped her hands. "But I'm terribly hot."

And she unbuttoned her white silk dress and let it fall to the ground.

"It needs to be folded up neatly," she said, "like Nanny said."

And she folded her dress and laid it neatly on a stone. Wearing only her petticoat, she laughed happily.

"Like this it's nice and cool," she said and sat on the moss looking up at the tops of the trees.

"You are incredibly big!" she exclaimed.

"We are old, very old," whispered the tree-tops. "We have seen many little princesses grow up, get old and die, and new ones always come here."

"You might be old, but you can't run and jump like me!" said the princess, jumping up and running further into the forest. But she stumbled and fell in her fine shoes, and so she sat down to take off her shoes and socks.

"They can stay here till I come back," she said, neatly putting her shoes next to her folded socks.

"What fun it is to run barefoot," she called and her little pink feet flew over the moss.

The sun still stood high in the sky, and the leaves of the trees made the rays dance like thousands of golden spots on the ground. Between the trees the silver sea shimmered. The whole forest was quiet. The only thing she noticed was the scent of the pines and the fir trees in the warm air.

"That's a lovely scent," said the princess sniffing the air. "Better than the scented water my mother has in her bedroom, better even than the incense in church."

Suddenly Bella stood before a slope covered with wild raspberry bushes. The berries were ripe, so she beat a path there and began to pick and eat them. Suddenly her bare feet stood on something smooth, and in the same moment an adder lifted its head, staring at her with its yellow eyes, its forked tongue darting in and out.

"And who might you be?" asked Bella in astonishment. "You stare at me in such a strange fashion. And you stick your tongue out at me. See I can do the same!"

And she stuck her little pink tongue out at the adder. The adder lay down flat again, and wriggled around Bella's feet.

"You're very nice!" said Bella kneeling down. "Your skin is so smooth and you twist and turn in such a curious way. Come on, let's dance together!"

It looked as if the snake was smiling, an odd kind of wicked smile, but then it began to sway back and forth on the moss. The little princess took the hem of her petticoat in her hand, and sang as she danced:

Cannot run, cannot walk,
Cannot go on tippytoes.
Cannot sing, cannot talk,
So come and dance around my toes.

Her little bare feet made funny jumps and her arms swung high over her head, while she laughed out loud. The snake was quite taken by the princess' dance and was soon swaying in the strangest twists and turns. Suddenly it seemed tired, twisted around and disappeared between the raspberry bushes.

"What, are you tired already?" cried the princess. "See. I'm not! I'm not!"

And she sang louder and louder while she twirled on the moss.

216

Cannot run, cannot walk,
Cannot go on tippytoes.
Cannot sing, cannot talk,
So come and dance around my toes.

At last she too had enough of dancing and ran to the bushes to pick more berries. When she had eaten plenty, she gathered more in her left hand.

"These are for Mother and Nanny," she said wandering on. She had not gone far when she heard something stamping in the undergrowth. "That will be Nanny coming to get me," she thought and stood still. But it was not the nanny. It was a big brown bear who stared at her with his little eyes.

"Look, what a clumsy fellow!" said the little princess. "You're really just a large dog! If only I had some bread to feed you, for you won't like raspberries, will you?"

She stretched out her hand with the berries. "Do you want them?" she asked cheerfully. "That's all I can offer you."

The bear ambled over to her and ate the berries. He carefully licked the princess' fingers, and then looked at her curiously.

"Do you not find the summer too hot in your thick coat?" she asked stroking his fur. "Poor old clumsy fellow!" she added and kissed the bear on the nose. "You're sweating and you can't even take off your coat and lay it on a stone like I did with my dress."

The bear growled gently, and rubbed itself against her, then he suddenly turned round and said something, which she could not understand. Two bear cubs leaped out of the undergrowth. They were like two lovely balls of wool, gawky and awkward in movement, and funny to watch.

"Oh, you're so sweet!" called the princess. She sat on her knees and embraced the two cubs.

"Are those your children?" she asked.

The bear grinned as if to say, "Of course they are."

"Now I don't have any more raspberries to give you," said the princess sadly. "But come along with me and I'll show you where they grow, and then you can pick as many as you want."

She ran on ahead until she came to the slope with raspberries. "See!" she said when they arrived, "Here are lovely ripe berries!"

She pushed the branches down for the little bear cubs, so they could see all the berries. The little cubs jumped around her legs so merrily that they almost knocked her over as they gorged themselves with berries.

"Gently, little ones," she warned them while she went deeper into the bushes.

The old bear went growling quietly alongside. It seemed to be saying, "You are a really kind girl to be helping my children pick berries."

Suddenly, though the two cubs were fighting over a branch of juicy berries. They rolled and bit and tore each other's ears, and in their struggle quite forgot about the food. The bear tried to get them apart, but they ran off into the forest with their mother chasing behind. The princess was left alone.

She decided to go on through the forest and sang a song to herself. Suddenly she heard something, which sounded like the conversation of birds, and she stood still to listen. But in the same moment she heard a flutter over her head and felt something brush against her head, and she noticed her crown was no longer there.

"Oh dear, my lovely crown!" she lamented, and when she looked up she saw a crow with her crown in its beak.

"Give me my crown back!" she called. "You can't just take it away from me!"

"Be quiet, silly girl," answered the crow who had laid the crown in his nest and now looked down at the princess. "I didn't pinch your crown for myself. At last my poor children have something to give them joy."

"Have you got children?" asked the princess. "Where are they?"

"They're here in the nest," cawed the crow, "for they can't fly yet."

"Oh, let me see them!" pleaded the princess and clapped her hands. "I love little children!"

The crow bent its head to the nest, and soon four little black heads peeped over the edge.

"Are those your children?" asked Bella. "Pooh, they are ugly!"

"Ugly?" repeated the crow angrily. "Well if you think that, it just shows you have no taste."

"I'm still so small," answered the princess, "only four years old, so I don't understand very much. Can your children sing?"

"Their voices are not yet ready for singing, but they're already showing promise," said the crow.

"Oh be so good as to ask them to sing a little song — I love to hear songs," the princess asked.

"Wait a moment, I will give them a note," said the crow. Then it explained to the fledglings what was wanted, and there came a long clamour from the nest. Finally all was quiet and the crow sat on the edge of the nest with two young ones and sang:

Caw, caw, caw,
Soon we'll sing a song,
Caw, caw, caw
It isn't very long.

"Is that all?" asked the princess uncertainly.

"We can sing it again if you wish," the crow answered.

"No, thank you," said the princess, "I can't stay that long. I have to get home before the sun sets." And she hurried down the hill.

The lake shimmered through the trees and looked more and more inviting, and soon Bella found herself at the shore. The sun made the water silvery and white water-lilies floated on the surface and in the reeds there were many swans.

"What wonderful white flowers!" cried Bella, and was about to hop out on to the water-lilies which looked like a carpet over the water. A swan shot out of the reeds.

"Don't go in the water!" it called anxiously. "You'll drown. But if you want, you can ride on my back, and I shall swim out to the flowers."

The princess longed to do this and climbed on to the back of the swan, took her long pearl necklace and laid it like reins round the swan's neck. Soon it glided through the water and as it went along the princess picked an armful of water-lilies. In the middle of the lake there was an island with great oak trees and juniper trees.

"That's where I want to go," said the princess. "I want to sit in the grass there and make a wreath out of the lilies."

The swan brought her to the island and let her jump ashore. She ran to the shade of the trees and sat down to make her wreath.

"But your pearl necklace ..." called the swan.

"Oh, you may keep it to remember me," answered the princess and waved a farewell to the swan.

Making a wreath was not so easy. Hard as the little princess tried, it just didn't work. For one thing she had no wire for a frame, and for another the water-lilies were only happy on the water and now let their heads droop. The princess threw the flowers on the ground and began to cry. And when she heard herself cry, she became even more miserable and cried all the harder.

Suddenly she heard the rushing of great wings and when she looked up she saw a gigantic bird which had settled down in front of her and looked at her sternly.

"What sort of a hen are you?" she asked. "Even in my father's palace I've never seen such a big hen."

"I'm not a hen," answered the bird and lifted its head proudly. "I am an eagle, the biggest and most powerful bird of the sky. I built my nest on the lonely cliffs, I thought that people would leave me in peace there, but now you silly little creature are howling so loud that my young ones are restless when they should be going to sleep. Go away from here. You've no business here."

"But how will I get back?" sobbed the princess. "It is so far, and soon the sun will set, and everyone will get worried about me."

"Well, I suppose I'll have to take you back, for you can't stay here. Sit on my back. But hurry, for my little ones don't like being left alone when it gets dark."

The princess quickly climbed on to the back of the eagle who rose gently into the air.

"I shall just fly past my nest," said the eagle and flew to a high cliff. In the nest were two featherless fledglings who opened their beaks wide when they heard the flapping of wings.

"Be quiet and listen," said the eagle to them. "You've had enough to eat for today. Just stay still until I return. I have to take this human fledgling home, so that we can have some peace."

Then the eagle rose high into the sky with the princess. She was a bit dizzy at first, but then she peeped down and soon found it enchanting to sit up there. Far below were forests and the high trees were like tiny bushes. Here and there were light patches which were villages, palaces and castles, and she saw little lakes glistening like hand-mirrors dotted in the landscape. The air was so light and clear up here, that the princess spread her arms wide and shouted for joy.

"What silly nonsense," grumbled the eagle. "Now you have to promise to hold on tight, for we are going down very fast to the ground. See, down there is your father's palace."

221

The princess looked down, but at first could not see anything. Then she saw that the tiny toy castle at the edge of the forest had four towers, and then she recognized the palace. They came to the gardens in a dizzying descent.

"So, now you're home," said the eagle after the princess had landed. "Stay here, and don't go and disturb the peace of the island again."

"But what can I give you as thanks for bringing me home?" asked the princess. "I know! She pulled off her petticoat. "That's the only thing I have left. But if you cut it and sew it you can make two little coats for your children."

The eagle did not answer. He took the petticoat in his beak, spread his wings and flew off. Now the princess ran naked through the garden, so glad to be home before dark.

In the palace there was great fear and worry since the princess had disappeared. Everywhere had been searched — the gardens, the forest, the hill — but all without success. Now the king and queen were weeping in sorrow that they would never see their daughter again.

The princess quietly opened the door and ran to them as bare as the day she was born.

"See. I'm here again!" she called and laughed.

"Dear child," asked the queen, "what has happened to you? And where are all your clothes?"

The princess looked down crestfallen. "I have no idea," she said in a carefree tone. "But don't be angry, for I had such a glorious adventure."

The Giant who Slept for
Ten Thousand Years

Einar Rosenborg

S kul was the name of a family of giants who lived by the Baltic Sea so long ago, that no one can remember exactly when it was. In those days it was very cold and snow lay for much of the year, but Skul the Giant and his family loved the cold. Skul was old and remembered the time when it had been much colder, and when not a single green leaf or shoot was to be seen far and wide. However, in the last few years the coast had become greener and greener. And what was worse, when Skul marched around, it sometimes happened that he saw swarms of funny little midgets marching through the growing woods. What could they be? Skul liked stamping his foot in front of them so the whole earth shook and the funny midgets ran away in terror. But before long, the swarm came back. No, Skul no longer felt at home by the sea.

Skul had five big, stupid, clumsy sons. One was a bit bigger, more stupid and clumsy than the others. When he was born, he was as big as a fully grown bear, and just as hairy. That is why he was called Björn which means bear, or Skulbjörn after his father. Every year he became bigger and hairier and moved so clumsily, that he was always in the way of the others or even stumbling over his own feet.

From time to time, the five Skul brothers would have hefty skirmishes with Vätter, the sea-troll. If Vätter was annoyed, he would slurp up sea-water in his enormous mouth and spray it like a fountain over the giants. And if there was one thing that bothered the giants, it was water. Furious, they would pick up the nearest boulders and rocks and hurl them at Vätter in the sea. That is why today there are places on the Baltic coast where Vätter and the giants fought which are now littered with little islands, called skerries.

One day Vätter and the Skul brothers had their usual battle with water and rocks. But soon the giants found a shortage of rocks on the shore, and one of the brothers went up the hills to find more that were big enough. He found a huge rock, lifted it and hurled it with all his might.

"Watch out!" he called to his brothers. But as always, Skulbjörn stood in the way. Bang! The rock crashed against his skull and Skulbjörn fell to the ground.

"Did you hear how hollow that sounded?" his brothers laughed. But soon their laughter stopped, for Skulbjörn did not get up nor even moved.

"Dead!" the brothers cried, and rushed off home weeping giant tears, to tell their father and mother of the disaster.

Old Skul heaped stones all round Skulbjörn's body, until he was completely hidden from view and a real hill stood there. Then Skul and his family moved far away from that sad place. It is said that he and his wife died soon afterwards of a broken heart, while the four brothers got together with the strange little midgets but soon came to a sorry end with them.

But that wasn't the end of the Skul family, for Skulbjörn wasn't dead at all. The blow on his head had knocked him out and he lay motionless under the stones. They were not too heavy for him, and let through plenty of air. So Skulbjörn just lay silent and still and as time passed no one even suspected he was there.

People wandered past the hill, settled on the coast, built farms and boats. And Skulbjörn slept. Summers came, each one warmer and greener than the last. Shrubs began to grow at the foot of the hill and slowly crept higher. Some little bushes grew into trees that dropped their leaves in the autumn, and new plants grew up. And still Skulbjörn slept. Hundreds and hundreds of years passed, the single trees grew into a forest, the villages became cities humming with busy life. And under the green hill Skulbjörn still slept his long sleep.

Ten thousand years perhaps had passed when, one day, quarry workers blew up Skulbjörn's hill. They had spent many hours preparing this, and now it was getting dark and raining. They were all looking forward to going home after the final explosion. This last blast was enormous, and there was an ear-splitting boom. Immediately there came an even louder deeper groaning, and the earth under the workers' feet began to shake. Frightened they ran off, crying out: "Earthquake! Earthquake!"

But it was no earthquake. It was Skulbjörn who had been woken and was stretching. The last blast had been close to his ear, and it had felt like a tap on his ear. He yawned, stretched and started to get up causing cracks to open in the hill. Then he shook off the stones and the earth, and felt the rain on his head. That made him angry. Of course he thought that Vätter was spewing sea-water in his face. He staggered to his feet, reached for a boulder to throw at the sea-troll. And then he stood with his mouth wide open.

Clouds had darkened the sky bringing dusk on more quickly. In the nearby town all the lights had gone on already.

"What kind of a big creature is that lying on the beach?" Skulbjörn asked himself. The giant could see the whole city from his lofty height. He saw a great mass with glimmering lights, and a huge number of dark objects with midget people moving among them. The clouds suddenly lit up with flashes and there was a rumbling and roaring in the air far worse than when Vätter was up to something.

Until now Skulbjörn had no idea what fear was, but now he felt a sudden panic. He made a few jumps inland. Then he looked back to see if the strange creature was

224

following him. No, it was still in the same place, blinking and shining as before. Only now did Skulbjörn notice that the sea was no longer covered in ice, that the snow had melted and strange fluffy things were growing all over the earth. And from the heavens there fell this dreadful lukewarm water that drizzled over him.

Gradually he felt a bit hungry, and so he broke off a fir tree to see if one could eat it. A bit bitter, but he chewed it anyway, still staring at the odd creature on the shore. He was trying to understand what had changed since he fell asleep last night. Eventually Skulbjörn decided that the thing there couldn't be a creature. There were so many of these tiny midgets moving along the narrow lit bands which criss-crossed the glimmering mass, that Skulbjörn grew quite dizzy trying to count them. And the dark bits were little stones neatly strung out next to each other. Funny thing was, they had little holes with fire inside. Possibly these midget people had hollowed them out and lived inside.

Once Skulbjörn had figured things out this far, he was no longer afraid. He tore up a second fir tree, and filled with curiosity went towards the city to have a closer look. He had hardly taken a few steps when just in front of his feet a fiery snake rushed out of the forest whistling and belching smoke, dashing over the ground until it disappeared among the lines of stones. The giant stared fearfully after the train (for that's what the fiery snake was), and then carried on to the city.

In the city there was turmoil and panic. First it was thought there was an earthquake, but then people reported seeing a terrible monster near the city. As Skulbjörn came nearer, news spread like wildfire, and soon the streets emptied as everyone sought shelter within. Doors and gates were closed and locked, only here and there an anxious face peered out from between the curtains.

With every giant's step the earth shook and the walls of the houses trembled. Skulbjörn walked very carefully, so as not to step on the houses. But everything he stepped on, streetlights, cars, trams, was flattened under his huge feet. Suddenly he tripped on some overhead cables he had not seen. With a terrifying noise he fell onto a factory which luckily stood empty at this time.

"What silly things these people put in my way!" he snorted with annoyance and went on.

He came to some barracks where there were twenty soldiers and an officer. The officer quickly placed his men in front of the barracks, and commanded them to shoot at the monster. The officer and his men were the first midgets he had seen close up, and he was just wondering whether he should try and talk to the officer when bullets whistled past his legs.

"Why do you tickle my legs?" called Skulbjörn in a huff, and leaped right over the barracks. No, there didn't seem much point in talking to these midgets.

His leap took him into a park where he paused for a moment, trying to make sense of these strange experiences. Now he noticed three midgets under a tree, staring up at him in terror. It was a woman with two little children, a boy and a girl. When the giant bent down, the boy fell on his knees and called, "Dear Goliath, don't harm us. We are so poor and Mother is sick."

"What's that, little one?" asked the giant, for he didn't quite understand this business with Goliath. "Why are you out there in this weather? Don't you have a stone to live in like the others?"

The boy did not understand what the giant meant with stones, but he understood the rest, and so he answered: "We are poor and Mother can't pay the rent. So we are not allowed to live at home any more."

"Poor?" asked Skulbjörn, "What's that? And rent? Who won't let you stay in your stone?"

"The landlord has thrown us out," the boy told him.

"Well, take me to this Lord Land, and I'll show him!" And he picked up the boy on his open hand. From there he could see the whole city, and it was not long before the boy had spotted his home.

"There!" he cried. "That's the house."

With one step the giant was there. "And Lord Land, does he live inside?" he asked.

"He lives in there and the door is locked," answered the boy.

"Don't worry. We'll get him out," said the giant, and he picked up the entire roof in his hand as if he were taking the lid off a box. Now he could look into the room from above. In the biggest room the landlord was lying on a sofa. Rigid with fear he had seen the roof disappearing and in its place appeared the face of the giant.

"Are you Lord Land?" asked the giant with a growl in his voice like a storm brewing.

The poor landlord could not open his mouth for fear.

"How can you be so wicked?" the giant went on. "Why can't you midgets be nice to each other? Now you must take this boy, his sick mother and his little sister in again and let them live in peace, so they don't have to be outside in this terrible wet weather."

He set the boy in the middle of the table in the big room and took a step back into the park to pick up the mother and sister. He put them down in the middle of the room as well, and saw how the landlord was hurrying to make the sick mother comfortable on the sofa. Satisfied, he set the roof back on the house which now was more or less repaired, apart from a crack in the wall to remind them of the giant's visit.

Skulbjörn stood in the dark and pondered. There was nothing to keep him here. The lovely cold had gone, everything was warm and wet ... brrr! And in any case there was so much unpleasantness among these midgets, blinking lights, fiery snakes, and everything was so confusing. Even among themselves they didn't seem to get on.

"No! This is not for me," he mumbled to himself. "I'll do better to look for a bit of space."

And he went on his way. The people in the city could see the black figure against the sky for a while before it disappeared.

Over the following days, there arrived from further and further north dozens of reports of broken electricity and telephone cables, trampled gardens and woods. Soon nothing more was heard of the giant, and no one knew exactly where he had ended up. Some said he had lain down under a hill to have another snooze and get some peace. What will things be like next time he wakes up?

The Queen

Anna Wahlenberg

Many hundreds of years ago there lived a young maiden who was famous in several kingdoms.

Adelgunda was indeed a remarkable young girl. She was slight, delicate, and pale as a lily, but it was not so much her beauty that people spoke of. Nor was it her good sense, though one and all could see intelligence shining on her brow.

No, what Adelgunda was renowned for were her two wonderful eyes, which could speak much more plainly than her lips. Her eyes could also see better than anyone else's; they saw what people were thinking and things that lay hidden deep in their souls.

Yet no one was afraid of Adelgunda's eyes which saw and expressed so much; rather, anyone who looked at them was glad. Adelgunda's gaze rested long on good and beautiful things, and when her eyes saw something ugly and evil, they said so, not with hatred and contempt but with sorrow and compassion. Adelgunda's eyes spoke a language that everyone understood.

Anyone who met the young girl became fond of her and left hoping to see her again. Only the really wicked and those with uneasy consciences shunned her. They never dared show themselves in the neighbourhood of the old castle where she lived with her father, Sir Hubert.

But one day a messenger announced the arrival at the knight's castle of a very special guest.

Prince Sigmund, who would one day inherit the realm from his father, the king, was wooing a handsome princess in a powerful nearby kingdom. This princess had already almost promised Sigmund her hand; now the two were to meet to see if they really suited each other. And since his road took him past Sir Hubert's castle, Sigmund decided to stay there a day and see young Adelgunda, of whom he had heard so many remarkable things.

Adelgunda was also curious about the prince, for she had heard how brave, handsome, and chivalrous he was, and how much his people loved him. But suppose she saw something in him, something that others did not see, something which was not beautiful, but which her eyes would nevertheless speak of, since she could not hide anything they saw? How terrible that would be! And how ashamed her father would be if such a thing happened to the young prince in his home.

At last Adelgunda decided what she would do. She would hide, and steal a glance at the prince before he entered her father's castle. Then if she saw anything that her eyes ought not to reveal, she would run into the forest and not return until Prince Sigmund had left.

Silently and alone, she slipped from the castle and walked towards the road on which the prince was expected to arrive. When she saw a cloud of dust at the top of the hill, she hid behind a wild rose bush, where she could watch without being seen.

The cloud of dust drew nearer and nearer, bringing with it a big wagon drawn by four horses and loaded with baggage. Two valets in gold-braided livery sat on top. The prince's servants were travelling ahead of their master.

After a while, however, another cloud of dust rose at the top of the hill. This time four riders approached at a fast gallop. One was taller and more distinguished than the others, and Adelgunda realized it must be the prince. Just as the riders reached the rose bush where she was hiding, the prince's horse stumbled on a stone and fell heavily.

His frightened companions reined in, dismounted, and gathered anxiously around Prince Sigmund to see if he had been hurt. But he was already on his feet examining his horse, which was trying to stand.

"It's nothing serious," he said, "but my horse has sprained a leg so I won't get back into the saddle."

"Will your Highness take my horse then?" asked the nearest knight, bringing up his mount.

But the prince slapped him warmly on the shoulder and refused. "Should one of you, my trusted and faithful comrades in peace and war, walk while I ride?" he asked. "No, indeed. That will never do. Let's ask at that farm cottage if they will lend us a horse."

The knight rode towards a nearby cottage, and soon he returned with a large, heavy drayhorse, shaggy, unkempt, and ugly, as such horses sometimes are. He dismounted, took the saddle from the lame horse and strapped it on the borrowed one, and was just about to swing himself on to its back, leaving his own horse for the prince when again the prince rebuffed him with a warm smile. "I am the one who fell," he said. "I shall ride old Shaggy." With that, he threw himself on to the saddle, caught the reins of his limping horse, and rode on at the head of his companions.

As Adelgunda watched him riding so tall and erect on the strong but homely drayhorse, he seemed as handsome as a dream. She knew that from then on she would think about him every hour of every day of her life.

She got up from her hiding-place and walked home in a dream. And she was still dreaming when she went to her room and braided pearls in her hair and put on a white gown with silver embroidery.

Only when a lady-in-waiting knocked on the door with a message from her

230

father to hurry to meet their distinguished guest did she come to her senses. She started in fright, for she had suddenly realized that she could not meet the prince and let him look into her eyes. They would tell him, plainly and clearly, that to her he was the finest man on earth, and that she would think about him every hour of every day of her life. A little noble maiden must never make such a confession to a man, much less to a prince who was so far above her in birth and rank.

Yet Adelgunda said, "Tell my father I am coming," for of course now it was too late to run and hide in the forest.

Instead, she ran to her mother's old room, opened a cupboard, and picked out the thickest white veil she could find. She had never worn a veil over her face before, because she had never needed to hide her face or her thoughts. But now she did. Quickly she threw the veil over her head and walked into the hall where they were waiting for her.

A murmur of surprise rose from everyone in the room as she stepped over the threshold. After she had greeted their honoured guest, her father asked, "Why are you wearing a veil, Adelgunda?"

"Forgive me, Father, but I am not used to the company of princes," she answered.

Sir Hubert smiled and turned to Prince Sigmund. "I am sure she will soon be more confident," he said.

They sat down at the table, with the prince between the knight and his daughter.

The prince had eyes for no one but Adelgunda. She seemed to him graceful and gentle; her voice was musical and her words were wise. When she lifted her veil a little to put a wine goblet to her lips, he caught a glimpse of her face, and that made him even more impatient to see it unveiled.

After the meal, they rose from the table, but Adelgunda slipped behind the other guests in the hope of being able to leave the room unnoticed, and then run from the castle. However, the prince still had his eyes on her, and suddenly she found him barring her way.

"I have heard about your eloquent eyes, noble maid," he said. "Won't you let me have the pleasure of seeing them, as others do?"

She bowed her head low. "I cannot," she whispered.

"Then I must believe you have seen something in me that you do not wish your eyes to speak of."

"Oh, no. No," she exclaimed in a troubled voice.

"Then lift your veil."

But Adelgunda stayed still, wishing she could die.

Her father joined them and looked at Adelgunda with puzzled brows. "What sort of childishness is this?" he asked. "Take off your veil at once."

"I cannot," Adelgunda replied in a voice so low it could hardly be heard.

The prince froze. He stopped Sir Hubert, who was about to tear the veil from his daughter's head, and bade the company a stiff farewell. He did not wish to force Adelgunda to obey him. He and his retinue rode quickly from the castle, and the girl remained standing in the hall, weeping bitterly and without a word of answer to all her father's reproaches.

Word spread quickly throughout the realm that Adelgunda had not let the prince look into her eyes. People asked each other what she could have seen in him that she could not speak of. And so strong was their faith in the girl's gift of reading people's minds that now they whispered that she must have discovered something wicked in the prince, although he had always been thought of as good and righteous.

The whispers spread farther and farther, until at last they reached the court of the powerful king whose daughter Sigmund was wooing. When the princess heard what was being said of Sigmund, she refused even to discuss marriage, and asked him to leave at once. Not until Adelgunda had lifted her veil, she said, and shown that her eyes had nothing evil to say of him, might he return.

The prince went back to his own kingdom angered by this insult, and yet even at home he saw only mistrust and suspicion in people's eyes. So his anger turned to sorrow, and he locked himself in his rooms, cursing the day he had met Adelgunda.

There was one person, however, who was even more grieved than the prince by all that had happened, and that was Adelgunda herself. When she heard how he had suffered for her sake, all she could think about was that she must do everything she could to absolve him from blame.

She went to her father and asked him to go to the court and request the king to call together all the knights and ladies of the realm on a certain day — as many people as possible from far and near. Then she would agree to say something about the prince which would dispel all their suspicions.

Sir Hubert set out at once to deliver his daughter's message, which was received with pleasure by both the king and prince. Adelgunda, they believed, would soon appear without her veil, and then everyone would see that her eyes had nothing evil to tell.

From every corner of the kingdom knights and liegemen were summoned, and their wives and daughters came, too. On the appointed day, half the throne room was filled with nobility, and the burghers and peasants so crowded the other half that no one could move an elbow.

When all the guests were assembled, a door was opened, and Adelgunda and her father entered.

But when they saw that Adelgunda was still wearing her veil, the faces of the king and prince darkened, and their guests were offended.

As she reached the throne, she curtsied deeply to the king, and even more deeply to Prince Sigmund. Indeed, she made such a long, low curtsy that the prince sprang up and offered her his hand.

She turned to the king, and then to the whole gathering. "I have heard that some people are suspicious of Prince Sigmund because I did not wish to lift my veil before him. I have come here today to tell you what my eyes have seen. They have seen that there is no more chivalrous, noble, and good man than he on the whole wide earth."

"Then lift your veil and let us see that your lips do not tell us one thing and your eyes another," said the king.

"That I cannot do," she answered.

"Then no one will believe you," said the old king, his eyes ablaze.

"No one will believe you," everyone called out angrily.

The little maiden stood where she was, with her head still bowed. Then she took one step towards Prince Sigmund, and slowly lifted the veil from her pale, beautiful face.

The eyes that rested on the prince shone like two wonderful stars and told him, plainly and clearly, what a young maiden must never say to any man, much less to a prince. And it was not only the prince who saw what they said; everyone present saw, too. Now they knew why she had not wanted to lift her veil, and suddenly the throne room was so still you could have heard a handkerchief flutter to the floor.

"May I go now?" asked Adelgunda. "Come, Father."

She took Sir Hubert's hand, and they walked slowly through the throng of people, who opened a path for them.

But before they had reached the door, a voice rang out over the heads of the guests. "Close the doors."

It was the prince speaking, and the guards hastened to obey him. Then the prince threw himself on his knees before the king.

"My Father," he pleaded. "Will we let the queen depart?"

"The queen?" asked the king.

"Yes, the queen. For is she not a queen among women? To me at least, there will never be anyone else."

The king looked at the upturned faces before him. "Do all of you, too, say that she is a queen?" he asked.

A roar of "Yes" rose from every corner of the room, from nobles and peasants, from young and old. It echoed and rang until the old castle walls reverberated.

"Since you all say so, so be it," said the old king. "We will not let the queen depart."

He rose, stepped from his throne, and walked the length of the room until he stood in front of the noble maiden. Then he took her by the hand and led her slowly back through the joyous crowd. Before the throne, he placed her hand in the young prince's. Then everyone saw that Prince Sigmund's eyes, too, could speak. They told Adelgunda something very similar to what her eyes had told him.

The two stood in silence, hand in hand, while cheers rose around them, so strong and loud, it seemed they would never stop.

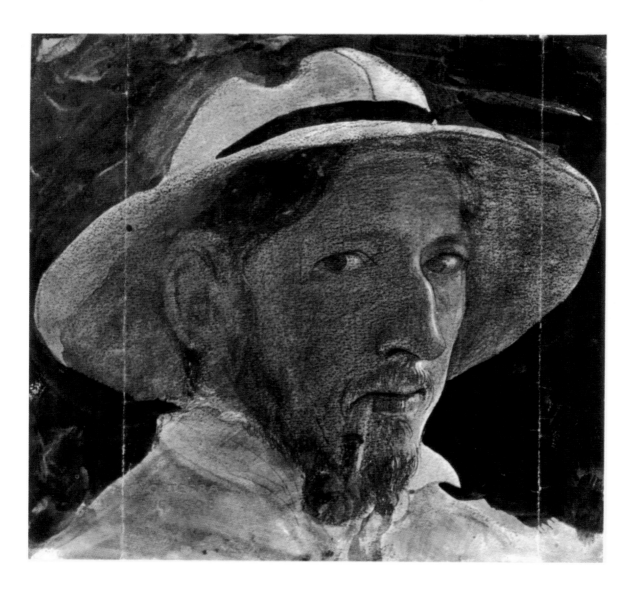

Self-portrait, Volterra 1908.

John Bauer 1882–1918

John Bauer was one of the world's greatest illustrators of fairy tales. He was born in 1882 in the Swedish city of Jönköping. His father came from southern Germany; his mother was Swedish. As a boy, he showed an interest in and a gift for drawing, and his school books are filled with caricatures. He also displayed a warm feeling for nature, and often made long excursions on foot, alone, through the deep forests that line Lake Vättern, on the shore of which Jönköping is situated.

When he was no more than sixteen years old he went to Stockholm, seeking to enter the Royal Academy of Arts; but while his great talent was obvious, he was too young to be admitted. He had to wait two more years, during which time he further improved his skill as a draftsman.

At the Academy, Bauer soon achieved a respected name, among both teachers and pupils. He drew with serene and sure strokes, with spirited detail, and with a pronounced feeling for form. The noted Swedish painter Gustaf Cederström later compared the preciseness of Bauer's student sketches with the drawings of Dürer and Holbein.

In his spare time Bauer studied historic costumes, weapons, and buildings, and the value of this research shows itself particularly in his later fairy-tale illustrations. These also reflect his strong feeling for his native land — the deep forests with mossy boulders, the smiling glades, the low houses, the tarns, the mountains.

While still a student at the Academy he received his first big commission as an illustrator of fairy tales: it was Anna Wahlenberg's book Länge, länge sedan (Long, Long Ago.) Three years later he made his real breakthrough when the annual Jul-stämning (Christmas Spirit), under the aegis of Cyrus Granér, began publishing the collection Bland tomtar och troll (Among Tomtes and Trolls) which came out once a year. Of the first ten editions, eight were illustrated entirely by Bauer, and his clumsy, strangely natural-looking troll figures were soon beloved by every Swede. During his short lifetime, he illustrated the work of almost every well-known Swedish storyteller, the best of whom are represented in this collection. Generations of Scandinavian children have been brought up among his pictures, both in their books and on their walls.

John Bauer did not wish to remain an illustrator of children's books forever. He had long felt a strong urge towards other kinds of painting but was never able to fulfil this ambition. With his wife and their two-year-old son, John Bauer was among the passengers on the steamer Per Brahe which, on a dark November night in 1918, sank in Lake Vättern, drowning all on board.

Authors

Elsa Beskow (1874-1953) was born Elsa Maartman in Stockholm. She started drawing at an early age, and was strongly influenced by the fairy stories told to her by her grandmother, Johanna Wilhelmina. In 1894, she started writing for *Jultomten*, a children's magazine. In 1897 she married Natanael Beskow, and in 1901 they moved to Djursholm where she lived until her death in 1953. She wrote thirty-three picture books and illustrated eight collections of fairy tales. She is considered to be one of the founders of Swedish children's literature.

Cyrus Granér (1870-1937) was both a writer and a composer. From 1907 to 1915 he edited *Bland Tomtar Och Troll* (*Among Gnomes and Trolls*), an annual Christmas book of fairy tales that helped make John Bauer popular, and in 1908 wrote *Burre Busse i trylleskoven* (*The naughty boy in the magic wood*). He is, however, best known for his music and was an accomplished organist.

Helge Kjellin (1885-1984)

P.A. Lindholm's books include *Lappfolk* (*The Lapps*, 1908, with illustrations by John Bauer) and *Hos lappbönder: Skildringar, sägner och sagor från Sodra Lappland* (*Lapp Farmers: Stories and Legends from South Lappland*, 1884).

Helena Nyblom (1843-1926) was born Helena Augusta Roed in Copenhagen, Denmark. In 1864 she married Professor Carl Rupert Nyblom and moved to Sweden. In 1875, she had her first short story published in the magazine *Ny Illustrerad Tidning* (*New Illustrated Journal*) and went on to be published widely. In 1905 she won the Iduns book prize with her novel *Högvalla*. In 1923 she was awarded the Swedish Medal for Art and Literature for a lifetime of service to literature.

Harald Östenson was a widely-published author. His stories appeared in the well-know children's magazine *Folkskolans Barntidning* (*School's Magazine for Children*), founded in 1892 and edited by Stina Quint. He was also the editor of *Till Föräldrar* (*For Parents*), a parenting magazine founded in 1897.

Jeanna Oterdahl (1879-1965) was a teacher, author, lecturer and poet in Göteborg. Her children's books include *Solhult* (*The Sunny Bushes*, 1901, with illustrations by Ottilia Adelborg) and *Blommornas bok* (*The Flower Book*, 1905, with illustrations by Elsa Beskow).

Einar Rosenborg (1882-1960) was a journalist and liberal thinker. In 1930, he and his wife lnge bought Carl Gehrman's music publishing business, and in 1950 they founded the Inge and Einar Rosenborg Foundation for Swedish Music which has provided scholarships for more than two hundred musicians and composers.

Alfred Smedberg (1850-1925)

Walter Stenström (1881-1926) was born in Målilla in the district of Kalmar. He was an author, comedy writer and a lecturer. His books for children include *Prinsessan som inte ville äta havresoppa* (*The Princess who wouldn't eat porridge*), *Pepparkaksgubbarna i pepparkaksskrinet* (*The Gingerbread Men in the Gingerbread Tin*) and *Drummelbergs husdräng* (*The Farm Hand from Dummelberg*).

Anna Wahlenberg (1858-1933) was born Anna Maria Lovisa Wahlenberg Kjerrman in Stockholm. She was the daughter of industrialist Adolf Wilhelm Wahlenberg and MariaTheresia Lunngren. A poet and author, she wrote many fairy and folk tales; John Bauer's first commission as a student was to illustrate a collection of her fairy tales called *Long, Long Ago*.

Cover picture of Sagoprinzessan, 1915.

Acknowledgments

The following stories are reprinted by kind permission of the respective literary executors: *When Mother Troll took in the King's Washing* by Elsa Beskow; *Leap the Elk and the Little Princess Cottongrass* by Helge Kjellin; *The Four Big Trolls and Little Peter Pastureman* by Cyrus Granér; *Stalo and Kauras* by P.A. Lindholm; *The Prince Without a Shadow* by Jeanna Oterdahl.

With thanks to the following for permission to use the images on the pages indicated: Bonnier Carlsen Bokförlag, Stockholm: pp. 15, 42, 46, 99, 111, 116, 123, 130, 133, 141, 142, 152, 153, 168, 172, 174, 176, 178, 218; Göteborgs Konstmuseum, Gothenburg: p. 58 (photograph: Ebbe Carlsson); 63 (photograph: Sixten Sandell), 161 (photograph: Jönköpings Läns Museum); Jönköpings Läns Museum, Jönköping (photographs by Göran Sandstedt): pp. 6, 8, 9, 11, 31, 102, 104, 106, 231; Malmö Museer, Malmö: p. 47; National Museum, Stockholm: p. 108 (photograph: Åsa Lundén); p. 120 (photograph Jönköpings Läns Museum); private ownership, most photographs Jönköpings Läns Museum, Jönköping: pp. 22, 56, 61, 67, 68, 72, 75, 78, 80, 83, 86, 89, 122, 136, 140, 143, 163, 164, 180, 183, 184, 187, 200, 202, 204, 206, 209, 221; Zornmuseet, Mora (photograph Jönköpings Läns Museum): p. 44.